DCS BOOKS PRESENTS

# A BREACH IN TRUST

### 2ND EDITION

DCS Books and Publication, LLC

# DAVID C STEWART

ISBN: 978-1-7360313-2-2



Library of Congress Cataloging-in-Publication Data

**A Breach in Trust: A Novel by David C. Stewart/published by DCS BOOKS AND PUBLICATIONS, LLC.**

**Printed in the United States of America**
david@dcspublishing.com
www.dcspublishing.com

Bootlegging this book is unauthorized and illegal. This work of art has also been revised and edited, meaning you may have the bootlegged copy if you did not purchase it from a reputable place of business or person. Please do not support bootleggers. It's unlawful.

# Acknowledgements

Completion of this project hasn't come without struggles. It's through those struggles and experiences-some I had clung to as handicaps-that I was able to accomplish what had seemed unattainable. Major work had begun once I began prayer and placed faith and trust in Him; only then was I able to remain focused on achieving my goals and conjuring the strength, discipline, and motivation necessary to press onward, slipping. Therefore, my first-of hopefully many other-praise rests with my Lord and Savior Jesus Christ for His ever-present Spirit in my life. Thank you, Lord, for choosing me.

To my daughters for accepting me despite my imperfection. Life teaches us when we don't even realize we're being schooled. Let my life stand as a beacon.

Thanks, Ikiesha, for holding strong with me throughout our adversity and family crisis. Thanks, Idriea, for always loving me, believing in me and wanting what's best for me.

You'll always be 'Daddy's Little Girl.' Thank you, David, for being that renewed strength in my life to stay motivated.

And to continue to be the better man.

I owe thanks to my parents, stepparents, grandparents, for sure. David C. Stewart, Sr., Ms. Hazel, Robert, and Darlene Williams, Bertha Brown (rest in peace), and Lula Canty (rest in peace). Thanks for the unconditional love and support. I am blessed to still be able to reach back into my childhood and embrace so many fond memories. To my sisters for all of their treasured wisdom, I thank you. Kim, I'm so proud of you that I may just allow you to keep telling people you're my twin. (It must be the dimples). Sis, you've truly come full circle, girl, and always impress me with your inner strength.

Tempie and Davina, it's been a long time coming. No situation will ever be able to separate us again. Dig me? And to Robin-I didn't forget about you, baby sis. You definitely have the mind to succeed. Hurry home. Uncle Sam doesn't love you like we do! Thanks for the support from day one. I know you're always there.

To my paternal brothers for…uhm…give me a minute. Okay. I got it. Thanks for all the butt-whippings, yall dragged me into. Whew! It's safer now that we're grown. Nevertheless, Rich, Dewayne, Lionel, and Fred (rest in peace), we've always been supportive of one another. Hopefully, my rise, fall, and rebirth, will be an example. Your brotherhood, I could never do without.

To my many aunts, uncles, and cousins of the Canty and Stewart's clan-especially those of you who've supported me (And you know who you are), much love. A special thanks to aunt Christine who's always been there for your nieces and nephews. Also, a special thanks to aunt Gerrie for your support, wisdom and understanding. You kept me focused on the "big" picture. Like you said: "When the student is ready, the teacher will come." Love you.

To my closest friends, brothers, and sisters on lock down (there's too many to name), keep your heads up and know that I'll never forget our bond…

A special thanks to you, babe. Patrice, thank you for always keeping the door open for me, not just the front door. Lol, but my mind, and my heart, my faith and belief. You've kept me as we all say.

I love you, babe.

There's always someone who feels forgotten. You aren't. We are all connected through the CREATOR.

PEACE & BLESSINGS,
***David C. Stewart***

# TABLE OF CONTENTS

# CHAPTER 1

# CAROL

I was already shaking loose beads of sweat dripping down the crease of my back, causing my thin cotton blouse to cling to my sun-warmed skin and my short, jet black doo to fall across my forehead. I peeked up at the blazing sun-more to God, then frowned. He knew my day would be hectic. He could've cut a Sista a break and not let it be so damn hot. The local news had said that the temperature would probably reach close to three digits. Judging from the rise of my thong underwear, it was already close to 90 degrees-and it's only 8:00 a.m.

"Don't cross that street!" I hollered to the twins. "And, Kevin, you be careful!" That boy...I swear...Even with those chrome wheels on his chair he's a handful. I watched my twelve-year-old son come to an abrupt stop at the curb and raise victorious arms at his seven-year-old sisters.

"Now who the man!" he hollered; his smile as bright as the morning.

Kevin is cursed with a frame filled with energy. In a way, I believe, that's a bad thing, considering he'll spend the rest of his life in a wheelchair.

William Dick Elementary School is just a few blocks' walk. However, for me, even one block is too long. Ever since Kevin's injury, two years ago, I've walked my children to and from school. I was through taking the chance that nothing would happen between here and there. Hell! My behind isn't bulletproof, but I feel a helluva' lot better knowing that they reach their destinations safely.

Kevin's situation is a bit different with him being enrolled in a different school. His social worker had helped to hook me up with a van service that carpools disabled children to a school out in Roxborough, a school where Kevin can receive the special attention he needs. Of course, I wasn't too thrilled about him having to pool out of North Philly, but my choices were few- plus, it was one step toward my learning how to cater my overprotectiveness around Kevin's needs.

I caught up with the children, yelled for the girls to hold hands while I waited to push Kevin's wheelchair across the pitted street.

Traffic wasn't much, a few cars-not many adults around either-plenty of children holding hands, yapping, and lugging notebooks. A stout, female crossing guard was directing traffic, and behind her, was a fleet of children, safeties-all with orange belts strapped across their chests and badges pinned on the belts. The safeties' arms were outstretched at their sides, preventing anyone from crossing the street. When their arms lowered, I wheeled Kevin's chair across the street and onto the sidewalk in front of the ruins of a burnt down cleaners.

"Mommy!" the twins shrieked as an alley cat scampered from the ruins. A small mouse dangled from the cat's jaws by its tail. The alley cat hunched its back, daring us to interrupt its fun.

"Get outta here, cat!" Kevin shouted, flexed as if he were our protector. The twins had wrapped themselves around my legs. I had to pry them loose-even after the alley cat had retreated.

"It's gone now. Stop acting so scary," I told the girls.

"Mommy, can we go over Grand mom's after school?" That was Kia, the oldest twin.

"If your daddy takes you, you can."

"Yeahhh!" Kia's hazel eyes were dancing.

"He not gonna take you," Kevin butted in.

I had let go of the wheelchair and allowed Kevin to push for himself. He thrives on his independence and hates when I baby him.

"Kevin, be quiet," I said.

The twins were dressed alike. Dun-brown below the knee dresses with chocolate ribbon-bows at the neck. Kia grabbed the hem of her dress with both hands. "Ha, ha. Mommy tol' you." She then scratched the quarter-size birthmark on her chocolate neck, the only way many can identify which twin is who. After seven years of raising the twins, I sometimes find myself still confused.

At the school's entrance, I kissed my daughters and waved hello to my former elementary school teacher, Mrs. Bullock.

She waved back.

Mrs. Bullock looks as if she hasn't aged since my tenor. She still looks elderly and intimidating with thick coke-bottle glasses bending at the bridge of her wrinkled nose. If she had been old back then, she has to be ancient now, but from what I have experienced during the PTA meetings, she's still as feared and demanding. Subconsciously, I rubbed the earlobe she had so loved to yank on.

With the twins gone, I hustled Kevin to the van

stop two blocks away. While we waited, I whipped his butt on his palm-sized, video basketball game and giggled like a schoolgirl, the way he always makes me laugh when he smiles the smile his father had mastered before dying in a car crash thirteen years ago, just after Kevin had been conceived. I had been thirteen then. A teen mom. I can still recall the subtle assaults from grownups. Nodding. Mumbling. "Babies having babies," some had said. Most just stared with "that's-a-damn-shame" faces.

After Kevin had redeemed himself at basketball and the van had scooped him up and whisked him away, I practically ran my 115- pound frame to 22$^{nd}$ and Lehigh. It was check day, and a sistahs pockets were famished.

By the time I made it inside of the check place, the sun had scorched my caramel complexion to a deep chocolate. There was no air-conditioning in the small atrium, and the inside and outside heats clashed with the many perfumes that clashed with the cigarettes clashing with the odors of two funky, homeless men camped right near me. I kept my mouth shut tight, pursed my lips and tried not to breathe. The last thing I needed was to feel queasy and have to run to the bathroom. I wasn't about to lose my place in line and have to deal with the torture all over again. Behind four plexiglass windows, tellers took their sweet ol' times processing ID's and kicking out cash and food stamps. I was ninth in my line and knew from the disgruntled looks on people's faces that to cut line could very well mean death, and that the superannuated guard way in the comer would most likely endorse the beat down.

My turn came to shove my welfare ID through the window. I glanced behind me-a habit of mine-to fend off all wandering eyes.

Just from the amount you receive on your check, people could count the number of children that you have.

"Carol Shavers?" asked the teller.

I nodded and gave the woman a slight smile. Thank God today is food stamps day for me, usually the second or third day of each month. I gladly counted out my stamps along with the seemingly uninterested teller. "-260, 300, 315, 345." I then watched her ringed fingers pluck up a huge stack of spanking new twenties, tens, and five dollar bills from a tray filled with cash. She expertly counted out my $295.00.1 pushed two stacks of eighty-two dollars back at her. "Can I have two eighty-two-dollar money orders?"

Without batting an eye, the teller hooked up my money orders and shoved them through the slot. "Next!" she called, dismissing me. I guessed, for her, counting money wasn't as enjoyable as she'd hoped it'd be when she applied for the job. I stuffed my jeans pocket with the check's results and stepped from the window-broke, in my mind-all but a hundred dollars mentally spent.

Outside the check place, scalpers roamed in full-force, purchasing food stamps at seventy-cents on a dollar. Like always, I stopped at a Muslim stand to buy my monthly supply of Blue Nile oil. I also bought dollar-packs of strawberry and coconut incense, two packs of assorted hair barrettes, and a pack of multicolored hair ribbons for the twins. Hot dog carts, street vendors, scalpers, hacks, all make walking Lehigh Avenue an adventure, I searched beyond the avenue's circus for Sonny, my usual hack, but he was nowhere in sight. An older man, whom I've seen hacking before, must've known I needed a ride. He was smiling at me like he'd hit the Lotto.

"Goin shoppin'?" he chirped. His lips were still moving even after the words were out. I listened for more, but that was it.

"You know it," I answered. I allowed him to usher me to his chariot, a dull-gray, '97 Regal with a soft, red leather interior.

The ride was going along smoothly, but my conversation forced. I'd lost interest in talking to Desmond, that's the name he gave, when I realized I couldn't get a word in. For the most part, I nodded all the way to Save-A-Lot—my mind breaking down what has already become a hectic morning.

I had been awakened this morning by a loud crash that had sent me stumbling into the living room to find my stereo cabinet face down on the floor, forty or so CD's scattered around it, and a teary-eyed Kelly—wrapped in a rainbow of clothing—trying to lift the cabinet from the floor. The fear her small face had shown struck a chord in me, made me wonder if my children fearing my response whenever they make mistakes are what I want. Surprisingly, instead of cursing her clumsy behind out, I'd found myself wiping her tears and rocking her back to sleep—unlike James, who'd ranted and raved about the cost of the stereo up until it was time for him to leave for work.

In less than three hours, I'd raided the aisles of Save-A -Lot for my canned goods, expanded my shopping to Murray's for meats, then had Desmond drive me across town to 9th Street for my produce. I figured, since I'd committed to paying him thirty dollars, I might as well make him earn it He must've decided that all he needs to do is drive and wait. Already I'd done all the loading the trunk with bags.

I piled the last of my groceries in the trunk then hurried into the Regal's air conditioning. It felt like a cool blanket had been wrapped around me. I let out a small "Mmmm…" then shivered, sunk into the leather upholstery and rested my head back.

"You ready?" he asked.

"Yep, all set."

My rowhome is "Around Back," everyone says- directly across the street from "The Tracks," another neighborhood moniker given to the railroad tracks guarded by a ridiculous fence. There have been countless occasions where freight cars have been stopped and looted. Old, young, it never mattered. When the boxcars' doors fly open, scenes like the L.A. riots are experienced all over again.

"Around Back" were two-story rowhomes, six squared blocks of fourteen units, each with their own poled-off front yard. Things are usually quiet Around Back for the most part. A majority of Raymond Rosen's gutter activities take place across the field where eight skyscrapers receive most of the attention. You could easily say that life is a bit softer "Around Back." But, make no mistake, project-shit still happens. It just lingers on like a dreary fog until the residual effects occur.

Desmond pulled the Regal in front of the ramp leading into my block. He couldn't pocket the thirty bucks fast enough, knowing exactly where he was and how not to entice the natives. We hadn't unloaded a single bag before three ashy-legged boys came to our aid.

"Hi, Miss Carol," one sang. He was one of Kevin's friends.

"Hi," the other two joined in, brandishing smiles. They've probably been planning this all morning.

"How much?" I asked.

"A dollar apiece," Kevin's friend answered.

"Just to take them to the front door? What happened to fifty-cents?"

"O.K., seventy-five cents."

"Fifty-cents apiece," I said, "take it or leave it."

The two nodded quickly like I'd change my mind while Kevin's friend sucked his teeth and rolled his eyes. "Come on, yall, grab the bags."

I still wound up carrying the two bags with eggs and bread in them after witnessing their roughhousing of the nine others.

Alone in my home, I stripped to my panties and bra, clicked the TV on the Young & Restless, and began putting away groceries. I was halfway through when the phone rang. It was Tonya.

"Hey, girt, whassup?" Her voice was dry. I knew she was bored. I was in no particular mood to gossip. I was still trying to cool down.

"Girl, they got me runnin' around here like a healthy eight-handed slave."

"Mmmm. I feel for you. You did laydown and have 'em, so, I guess a bitch gotta do what she gotta do."

I sucked my teeth loud enough to convey my mood. "Tonya, I'm busy. What is it? I know your broke ass just callin 'cause it's check day."

"Puh-lease, honey, don't nobody want none 'a your tired-ass

check."

I put the last of the bag of groceries I was digging from on the shelf and stepped closer to the TV. "Tonya, you watchin' Young & Restless?"

"Everyday."

"Who's this hoochie all up on Malcolm?" Tonya's my foster sister, my vagabond, extra-fifty-dollar-a-month-needing sister.

"That's Phillis. Some skin-and-bones is playin her part today."

"Oh, I was about to jump through that TV and, honeyyy…"

I gossiped with Tonya for nearly an hour, until Y&R's credits flowed up the screen and she was able to talk me out of fifty dollars until "her" check day, a few days after mine. Tonya's babies' daddy had taken on the task of raising her two sons. I was still trying to figure out how she'd gotten to keep the DPA checks.

After showering, I pulled on tom jeans and a blue

sleeveless T-shirt that clung to my 36 B's. I mashed together a meatloaf, put it in the oven on low heat, and ventured back outside, into the afternoon Eyewitness News had warned about.

"Hi, Miss Carol," a child greeted me on my way down the ramp. He was flipping on the knee-high pole that surrounds his mother's yard, another child who should have his ass in school. The other three were the boys who'd helped me with my grocery bags.

"Ain't you supposed to be in school?"

"I got suspended." He was out of breath, but kept flipping over the pole.

I stopped walking. "For what?"

"Cause my teacher stupid."

I walked away shaking my head, but the image of him in prison at eighteen forced me to stop again. "Where's your mother?"

"She not home."

"Do she know your little behind out here swinging on poles?"

The child was every bit of 11-years-old. He took one last flip and backed away with a scowl. My fury must have made me seem wicked. He backed up some more. All the way into the doorway where he lived then went inside. Children somehow know when not to disobey an adult other than their parent. He'd only wait until I was out of eyeshot to again defy the punishment his mother had probably placed him on. The way he'd backed away convinced me that my assumption was right, it also hints that we're adhering to a different generation of parenting, not the kick-ass-take-names later parenting of the 19th Century, but today's 20th Century parenting, one which is far more parent-child friendly and open. More understanding. Even I've fallen into the mold of disciplining my children with verbiage and psychologists' remedies to parenting. Simply, because nowadays, it has become common for children to call the Department of Human Services on parents if the child even suspects an ass-whipping is imminent. James, my twins' father, is always giving me grief about how soft I am with the kids. I wondered how his trifling ass would know. I've been spoiling him for twelve years now and lately, all he's been giving me is his ass to kiss.

When I reached William Dick, I wasn't the only parent stalking the school's entrance for her child. My so-so girlfriends-Pebbles, Lisa, and "Big Booty" Elaine-were camping out, too. I only sashayed to the group because Lisa has been my girl since grammar school. We've even carried to term together and sometimes joke that we may have gotten knocked up on the same night. Pebbles and Elaine were all right and all that, but Lisa was my homegirl, one of only two females who I actually socialize with.

Lisa had her youngest of two by the hand. A yellow 7-year-old girl with a long forehead named Mira. Scores of ghetto children were pouring from the school's doors already. Teachers were hurrying to the parking area to escape what I was sure had been a day's madness.

"Carol, you out in this heat, too?" Lisa asked.

"For the last time today, thank God." I said hello to Elaine and Pebbles then scooped up Mira. She was a tiny seven but still weighed heavy on my hip. "Heeyy, bad girl. Mommy got you out here in this heat?"

Mira rubbed a red eye with the back of her hand and nodded with a poked out bottom lip. Even with her long forehead she was cute.

Pebbles left to collect her six-year-old son who'd emerged from the crowd.

"What's the matter, boo?" I asked Mira. She was staring at me like I had no nose. I set her back on the ground and smiled as she ran to grab her mommy's hand. "Dang. Lis', you done spoiled that child rotten."

"Don't blame me, blame her father. We going through something about that now."

"Don't I know. Only it's the exact opposite with me and James."

"It'll catch up to you down the road. You got twins, too…"

She shook her head. "You better recognize, girl. Shit start when they asses is young."

On cue, Kia and Kelly broke away from the crowd with hair as wild as Macy Gray's, they attacked me with a barrage of questions on our way to the van stop to pick up Kevin: Mom when are we going over Grand mom's? What's for dinner? Is daddy home? Did you go shopping? Can I ride my bike? On and on the questioning went. When Kelly asked whether I'd bought Fruit Loops or Fruity Pebbles,

I thought, "Damn. They must save all their energy till they get out of school." A parent would hope that a child would be exhausted after expending their brain cells all day.

The van arrived thirty minutes late, forcing me to extend my strides to quicken my pace at the thought of my meatloaf burning. When Kevin began with his assortment of questions, I felt like hopping over a gate and leaving him right on the spot. Did I buy something for him? Did I get the sardines he likes? Do we have to go over Grand mom's? Do I have to do my homework right away? Yadda, yadda, yadda. The questions kept on coming.

I was relieved the meatloaf hadn't burned. It wasn't as moist as James likes it, but it was edible. I supervised the girls' homework then screamed at Kevin for the third time to turn that damn Sega off. I'd figured out Kevin's problem long ago. He thinks that because he's in a wheelchair, I won't kick his skinny, little ass. "Just because I haven't, yet," I told him, "don't think that I won't!"

I put the rest of dinner together-Kraft macaroni & cheese and string beans. I kept the meal warm on the stove until James got home an hour later, asking just as many questions as the kids had. I praised God when James had shut up and went to shower the construction dirt from his body. I set the table for us all and made plates of food.

"Baby, you coming down to eat?" I called upstairs.

James didn't answer.

I huffed and dropped the oven mittens to the countertop. "Yall go ahead and eat," I told the kids. I had a feeling James was experiencing another one of his recent mood swings.

James' six-foot, 195 lb. frame was sprawled across the bed with just a maroon towel to hide his package. I've always been crazy about his body. Chocolate. Hard. Sexy. Both hands were cupped behind his head, displaying black bushy armpits.

"What's wrong with you?" I asked. I'd stopped at the room's entrance and leaned against the doorframe.

"I'm just chillin."

"Well, can't you just chill at the dinner table with us? We're all downstairs waiting on you and you up here chillin'."

"Bring a plate up for me."

"Nope. Uh-uh. You've been doing this for weeks. You come home, lock yourself in this room, or you run the streets. Your kids need to see you sometimes, eat supper with their dad."

"I spend time with 'em."

"Then you know they wanna go over their grandmothers?'

"You take 'em."

"I'm tired."

"Tired? You ain't did nothin' all day. I'm the one who works."

"Don't even go there, James. I been running around here all day taking care of your kids. I ain't even have the time to pick up Kia's ear medicine."

"Probably 'cause you and Tonya was runnin' yall mouths on the phone all day."

I stared at him and wondered if my phone line had been bugged. Anyway, Tonya and I had only spoken for an hour-plus, I wasn't about to feed into his dumb stuff. He was aching for an excuse to run with his boys. I spun from the doorway and stomped back down to the kitchen. Ten minutes later, I heard the front door slam.

"Asshole," I mumbled.

It was well past 11 o'clock when I heard James return to the house. I had long ago sent the children to bed and only knew what time it was because the red digits displayed on the nightstand's dock shook when he'd slammed the door.

He was drunk.

Sounds of pots dinking in the kitchen, water running, icebox slamming. Like always, he had the munchies. But tonight, I had the munchies, too-and chewing his ass out would be the only way to get my till.

I entered the darkened living room where James was stooping with a plate of food resting in a palm while fidgeting with the broken stereo. The glow from the kitchen's light illuminated the room, cast a glow onto the bottom-half of his body, so I couldn't see his face.

"I don't appreciate you walking out on us the way you did."

He didn't budge, just continued acting like he knew how to fix the stereo.

"You don't hear me talking to you, James?"

"Yeah, I hear you."

"Well?"

"Well, what?"

"Where have you been and why'd you leave? You

knew the girts wanted to go to your mom's."

Giving up on the stereo, he flagged it, flopped down on the sofa and shoved a fork-full of food in his mouth as if I hadn't said a word.

"Well?" I pushed

He darted toward me with the fork enclosed in a fist. He stopped within kissing distance, dose enough for me to see the dip in his bushy eyebrows and his wrinkled forehead. His coal-black eyes held fire. "Gotdammit, Carol! Why the fuck you sweatin' me 'bout this bullshit! I'm back, right!?"

Spittle of food flew from his mouth onto my cheek. I wiped it off.

"That's not the point. And lower your voice, the kids are sleep."

His string-like sideburns and goatee flexed when he chewed. He chewed, chewed, and chewed until evil thoughts of him contracting mad-cow disease invaded my mind. I remembered we all had eaten the meatloaf and regretted thinking such a thing.

"What's the point then?" he barked.

"If I have to tell you, then you're dumber than I thought." I turned and stalked off upstairs-flaming mad. I didn't want the children to hear all the filth that would be said if I continued to look at his sorry-ass face.

I'd just dosed off when my aura was invaded.

James had slid between the sheets next to me, his nakedness warm against my back. I scooted over to avoid his touch. I was steamed.

He slipped an arm around my waist and pulled me against him.

Again, I scooted away.

He followed. This time, I not only felt James's stiff member against my rear but inhaled the scent of stale liquor and cringed at his hot breath against my neck.

"I'm sorry, baby," I thought I heard him mumble while grinding against me.

I bit my bottom lip and laid still, unwilling to participate, not wanting to turn to see his lying face or respond to a drunken, rehearsed touch. My anger was steady, dormant at the core of my being. Even if that were an apology, he'd given moments ago, he wasn't sorry at all, just homy. I pushed away his arm and felt it slither right back around my waist.

He tugged the band of my panties.

"I said no, James."

"Come on, Carol, stop playing."

"I'm not playing," I said earnestly.

He continued to probe, reached between my thighs from behind and fingered my nest. His touch was coarse and his breathing, animalistic. I spun onto my back and stared daggers at my man. "James, I said 'no'!"

"Just once," he whispered, never stopping his kissing and fondling and murmuring and disrespect.

He climbed on top of me.

I pushed his shoulders back.

He must've thought I was pushing him down to taste me because he was there, planting kisses, trying to shimmy down my panties.

"I mean it, James. Stop!" I hollered, thought about the children hearing me and lowered my plea. I closed my thighs to limit his access then felt them being pried open again. I tried sitting up, but his arm kept me pinned. He was bear-like in his assault

I was pinned beneath his body weight when he stuck his head in the crook of my neck and moaned. When he captured my arms above my head, all I could think of was him not wearing protection and me getting pregnant again.

"Don't do this, James," I pleaded softly. My tears were beginning to swell. My plea carried the weight of a paper mallet as he steadily invaded my body, mind, and spirit. I finally succumbed to his aggressiveness and shut my eyes, now just wanting it over with. The sting of not being prepared for him forced me to cry out.

James sank into me with brutal strokes, more brutal than the act itself. He slammed into my body with unimaginable hatred, and every grunt he released sounded like "fuck you." He tried pulling his entire body inside of mine when he climaxed, making certain he was in as deep as possible, squeezing our bodies so tightly together that I could barely breathe. With that same intensity, he pulled himself from me, snatched a bedspread around himself, and stomped from the room.

That quickly he was through.

We were through.

I stared into the darkness of our bedroom for answers, wondering how our relationship has come to this. I knew there were problems, but not to this extent. All I could ask myself if: why? Why had James-my man of twelve years-my children's father just raped me?

# CHAPTER 2

## CAROL

The front door closed, signaling James' departure for work. I stood up from the sofa and touched my toes, tried to loosen the cramp in my back. James would usually wake me up before leaving. Last night was as freshly etched in his mind as it was in mine-and will most likely always be.

For a long time last night, I contemplated leaving him-just pack up the children, a few clothes, whatever-just say "fuck it." I had no idea where a 26-year-old Black woman with three children-one a handicap-would go, but, I'd seriously debated dealing with that obstacle once we were out the door, then thought, why should we leave? He's the one who deserves to be uprooted, not my kids.

I snatched the bedding from the sofa and shuffled up to the bedroom, stripped the soiled linen from the bed then remade it before climbing in. For a long time, I eyed the yellow stain on the ceiling that's proved to be so therapeutic for me over the years. Never has James done anything as disrespectful to me as he'd done last night. Ifs not as if I'd closed the playground to him, at least four or five times a week we'd sweat through sessions. But lately, James's behavior has been strange and unpredictable, and last night only adds to the list of absurd behavior.

I was too keyed up to lay still any longer. And now that James has left for work, I felt a bit freer to roam within my own home. As pitiful as it sounds, ifs how I felt, as if I were living life beneath some kind of Taliban regime. I knew soon I'd have to face the optimistic me that tries figuring out why someone does something wrong. I fight to admit and deal with the fact: there are just some "fucked up" people in this world who needs little excuse to do dirt. Ifs in their genes.

I traipsed down the stairs inventing excuses for James' recent behavior, poured myself a glass of orange juice and downed half of it, allowing the juice to fulfill my palate's yearning for sweetness and distract my thoughts. Before finally closing the fridge, I'd already devoured a banana, two slices of turkey loaf wrapped in American cheese, and two spoonful's of cold macaroni & cheese.

I scrambled eggs and fixed bowls of Fruit Loops for the kids' breakfasts. Kia was already woken. She was at the room's window with her stuffed bunny clutched by one ear. I eased my face beside hers and looked.

"What's out there, sweetheart?' She'd dressed herself in a collage of colors and her hair was scattered every which way.

"Birds."

We watched a small flock of pigeons peck at the ground. Neither of us noticed Kelly until she was beside me.

"Yall watching those dumb birds," Kelly, mouth around her thumb.

I pulled her hand down from her face.

"They not dumb," Kia whined.

"Uh-huh, yes they is."

"No, they are not."

"Uh-huh."

"Mommy, make Kelly stop callin" the birds dumb."

I felt compelled to referee. "Kelly, birds aren't dumb."

She pointed to the pigeons. "Then why they keep

bumpin' they head on the ground?"

"That's how they eat," I said.

"See, you the one dumb," Kia said accusingly.

I couldn't help but smile. The similarities do not astonish me, but my daughters' differences do. They were so much alike, but yet so different. Opposites.

Kia's the shy one-except around her father, who she always tries catering to. I think she's adopted that trait from watching me, but now, I'm not so sure if catering to any man is a habit I'd like to instill in my girls. Kia's eagerness to help me with domestic chores is certainly more refreshing than Kelly's, who's becoming a straight-up tomboy. Occasionally, she too, has her moments when she wants to participate in housekeeping. But for the most part, her loves are sports, fighting boys, and the TV show C.O.P.S. James' mother believes that she'll outgrow her tomboyish ways. She even refers to the transformation of her wish-daughter, Tyra Banks, as an example of an admitted tomboy.

The sound of running water pulled me from the window and signaled that Kevin was awake. I still carry an urge to help Kevin with some of his morning routines, but now that he's older, he never allows it. Ifs been close to a year since he had. We were still trying to adjust.

"Come on, girls, your breakfast is downstairs. I made eggs."

"Yuck! Dead bird!" Kelly shrieked.

Panic settled on Kia's face. She shook her head frantically. "I'm not eatin' no dead bind." Her tone was definite.

I looked at Kelly's mushed face. 'You see what you did?" I turned back to Kia. "Boo, you don't have to eat eggs, sweetheart. You can eat cereal."

I sent the girts downstairs for breakfast then laid their matching short sets out on the bed. I left the room and knocked on the bathroom door.

"You okay in there, Kevin?"

"Yeah."

"Your food's downstairs, so hurry."

"I'm cornin'."

I helped Kevin downstairs to his first-floor chair. It's easier to keep a chair downstairs as well as up. Whenever I'd help him up or down the stairs, I'd wish for the transfer I'd placed with Housing Authority for a single-floor, 3-bedroom apartment. I've been waiting fourteen months already since doctors' have broken my heart by telling me that Kevin will never walk again. The neighborhood grapevine says that it takes at least two years before an application is processed. I still have another ten months of waiting.

After breakfast, my clan and I crossed the project's plaza and was at William Dick in minutes. I waved goodbye to the twins and realized how, this morning, they looked so much like their father.

Kevin had been quiet throughout breakfast, and during our walk so far. I could always sense when something was wrong with him, he'd never look me in the eye or he'd chew his pinkie.

"Okay, what's wrong?" I asked. I was behind him, pushing the chair around a roped-off section of sidewalk. All around the area were chips of concrete that sent vibrating through my hands as the chair rolled over them.

"Ain't nothin' wrong."

"Don't lie. You think I don't know when something is wrong with you?"

We stopped at the corner and watched the traffic roll by. When we'd crossed the street, he looked back and up at me. "I heard yall fightin' again last night."

I didn't try denying it, just hoped he had no idea why we were fighting. 'We're okay, Kevin. Don't let it bother you."

He faced forward. 'Was it over him never being home?"

"Partly."

"Did you win?"

"Nobody won, Kevin. It's not like that."

"I know that. I'm hoping you kicked his butt."

I had to smile. It felt good to have an ally. "No. I didn't kick his butt."

"Well, did you at least black his eye, buss his lip or something?"

"Stop it, Kevin. We don't fight like that. And I don't ever wanna hear about you fighting a woman like that either. You hear me?"

He didn't answer. I playfully popped him upside the head.

"Ow!"

"I asked you a question."

"I heard you. Dag!" He rubbed the place where I'd popped him.

I bent over and kissed his cheek. 'You don't have to worry about me, sweetheart. I'm fine."

Even I wondered if that were true.

Kevin and I shared a goodbye wave as he was being driven away. His eyes were sad, made me wonder if he believed any of what I'd said about last night. The way he looked made me think that he knew what James had done to me, and that he'd never tell a soul. The idea of him knowing, stirred my inside and caused my first few steps to drag like my feet were cement.

My entire walk back to the projects, I mumbled to myself, wrecked my brain, trying to think about anything but the issue controlling my emotions-my relationship with James. I had some time to kill before Diamond Medical opens and I could refill Kia's ear medicine. I decide to drop in on Liz, my party-happy advisor.

Liz not only didn't own a screen door, but no doorknob either. There was a hole where the doorknob should be, but a gray T-shirt filled the void. Liz's reluctance to buy a doorknob amazes me. She relies on an extremely strict house rule that states: If you're not in the house by 12:30 a.m., then a slab of wood would be placed at the base of the door as a makeshift lock.

Liz's kids should have already left for school, so the door shouldn't have been locked. I knocked twice before walking in and surveying the home.

Right away, my nostrils stung from the stench of mildew, smelled like old mop heads just sitting around rotting. My face cringed and I dared myself to step inside.

The walls were bare. A dingy creme. The furniture-well, a tattered couch and a dining table were littered. The couch: books, blankets, clothes. The table: dirty dishes, cups, old cartons, and lots of aluminum foil that had been torn away from some foods. The black-tiled floor was home to a mass of dust and scars. The downstairs was a mess as always.

I felt bad for the six children growing up in the house, but not sorry. I only felt bad because Liz could do a better job of housekeeping.

I didn't feel sorry because all of her children are healthy, high-spirited, and doing well in school. I have to give it to my girl; she sees to it that her three teenagers stay draped in the latest fashions and eats well—as far as take-out food goes. She instills values and morality in her children by a different standard. Her project home just isn't priority.

I climbed the stairs to Liz's bedroom. She was propped up in bed, on the telephone, with a Styrofoam plate filled with eggs and sausages balanced on her lap. She always looks pleasantly surprised to see me. She may wonder how anyone who'd visited her home once would visit again. After growing up a foster-child, I've learned to play out the hands I'm dealt. Liz is one of the few people I could confide in-even so, I was still nervous to tell her about last night.

"Heeyy, Carol," she sung. "What brings you out slummin this morning?"

"The clinic. That place takes forever to open. Ooohh, look at you all laid up like 'a queen.'" I scanned the messy room for somewhere to sit.

Her room was a clutter box.

The pieces of furniture that were missing from downstairs were in her room, a couch, floor-model television, a recliner-but clothes mostly. Everywhere. Liz could easily be the ghetto's female Fred Sanford.

"Let me call you back. I got company, okay?" she asked whomever she was on the phone with. "Mmmm-hmm. Okay. I'll call you back." She hung up clutching a bedspread to her large bosom and set aside her meal. It took an effort for her to adjust her big body toward me. "So, how you been, Carol?"

"Tryna make it"

"Where those two pretty girls at?"

"Girrrl, they bad asses in school."

"Don't even try it. Compared to mine, yours are angels."

"That's because they're young. As soon as they old enough to start their shit, I'ma send those little angels you talking about right around here to you."

We both laughed.

"I saw you the other day goin' in Butch's."

"And you didn't call me?" I asked.

"I was with some man, chile." She stuck a forefinger in her head-scarfs opening, right above the knot and scratched.

I sat on the front edge of a straight-back filled with clothes. "Who?"

"I can't say."

"Somebody's man, huh?"

"Nope."

"Then who?"

She shook her head. "I promised I wouldn't say anything."

"Not even to me? You know I don't gossip."

"Ha! Imagine that."

I twisted my fingers at her. "Forget you then. He probably butt ugly, that's why you creepin'."

"Don't you wish. Anyway, how's my baby?"

"Kevin?"

"Who else?"

"I'm still trying to adjust to a teenage son. All he wanna do is play that effn video game."

"Is that a bad thing? Ain't that what guys do? I don't think boys ever grow outta that stage. Just look at all the grown-ass men that still play 'em—professionals and shit. Ya feeling me?" We were leaning over to high-five when the bathroom door slammed shut. Our heads twisted in the direction. Liz must've read my mind.

"That's Michael's girlfriend, Niecy. She been stayin' here for about a week already-ever since her drunk behind mother threw her out."

"Since when you start doing charity?"

"You know I don't-but, Carol, Michael done got this child pregnant."

"Stop lyin'!"

"I wish I was."

"You talking about little Michael…14-year-old Michael?" I measured about four feet from the floor with my hand.

"The one and only."

I rolled my eyes and shook my head the way old women used to do to me when I'd carried at thirteen. Now that I've matured, I understand why it had been done.

"Tell me about it. Shocked the fuck outta me," Liz exploded.

"I didn't even know he was out there gettin' his groove on."

"That goes to show how fast kids are growing up nowadays."

"But thirteen, though?"

"Hell, Liz, I was thirteen in case you don't remember?"

Liz huffed and shook her head dismayed. "But this girl is dumb as a blind donkey."

I laughed.

"I'm serious, Carol. She don't know if she cornin' or goin'. You should see the way Michael boss her around. I told her about it, now all she do is try to suck up to me, like I got the time to police their shit. I hope she don't think that when that little sucker get here I'ma take care of it."

"You will."

"Shhittt, I gotta trick for both of the asses."

Liz and I laughed about her being a Grandmom for a while and I gave Niecy, her pregnant border, the eye when she walked past the room's door.

She was a short petite thing with a six-month belly and looked her age. I found it hard not to be judgmental, even with my own soured past.

Somewhere our conversation turned to James, a place I didn't want to be. My womb was still raw. "Girrrl, I don't even wanna talk about that fool."

"Don't tell me he actin" up again?" She lifted a cold sausage from the Styrofoam plate and damn-near swallowed it whole, brought to mind a joke comedian Adel Givens had told at a Def Comedy Jam-about big lips and little wands resembling whales swallowing Tic-Tacs.

"So, whassup with you today?" I asked.

"You lookin' at it." She inhaled another sausage.

I considered us tight, so I didn't see a problem with being straight up with her. "Have you been downstairs?"

"Puh-lease. Eff that downstairs. Why clean it when all they gonna do is tear it up again? They be down there dancin and carryin on like they are crazy. Let them clean it."

"Well, it smells like something died down there."

I was surprised that Liz dragged her 5'5", 250-lbs out of bed to investigate. She'd wrapped herself in a bedspread, bounded at the chest, and sniffed while she tiptoed around the house.

That's where I left her. The stench was too much for me.

By now the sun was high. Many of the project's residents had begun to venture outdoors. I was able to get Kia's prescription filled, drop off the fifty dollars to Tonya that she'd asked me for and fend off two proposals from maintenance men loitering in front of the rent office where I did some business. I dropped my telephone payment in the mailbox and felt relieved to be broke again. I knew I'd taken care of all my business, because my earlier tabulations of what I'd have left matched the emptiness of my purse.

Back at the house, I collected my mail from the floor as I walked in and stared at the thick, plain white envelope addressed to "Kevin"-no last name, or address, no return address-no nothing-just Kevin's name in black ink. One just like it has arrived each month since Kevin was shot two years ago.

I turned the envelope in my hands and tried to stop my heart from racing.

I opened it.

Like before, it was filled with money. Always the same amount-five hundred dollars-always in crisp new hundreds. I fingered the bills and closed the envelope like always. I peeked out of the windows, trying to rid myself of the eerie feeling receiving the envelope instills in me. I felt like the nightmares will never end. I was being haunted by the past, always forced to remember the thing that pains me most.

# CHAPTER 3

# WESLEY

I never had asked my parents why they named me Wesley Rhodes. My two younger brothers, Benny, and Stacks, say that my moms had a crush on Wesley Snipes, the actor. But that doesn't add up. Hell, he wasn't even famous when I was born. I'm twenty-four, so Snipes would've had to have been in acting school. My brothers were always talking crazy smack. Overtime, I've become immune to most of their bullshit statements, and more now than then, they'd say something even crazier.

The clock in my Volvo read 7:45 a.m. Although my first class doesn't begin until 9:25, I'm absolutely compelled to get my behind out of bed, Mondays thru Fridays, and venture the few blocks it takes to begin my morning right.

The traffic light changed to green. I pulled off with a heavy foot on the gas, not wanting to miss my source of inspiration after a weekend of backsliding.

I slowed down. Schoolchildren were everywhere.

I could never fathom why ignorant asses would spray through stuffy noses that "Black folks don't want to learn." Sometimes, when I hear those preppy assholes, talk from their necks like that, I feel like kicking shit over, like a building—or a bus. I hadn't enrolled at Temple College because of what some nay-sayer had said, but because my insides had been shaken by the reality of death or imprisonment.

As a young Black man, I'd been faced with the decision to either: rot in the ghetto's jungle or try and make amends for the wrongs I'd done to others. I'll admit it's been hard trying to break from the mold of drug dealing, but the one thing growing up in North Philadelphia has instilled in me is resiliency. Each morning, I tell myself that my time has passed. My dealing days are over. I've even sprouted dread locks as a symbol of my changing values and priorities.

I pressed the brake at a red light and eyed another pack of children. The ghetto's future will arrive in many flavors, sizes, and shades. But for the moment, each child who strolled by, probably did so without a clue of what's expected of their lives. Many may end up just like me; still trying to make up for lost time spent, hustling on the drug infested comers.

When the people-parade ceased, I turned onto Diamond, just a block away from Raymond Rosen projects. I drove by Mr. Adams then Butch's grocery stores, past oh-hundred, oh-eight, and oh-nine buildings, with William Dick school now in sight. I passed that, too, pulled the Volvo into what I'd long ago designated as "my spot," my place of refuge. I knew their names from the newspaper clippings I'd collected two years ago.

A terrible tragedy. "A Horrible Accident" the Daily News had headlined it.

Kevin and Carol were quiet this morning. Neither spoke much. Usually, they'd laugh and talk until a blue van arrived to pick the boy up, but, this morning, there was a coldness in their postures.

I flicked a Newport from the pack and pushed in the car lighter.

Smoking.

Another bad habit I hope to rid myself of during my quest for moral recovery. Already, I'm sifting through spoils trying to fend off temptation. And when the temptation seems too much, I usually find myself sitting right where I am, needing to reinforce the wall I'm in the process of building.

I dragged from my smoke, blew a plume out of the window and watched-witnessed the boy's bond with his mother, something I'd never experienced with mine. A brain tumor robbed her of her life shortly before my fifth birthday. Her absence could possibly justify why I find Carol so appealing. In her, I've discovered similar qualities that my aunts and uncles say my own mother had possessed. Strength. Commitment. The more I've watched her, the more I understand who she is and who my own mother was. I was connected to Carol in ways other than admiration-is and will always be-in one way especially.

A large Wonder bread truck pulled beside me and blocked my view. I stretched my neck, tried to peer around the impossible. Seconds later, the driver leaped from the truck's cab and raised the hood.

"Now what?" I mumbled. I sat back and closed my eyes, needed to clear my mind of suppressed profanities I felt bubbling inside of me.

The truck was still there when I reopened my eyes. So were the profanities. I needed the truck gone or at least out of the way. Angrily, I plucked my smoke out of the window and stepped from the car. I stomped to the truck's hood.

The driver raised his eyes from the engine. "I'll only be a minute. It always does this."

"What's the problem?"

"I don't freakin' know. This piece 'a crap. You jiggle it here and there and…" He stuck his entire arm into the engine's depth and turned an agonizing face to me. "…Yeahhh!" he groaned. "Got it!" He refracted his arm and slammed down the hood. "Thanks anyway, buddy."

His appreciation pulled my eyes away from hers. She'd been watching us.

I tried playing it off, mumbled to the man that I'm a mechanic, but internally, I was melted ice cream.

She was still watching. I sensed her hazel stare on us, a stare that easily tugged at my soul. All my skeletons seemed to reveal themselves. I became so worried about what she'd find in me, I nearly ran back to the car.

Safe behind the wheel, I kept my eyes in check when the bread truck pulled off, didn't so much as cut an eye in Carol's direction when I nervously pulled into traffic.

I was still kicking myself when I turned onto Van Pelt Street, a few blocks away. I parked in front of Benny's crib, behind his dented LeSabre and thought about changing my Mr. Smooth moniker to Mr. Clutz, after my lame reaction to Carol.

Benny rents a three-story, now-home, the street's ugly duckling without question. Every other house had been remodeled to look almost exact-Colonial windows and doors, redbrick face, with black lining and aluminum sidings. Eighteenth century lamp posts line the curbs, giving the small street a yellowish glow during the nights and a show of unity. But the lamps were off after sunrise, and now the night's shadows weren't enough to obscure the plain off-white of Benny's place.

The rusted, gray screen door screeched when I opened it, and the unpainted, wood door slipped from the hinges when I jiggled the doorknob. "What the hell-"I cursed while dancing to keep the damn thing balanced.

I struggled to put the door back on its tract, then did. I looked around the home's emptiness, with its content's worth of emotion. Legend says: 'You can take the man out the projects, but you can't take the project out the man." In Benny's case the saying is true.

My brother's living room was bare-except for rust-colored carpeting and an office phone. No chairs. No pictures. Nothing. The walls were the same plain, ugly as the exterior.

I jogged my 5'10", 200-lbs up to the third floor. All of the rooms I'd passed were empty except for phones, as had been the last three houses Benny had lived in. He tends to change residency as quick and often as a field mouse fleeing a brush fire.

Not working out caught up with me after the

third flight of stairs, I was winded and coughing up Newport's.

"Whassup, my nigga?" Benny called from behind his bedroom door. He had to have seen me park. My coughing wasn't that loud. "It took your college-ass long enough to show thru."

I pushed open the door to a blast of cool air and entered my brother's hideaway. He was standing beside a new 52-inch television.

"Okay, player, I see you stepped your game up."

Benny's broad shoulders bounced as he sang in a pimp's tone, "Ya-know, same-o, same-o."

I plopped into a Lazy-boy and let loose a sigh. My morning dose of inspiration had been sliced in half.

"Nigga, don't bring that drama all up in here. Just 'cause you fam don't mean I won't kick you outta my spot."

"Cool out B. I ain't stressing. I'm only tired. My morning ain't go like I wanted it to."

Before I'd allowed my dreads to grow out, people would confuse Benny for me and vice versa. We have our mother's square chin, thick lips, and brown eyes. Benny has a jagged scar across his right cheek. While he spoke, I sat remembering the shoe fight we'd had to put it there.

"I thought those Temple chicks kept a brother

motivated. You playin' hooky or what?" It's just like Benny to associate everything with women, one reason he surrounds himself with telephones. The other was the business.

"Nope. I don't do the hooky thing. My first class don't start till later. I wanted to drop this off." I pulled the newest P. Diddy CD from my pocket and shook it at him.

"Oh, snaps! You got it, huh?"

"And I ain't pay a dime either."

He snatched the CD and hustled to his digital system, pushed a few buttons until an explosion of beats and rhymes engulfed us. The music was loud, but P. Diddy evened the discomfort with tight lyrics.

Benny was pacing the room, reciting the lyrics. He was shirtless, in jeans sagging just below the waistline of his St. Johns Bay underwear. He rapped the spiel with fiery hand movements and head faints.

I sat there, nodding to the dope beat.

Benny and I left his house twenty minutes after I'd arrived. I tailed his LeSabre to Stacks' second home, his new girlfriend, Sheila's, two-story section 8.

I still had some time to kill before I'd have to jet to campus, so we lounged around the living room discussing women. It wasn't long before the conversation turned raunchy.

"Come on, man, you can't tell me bitches like that shit."

That was Benny's ignorant ass. He's always saying stupid shit.

"They do. I swear to beans," Stacks said.

I was staring at Benny like he was the only brother who didn't appreciate OJ's freedom. "Why you have to call our queens bitches?" I asked.

"Man, that shit's a habit. Don't start that righteous shit. We just kickin it."

I shook my head, sat back, and listened to them rambling.

Benny was into it. His pupils were dilated and shiny like he'd discovered canned pussy. "So, you sayin all I gotta do is pour honey and strawberries and shit all over 'em and they'll cum. Just like that."

Stacks' smile was sinister as he nodded. "And you don't even have to touch 'em. Them anticipatin' the sex get 'em off-plus, ain't no niggah probably ever did no shit like that to 'em before. She'll be your sex slave forever. I'm feelin' you, B, bit--" They both looked over at me. "My bad, Wes. Women be eatin shit like that up."

They gave each other a dap.

I shook my head again, concluded that my baby bro' was shot the hell out. He was wearing a WWF Royal Fumble T-shirt with the Pock's face on its front. We only share the same mother, so his complexion was lighter than ours. He's more on the tan side with a long nose, lean frame, and our mother's eyes. "What?" Stacks asked.

"Yall dumb as hell, that's what. Who told you that bullshit?"

"I read it in Blacktails."

"Aw, man!" Benny frowned. "You talkin 'bout go-go girls?"

"So what? They still females, right?"

"I give up," I said. I shot Stacks one of my "yeah-right" looks while I stood up.

"Oh, you too good to hang out with the help?"

"Nah, little bro'. I got class in a few. Plus, you know how I feel about yall still slinging. It's hard enough already trying to stay focused."

Benny gave me some love-a handshake and a hug. "Man, that niggah buggin. You do your thing. At least one of us got out."

"Thanks, B." I turned to Stacks. "Stop reading that garbage."

He gave me the finger along with his boyish grin.

The walk across Temple's campus continues to be one of my life's most gratifying and tranquil experiences. I grew up believing that the reality of achieving the "college experience" did not apply to individuals like myself. As a child, conversations about college had never surrounded me. Hell, I didn't even know anyone who'd been to college or had the inkling of an idea or the money to get there. The click I'd run with, hadn't been big on planning any futures. Our misguiding led us to believe that we'd go as far as the money in our pockets would take us, and not a step further. At fourteen, I wouldn't have considered us bad teens, defiant maybe. Still today, I believe that we'd been pushed through high school just to save school faculty members from early retirement. Thankfully, I'd been wise to pay just enough attention in class to ingest the basics, brush up on them two years later, and barely pass my entry exam. Being in college has changed my entire outlook on life. My only regret is the path that has led to my transformation.

I made it through the day's classes reasonably comfortable with the assignments I'd been given to do. As soon as I stepped off of campus and onto Broad & Susquehanna, my pager went off. It was Pam, her third page today, her second with 9-1-1 behind her cell phone number. I'd have answered her previous pages, but I'd left my cell phone in my car's glove compartment. I hurried to the phone booth before my girlfriend burned out my beeper's battery.

On the second ring, she answered. "Where are you?"

"Is it necessary for you to clock a brother like this?"

"Is that what it seems like?"

"Yeah."

"Well, too bad."

I imagined her slim neck churning while she spoke.

"Are you coming over or should I meet you at your place?"

"And it took you two 9-1-1 pages to ask me this?"

"You didn't answer."

I don't think Pam even realizes her insensitivity and selfishness. They came so natural to her, having been spoiled by her parents her entire twenty-three years.

I sighed. "I won't be home until after six."

"Fine. I'll come by around seven. Should I bring something?"

A huge rottweiler whipped by, dragging a small boy at the end of its leash. I closed the booth's door. "Maybe something to eat."

"Won't I be enough?"

"Only if dessert's a main course."

"I can't wait."

"Neither can I."

I hung up and did a double-take for the

rottweiler. The coast was clear. I pulled my backpack over my shoulder and stepped.

Dinner consisted of Chinese takeout. Shrimp fried rice and egg rolls. My contribution to the meal was a bottle of Spumante that was vanishing fast. Our legs were curled beneath my coffee table, atop of the burgundy shag carpet. Pam was feeding me shrimps from her fingertips and teasing me with seductive looks.

"You trying to make it a long night, huh?" I asked.

A sly grin surrounded her pearly whites. "And morning, too." She ran a wandering finger around the rim of her wineglass.

Euphoria allowed her sexual scent to carry over the foods'. Several cinnamon incenses she'd stockpiled in my home, combined with the candlelight, set the mood exactly right. I welcomed the memories and the pampering.

"I'm ready for dessert," she teased. She crawled around the table and entered my space, leaned in for a kiss. Her lips were moist, brown pillows where I was willing to rest upon all night. Our eyes were locked when she tugged me up from the floor. "Where we going?" I asked.

"To the bedroom."

"Why not here?"

"The bedroom's nicer. Softer."

I didn't argue, just followed her 5'9" frame, let her slim fingers be my leash, and allowed the sway of her slender hips to lead the fire in my groin to a safer place.

Her ankle-length dress exposed a toned back. I sprinkled my fingertips across her satiny, cocoa skin in anticipation of the flight we were about to embark on.

At the bed we met like two thunder clouds, tried releasing all of the evenings teasing with probing tongues and flesh-filled palms. It took willpower to pace our fervor, to pause for a breath between tastes. There was the scent of berries in her shoulder-length curls when she spun her back to me and encouraged my member to rest against her.

She reached back and pulled my kisses to her nape and shoulders. Her skin was, silky warm, unsalty to the tongue. I was quickly lost in desire for this sensual creature I was hungrily tasting. I slipped the dress' straps from her shoulders and sighed joyously when the flimsy material hit the floor.

Pam faced me glazed-eyed, with hardened breast-a mouthful in size. She lifted my T-shirt and forced my Kani slacks to hit the floor in a heap. I was rigid when I slipped from my boxers, comfortable with my size. Pam had to be comfortable as well because she reached for me immediately, squeezed me hard, sent quivers the length of my body that could easily entice me into anything that she pleased. She kissed my chin, neck, and chest-devoured me with her sexy brown eyes and an active tongue. I broke away to the nightstand and quickly found what I needed.

Like always, Pam took the packet from me, tore it open, and placed the contraceptive between her lips. She pulled me into the warmth of her mouth, slipping the Latex snug around me. My toes curled upward and my legs nearly buckled. I closed my eyes and howled a long encouraging moan.

She pulled away from me and smiled. "Not yet, baby," she teased.

We met again horizontally-me kissing her navel down to the warmth where her scent loomed enhancing. Her small hips rose and fell in a rhythmic passion that forced me to lock my arms around her thighs so she wouldn't slide away from my tasting. Pam's small moans became pleas to God, and suddenly, I felt her spasms in the tightening of her thighs around my dreads. I refused her from slipping from my lips until I'd the chance to taste the explosion that I had built within her. I reached up and cupped both breast, pinched the nipples and enjoyed the sighs that escaped her. I felt like the maestro coordinating the perfect song, pushing for a finale where the feverish pitch from perfect direction sends his instrument into a frenzy of effort and reward. Finally, Pam's body collapsed in a fit of shivers, giving me the taste I desired and the opportunity to gather my bearings.

I slid the length of her nakedness, leaving a trail of love bites and kisses behind. I continued with her breast, two mounds of chocolate with inch-high treats, responding to being devoured. I nibbled each tip, bit, and tugged with my lips, thumbs, and forefingers.

She reached for me. Found my stiffness and guided me into her with just a lift of her hips.

A moan escaped us.

She sucked in a mouthful of air and released hot breath across my neck, firmly grabbed my rear and pulled me even deeper into her abyss, made us one. Our ecstasy was heard in our purrs, and roars, then in our whispers.

My body was soaring, a belly-ride on a fifty-foot wave of ocean. Our breathing was erratic or choppy, whichever leaves a person suffocating. I lifted into a push up and reeled off quick, long strokes. Her intensity was equal. Our passion in a tune as we wiggled and fought each other to a sweaty and pleasurable end.

When we'd been sated, I checked to make sure the rubber hadn't been lost before collapsing onto my back. We were both winded, me especially. I scrambled to the nightstand and lit a Newport.

Pam snatched it from my fingers after the first

drag and stubbed it in the ashtray. "What did I say about these things?" she scolded.

I was too tired to argue, so I laid back and rested, measured my heartbeats before I spoke. "It's not the cigarettes killing me. It's you. Whew, you put a brotha to work."

"No pain, no gain." She lifted to an elbow and leaned over me, staring.

"What?"

"Why didn't you return my pages earlier?"

Her question surprised me. I'd expected it earlier when she'd arrived all belly warmed. "My phone was in the car. You know I don't carry it around campus."

"Aren't there phones on campus?"

"Come on, Pam-"

"Oh, that's right. You don't want to be sidetracked, especially by me, right?"

"Not just you, but anybody."

She huffed then began twisting my dreads. Something was on her mind. "I think we should stop seeing each other," she blurted.

It was my turn to raise up, the speed at which I had made her flinch. "What?" I tried to sound under control but was certain my surprise lingered in my tone. "Stop seeing each other for what?"

She wet her lips and held the bedspread to her

breast. "Because, I think it'll be best before my graduation. This way, things will be less complicated before I leave for Atlanta."

I'd forgotten all about her returning home. I flopped back down and stared at the ceiling fan. "Back to Atlanta, huh?"

"Yes."

"Why break up at all?"

She laid as I did, stared where I was staring. Somehow, I minded her looking at my spot. She entwined her fingers with mine.

"You can come, too, you know?"

"Yeah, I know."

"Then come," she prodded.

"I can't do that."

"You keep saying that. Why not?"

I faced her then wished I hadn't. Her eyes were pleading. "I still have unfinished business here."

"Like what?"

"Things I can't talk about."

Pam tsked then turned her back to me. The two years we've been together, she's never been the beggar, the quiet treatment, disgusted looks-just examples of her typicalness.

Pam and I met during a Temple/West Virginia football game. It was Temple's home opener, a game that could've and did set the tone for the rest of the season, a game they'd lost.

Pam was a sophomore then. I was struggling to keep focused during a freshman year of torturous inconsistencies. Grades. Attendance. Things I'd struggled with during my high school days that I'd thought I'd overcome. It was Pam who'd pulled my coat to the disciplines of college life, the nots-and-whens-to-dos that decide a student's fate. I owe her much for helping me through my transition. I'll miss her when she's gone. Selfishness and all.

Later, Pam and I cuddled on the sofa with a large bowl of buttery popcorn, checking out the Wayans Brothers' flick, "Scary Movie 2." Her small frame was hidden beneath my oversized Owls T- shirt, and she was cracking up at stuff that wasn't even funny. I hate when she does that-force her laughter. I hate the way she flosses after every meal; her tiny, size four feet; her choice nail polish-red, a hooker's color-at least that's what Stacks says. I especially hate her for planning on leaving me behind to graduate into her corporate world of fashion-of all things. That's the jest of her plan-high design-whatever that field of work consists of. I was extremely bitter already, and her laughing annoyed me just enough to add to it. Her cackling made me assume she has little remorse about having to leave soon.

I'd nodded before the movie had ended, awakened this morning barely remembering Pam guiding me into the bedroom. I could swear I'd heard Pam crying in bed next to me last night, but this morning she was nowhere to be asked if that were true.

I showered and dressed. Dotted the "i" in my routine until I wound up parked in "my spot" on Diamond Street.

They were already there-like always-him in his chair, smiling, her at his side, waiting. It was bright, and I had my sun visor down. Today, I'd let nothing disturb my inspiration.

I sat and waited, too.

# CHAPTER 4

# WESLEY

Magic's the uncle of uncles, kind of a mentor to me, my confidant-oh, and my boss. I've been working at Magic's garage since I'd about-faced from the drug game, two years ago. We'd always been tight, even before I'd started working for him. Magic was in his closet-office, screaming at someone on the telephone. "You damn skippy. I needed it yesterday!" he barked. "The thing can't be fixed without it!"

The caller must've said something to piss Magic off, because his voice rose three octaves. "The whole damn thing fell apart! Use your gotdamn head!"

After a few more "damns," I realized that he was arguing about the Lincoln we'd worked on over the weekend. The same Lincoln still parked in the yard with a crippled transmission.

I wiped some sweat from my brow with the sleeve of my overalls and pulled the trigger on the solder gun. For the last half hour, I've been piecing together a fuel inject engine Magic and I had taken on as a project. I heard the phone slam to its cradle. Magic stormed into the garage, mouthing curses.

"That was about the Lincoln, wasn't it?"

He glowered while he snatched a Phillips screwdriver from his tool belt. "I could kick Willie's sorry ass. He know he s'pose' to had that daggone thing here yesterday."

I kept quiet, concentrated on the three wires that needed soldering. I'd been quiet throughout the afternoon-too quiet for Magic's fifty-four-year-old sensors. He pulled a white hankie from his pocket and wiped sweat from his George Jefferson hairline. Concern was in his soft, walnut eyes. 'What's on your mind, Wesley?" Magic's one of a few people who calls me Wesley.

"Can I ask you something?"

He gave me his don't-ask-me-no-stupid-question look.

"Can a person love and hate a woman at the same time?"

His bushy brows dipped into a frown. "What's goin' on wit' you and Pam?"

"Nothing. Same as ever."

He nodded. "Mm-hmm. I get it. You think I been suckin on these here fumes and can't see through the bullshit."

I smiled and wiped my hands on my overalls. It was hard to pull something over on Magic. He'd grown up running the streets just as I'd done. Game recognizes game.

The garage door was open. I saw the blue Chrysler before it drove across the rope alarm and the two dings grabbed Magic's attention. He left to service the customer and returned counting bills, stuffed a wad of them into his pocket. He smiled when he saw me watching. "Hell, Gloria don't know what we charge 'round here. Long as business up and runnin', my wife could care less. When she inherited the place from her dead ex, she tol' me so."

"Then why you looking all sneaky?"

"Boy, you not only a liar, but you nosy as hell, too. Never mind me. What you done did to that cute girlfriend of yours?"

"Why do I have to be the one who did something?"

"'Cause, you be you."

I told Magic what was troubling me. I explained about Pam returning to Atlanta after graduation, how I felt about it, and her wanting me to leave, too. Spilled it all in his lap while he nodded and rubbed battered hands over his potbelly. When I was through, he clasped his hands together, psychologist-like, and eyeballed me. "You know you fucked up in the head, right?"

"What did I do?"

He halted my protest with a raised hand. "No, no, no. Hold it. Here you are-doin' good never mind-and you still got dat drug dealer mentality." He scooted to the edge of his chair. "So, what your woman gettin ahead 'a you. She your woman. Your tum'a come 'round. If you asked me-which you did-l think you jealous."

"Jealous? Now I know you been sniffing fumes."

"Say what you want. You tryna keep dat girl down till you come up. I hope it ain't da case, but if it walk and quack like a duck-" He shrugged.

"I come to you for advice, and you talking about ducks. You getting old, Magic."

"Age ain't got nothin 'a do wit' it." He leaned back in his chair. "Let me tell you somethin, Wesley...I been there right where you sittin', thinkin' what my pappy had to say to me was bullshit, too. Now that I'm older, I can see how right a lota the things he said were true."

I let loose an exasperated gasp. "I'd asked for it," I mumbled to myself. Magic was probably right, though, just a little long winded. I just may be a little jealous, but Pam wanting to break up was extreme.

I left the shop as tight and unforgiving as the OJ glove. I punched the gas pedal as I drove 32nd Street north, puffing hard from my Newport on my way to Joe Frazier's gym. Like I'd said, I hadn't worked out in a while and was overdue to get back into some sort of shape.

I'm unsure if Joe Frazier's gym has officially been named a Philadelphia landmark, but in and around most of Philadelphia, that status had been achieved a long time ago.

I entered a near empty gym. The patter of speed bags and thumping on punch bags lifted my chest a bit. Each time I enter the gym without fail, my nostrils flare from the scent of testosterone. In opposite comers, two trainers were hollering instructions to shadowboxing fighters. Off to the right, a couple others molly-whopped heavy bags and skipped rope. In the center of the gym, a 20x25 foot ring, raised four feet high. I picked a spot that would obscure me from eyes during my workout. I dropped my gym bag at the front desk just as Clyde lifted his eyes from some papers. He broke into a crack toothed grin. "Well, well, well. If it ain't ol' Wes."

"Whassup to you, too, Clyde?"

"Mm-hmm. Where you been?"

"Busy."

"Still in school?"

"Yep."

He nodded his approval then snatched open a drawer and tossed me a key. "As long as you keepin' your part of the deal. Locker 12. You got forty-five minutes 'fore we close shop."

"Great." I rushed to change into my workout gear. Shorts and a tank top. I hit the speed bag first-fifteen minutes. Worked the heavy bag for twenty and skipped rope for ten-huffed and puffed throughout the entire workout. My throat and chest had been on fire, but I'd done it. I was bent over, sucking wind when Clyde flicked on and off the lights, indicating closing time in ten minutes.

After I toweled off and put on some sweats, I met up with Clyde at his desk. "Did you get it in?" he asked.

"Somewhat. I need about a month of straight training."

"Try two."

"I looked that bad, huh?"

He gave a disappointing nod. "Afraid so."

Clyde had been a drinking buddy of my dad's

before alcohol took my pop's life. I believe Clyde still drinks at the pace he did then, only now, he may drink for the purpose of joining his old friend.

"Here, take some 'a these." He handed me a pill bottle.

"Vitamins. They'll help wit' stamina."

I dropped the pills in my bag and gave back the locker key.

"Thanks."

On the way out, Clyde grabbed a handful of fliers and handed them to me. He locked up while I read. The fliers were promotion for a fund-raiser to be held at the gym. Sickle-cell awareness.

"Pass them out to your college friends. And leave those ghetto-ass brothers of yours home."

"You got tickets for me?" I asked.

"I might be able to squeeze a few floor seats for you."

"Then it's a deal."

"A deal?"

"You know what I'm saying."

"Yeah, I know. Anyway, Wes, I gotta get goin'-business."

"Yeah-business," I echoed, only my words were drenched with sorrow. We shared in daps before I headed to my car.

The night was warm. Painted against a black canvas was a bright moon accompanied by tiny white specks. I thought about calling Pam and asking her over for the night but ruled against it. Getting Pam to her peak takes time and effort, things I have little of left. I tightened the Eagles cap around my dreads and lit up a Newport, coughed through the first puffs, so I stubbed it even before reaching the Volvo.

The ride home had taken twenty minutes. I tossed my keys on the coffee table and walked straight to the bathroom, stripped on the way there. I could barely lift my arms to pull my sweatshirt over my head. I grimaced and thought about the soreness I knew would be there in the morning.

The hot shower felt good beating against my body. I let it run a little longer than usual, until I felt a sleepiness pulling my eyelids shut. After drying off, I applied some Polo lotion Pam had treated me to for Christmas. I crawled in bed naked and exhausted, was nearly asleep when I remembered something, stumbled to my gym bag, extracted the usual amount of my pay, and went to the closet-dug deep in the back among the many shoe boxes and pulled out the one I wanted. I put what I'd separated inside of it before stumbling back to bed.

# CHAPTER 5

## CAROL

Kevin, the twins, their cousins-Monica, and Arnold, was outside playing King Ball. From what I could hear, Kevin was the referee. His big mouth carried clear through the house and into the dining room, where us grownups argued just as loud over our Pinochle game. We were at James' parents' house. James and his father, Clarence, were in the living room, glued to a widescreen, roaring at the Eagles/Giants game. They were worst of us all. "Big Kids," Janice, James' mother, had commented earlier.

Janice and I were Pinochle partners. James' sister, Gloria, and her husband, Calvin, had taken the bid for seventy-five. "Do you have any meld?" Gloria asked Calvin.

"Fifteen."

"If that's it, then we're set."

"Good. That's just what your greedy behind get," Janice said. She was keeping score and snatched up the pen and pad.

While Gloria and Calvin exchanged hands, I shuffled my cards and shot a daggered stare across the room at James. If he'd a clue to how close, I'd come to packing up and leaving his smug ass, he wouldn't be so damn joyous. He was damn near inside the TV, laughing and giving his dad high fives.

I refilled Janice's glass with Colt 45.

"Thank you, Carol."

"You're welcome."

Janice shuffled the double-deck and passed them to Calvin to be cut.

He did with grossly large hands resembling cranes. Calvin was thuggish looking with a wide nose and beady eyes. He's also one of the sweetest men I know, an opposite of his wife. A real snob who treats him as if he were one of the children.

Gloria and I have had our fair share of fallouts, spats mostly. Overall, we're cordial, but I was certain that, behind my back, she dogged me out to anyone in an earshot. That's what she does, talks about everyone. She hadn't yet started her shit today, but my radar was beeping like crazy.

"Carol, can you get me another beer, hon?" James called.

"Huh-ell no!" Janice barked. 'You got hands and feet, get it yourself." She was always taking up for me, calls me the daughter she shouldn't have had because she couldn't fathom what I see in James.

"She can speak for herself," James retorted.

"Man, we playin' cards," Gloria added dismissing him.

"I'll get it," I answered.

Every Sunday, Gloria and James would find some reason to argue and mess up everybody's day. I wasn't about to be the reason they argued today.

I hurried around the wall into the kitchen, my blood percolating enough to make my hand tremble when I pulled the can of Heineken from the fridge. On the return trip, I shook the can like I was at a Vegas crap table, made certain I couldn't feel the moving around inside. I strutted past the card table, smiling like a Miss America finalist, smiled all the way to James, and even said, "Here you are, hon," before returning to my seat. Janice and Gloria's eyes were pools of fire.

"Where are we?" I asked, collecting my cards.

Gloria rolled her eyes and straightened her hand.

Janice sipped from her glass and glared over its

rim.

I kept my head down, my eyes on my cards and cleared my throat. I was about to send my meld to Janice when James hollered out. "Shit! Aw shit! Somebody give me a rag!"

Everyone's head snapped toward him, but nobody moved.

James was dancing around like a Cherokee, trying to capture beer suds with his mouth and hands. It was all down the front of his brand new warmup suit, and his chocolate face was drenched. He finally managed to calm the suds and turn a pissed stare at me.

The room was graveyard quiet. Even the football teams had taken a time out. Eyeballs rolled from James to me, then back to James.

I waited for the whistle heard during the Clint Eastwood westerns. Instead, Janice broke the silence with a long snicker that erupted into a gut-wrenching laughter, a contagious howl that enticed everyone else to start cracking up. Soon, we all had tears of laughter streaking down our cheeks, all but James. His blue-black face showed contempt. But for the life of me, I couldn't stop laughing. Didn't even try. All Clarence could muster was, "Get me a beer. Ha! I guess she showed you." The rest of the card game went uninterrupted.

Later, I was helping Janice with the dishes. She

was washing. I was drying and putting away. We were discussing men. "-don't think it doesn't get worse," Janice was saying. "One day you look up and find yourself still stuck in the same place you've been your entire life. And do they appreciate you not leaving their sorry asses? No…" She just kept going, yadda, yadda, yadda. Finally, I was tired of her rambling and cut her off. "I think James is cheating on me."

She stopped her washing, but kept her pudgy arms dangling in the soapy water. Her jaw dropped open, and for a second, she only stared. I'd surprised her.

"Don't tell me that, Carol."

"Why not?"

"Because, chile…the one thing I'm sure about is, James loves you and those children."

"That doesn't mean he won't cheat."

"Honey. James loves you."

"The signs are all there."

She tsked then resumed washing. 'What kinda signs?"

I told Janice about James' dusk to dawn trips to the store, his recent erratic behavior, the extra showers, the shortage of money. I confided in her all except for him raping me. I'm still unsure if that's what to call it, if such a thing could exist when you live, sleep, and breed with a common law husband-which in Pennsylvania is seven years of coupling.

With every example I'd given about James' possible infidelity, Janice's usually bright, brown eyes became dark and saddened. She wiped her hands on a dishtowel and grabbed me by the shoulders, squared her eyes with mine. "Carol, you're like a daughter to me. If that no good…if he…Ooohh, chile, I swear—" she gathered her words. "Carol, you are too good a woman to let some man-my son or not—run all over you. Sometimes you have to do what's best for you and you only." She paused. "Honey, I know you love them kids and want their daddy around, but if you think his lying ass is cheating, then pack his shit. Put 'em the hell out."

My eyes dropped from hers. "I don't wanna do that."

"Girl, you better make a stand. As long as he know you gonna put up with his shit, a dog gonna be a dog."

"A minute ago, you were telling me how much he loves me." "Carol, be for real. What's love got to do with this? This is lust we're talking about. You don't have to kick him out forever, just until he realizes his stupidity, and that won't be long, dumb as his ass is."

We laughed.

"I'm not even sure if he's cheating."

She sandwiched my hand between her meaty

paws and smiled. "Then do it for everything he's done to me."

I rolled my eyes and laughed, hugged her for showing me so much love over the years, then cried on her shoulder.

We were heading home. James was pushing the minivan through the city streets like he was catering to a crazed plan of suicide. I'd already asked him to slow down—twice. Two times too many, considering the children were in the back seats. James was still fuming over the beer thing I'd pulled. Kia was upset with me, too. Her tiny lips were poked all out because she'd wanted to stay the night with her Grandmom, even though it was a school night. She knew better, and her attitude was starting to sit under my skin. "Kia, you can sit there and mope all you want. You're taking your behind to school tomorrow."

"Grandmom would'a took me to school," she reasoned.

I ignored her while my body tilted during a quick right turn. The van straightened, and so did my body. If I didn't think James would crash, I'd slap the shit out of him. The children didn't seem to mind the wild ride. Kevin and Kelly barely took their eyes from the scenery. They'd been quiet throughout. "Kevin, is your homework done for tomorrow?" I asked.

"Yes."

"I mean all of it. You had the weekend to do it."

"Yes." He never turned from the window. Something was on his mind.

I let it go at that. I wasn't about to take my frustration out on the children, when I knew James was the source. I clicked on the radio, hoping that the music would ease my frustration. I was wrong. Not even the smooth tunes of Carl Thomas could crack the icy barrier between me and James.

At the mouth of the ramp in front of our block, James helped me unload Kevin's chair, the twins, then climbed back behind the wheel. I looked at him like he'd lost his mind. "Where you going?" I asked.

"I'll be back in a minute."

"Uh-uh, no you don't." I sent the children up to the house. "I wanna talk to your dad," I'd told them. When they were gone, I turned to James, folded my arms across my body and stared.

"What?" He had the nerve to ask-and with all sincerity.

"How you gonna just drop us off and go?"

He stroked a palm across his wavy hair and licked his lips, something he'd mastered to try and sweet talk my favors. "Come on, Carol, I been chillin' with those kids all day. It's my time."

"So have I."

"That's different."

"How?"

"'Cause, you don't go nowhere anyway."

"That's because I take care of my responsibilities."

"And I guess I don't?"

"Not lately."

He looked down the vacant street at nothing and puckered his lips. He turned back to me and took a breath like he was tired of my shit. "Look, I don't wanna argue."

"Then come in the house."

"I told you I got something I gotta take care of."

"Like what?"

"I told somebody I'd help him tear down a banister and put up some doors."

"At night? You think I'm stupid or something?"

"Oh, you think it gotta be daytime to fix shit?"

I weighed James' bullshit story and decided that his mother was right. I am too good a woman to have to put up with his shit. I turned and stomped away without another word, half expecting him to stay because of my seriousness. Before I made it to the house, the bastard sped off.

Getting the twins to bed had been easy. Kelly had

passed straight out. And Kia-I don't think Kia wants to see my face unless I can offer her Disney World tickets. She's funny like that-has an "on and off" personality that keeps you guessing whether she suffers from some kind of birth disorder. At age seven, she could lockjaw grudge like a starving pit bull.

I was on my way to bathe when I heard beat box noises and rapping coming from Kevin's room. I knocked thrice before opening the door, had to push really hard to dislodge what I discovered was a mountain of Kevin's clothing, against the base of the door.

Kevin's room was a wreck. I wondered if the whole family's gone mad. Kevin having a junky room certainly wasn't unusual, but even Theo, from the "Cosby Show," would be ashamed of him right now.

Every dresser drawer sat wide open and emptied, contents strewn across the floor. The open-closet's hangers were all bare. I was certain those items were also being used as carpeting. Kevin was across the room, bare chested in his chair. He was topped with a Kangal and wearing dark shades. He also had on matching leather gloves.

"Boy, what the hell did you do to this room? And who you supposed to be?"

He crossed his arms, B-boy style and smirked. "L. L."

"L.L., huh?" I had to laugh. He looked too silly for me not to. I surveyed some of the posters on his walls. Jordan. Iverson. Destiny's Child. Biggie. Tupac. Malcolm. Jesse. The latter two I'd hung up, I didn't think he should limit his inspirations to musicians and athletes. I kicked through the piles and sat on the bed. "I'm not cleaning this up," I informed him.

He nodded, pulled off his gloves, the shades, and dropped them into the Kango, tossed the hat on the floor with everything else.

"Mom, I wanna move."

"Move where?"

"I don't care. Anywhere."

To move anywhere meant something was wrong. His long face verified it. "Is somebody picking on you?"

"NO."

"Then why would you just want to up and move?"

"To get out the projects…and away. Never mind."

"No, go ahead and finish. Away from what?"

"Away from him."

"Who?"

"James."

I looked at my son as if I'd missed something. I thought the two got along fine. "Did yall have a fight about something?"

He put on his tough guy face and swelled up. "He ain't do nothing to me."

"Then tell me what's wrong."

He wouldn't look at me, just at the mess he'd created on the floor. "He playin' you, Mom."

Bits and pieces are how Kevin was feeding my curiosity. I wanted it all. Now. "I wish you'd tell me what you're talking about."

Kevin broke his face up like he was about to cry. His eyes revealed confusion as he continued. "Ms. Wanda son, Jay, told me how James be over his aunt house all night and stuff."

"What stuff?"

"I don't know." He shrugged.

"That ain't enough?"

For a normal person it would be enough to confirm their suspicions, but somehow, I needed more. I needed the smoking gun, DNA, and a videotape to get a conviction. I searched my soul for the strength to face my 12-year-old son for answers. He seemed to be the one with the common sense, because with me, it didn't seem as if common sense was all that common. "Is that all this…Jay said?" I pried.

"Yeah."

"What did he say his aunt's name is?"

"I didn't ask."

"Then how do you expect me to check out his story?"

"Ask James then fire his butt."

"Fire him?" I joked. Although I was smiling, my heart felt as heavy as brick. I wasn't about to let Kevin glimpse my pain. "Well, do me a favor, sweetheart."

He nodded.

"When your friend comes around you again, ask him his aunt's name, address, and phone number, okay?" I stood and waddled back through the ocean of clothing. At the door, I turned back to him. "I told you before that everything was okay, didn't I?"

Again, he nodded.

"When ifs not, believe me, you'll know." I looked at the mess. "Maybe then, you'll do a better job packing?"

Kevin smiled.

I walked to my bedroom, lightheaded, smothered my face in the pillow and screamed as loud as my lungs would allow, over and over. I screamed until the hatred and frustration stored inside of me lessened and my puffy eyes were all cried out. I've never cried so much in my life during a week span. Lately, my emotions have been raw, made me wonder if the night James had boggarted me could have possibly left me pregnant. I quickly ruled out that possibility in favor of being plain-old, unhappy. There had been other men in my past whom I've cared deeply for, Kevin's biological father being the most notable.

His name was Langston Burgess, a Capricorn-the same zodiac as me. We'd known each other since grade school, before James became his so-called best friend during the six grade. Langston had been tall and lanky, with warm brown eyes, bronze skin, and curly hair. His smile had been broad and bright, and he used to be able to make me laugh until I peed myself—literally, one reason I loved him so much. Another was because he had never looked down on me for being a fostered child. I loved him enough to give up my virginity to him in his grandmother's basement one Sunday morning while she was in church. That Sunday morning, I couldn't have been happier to cross the threshold of womanhood. That Sunday, the next Sunday, and every Sunday of that summer, Langston made me feel like a woman. I was only thirteen then, but I remembered it as if it had occurred just yesterday.

The day Langston had died in a car crash on 1-95, my insides had exploded into a million pieces. I had cried much like I did tonight, only harder, and not for a half hour, but for a week. I couldn't eat a bite then, had felt faint, vomited, then had cried some more when I found out that depression wasn't the cause of my illness-my pregnancy was. Strange as it seemed, shortly after realizing that I was carrying Langston's child, my depression ended. I'd found relief in keeping a part of Langston alive, preserving his spirit in my child and in my heart.

I was four months into my pregnancy when James had entered the picture. He'd been the stone I'd needed to get past my foster parents' verbal assaults. It was because of James' kindness and comfort that I was able to overcome, my grief and ease the suffering that had plagued me. By the time Kevin arrived, James had succeeded in making the two of them my main priorities—and priorities they were, up until the twins arrived seven years ago. Since then, our relationship hasn't been the same.

I picked myself up from my bed and trudge to my sanctuary, mixed truly little cold water to my bath and dumped damn near the entire bottle of moisturizing crystals into it. I turned the bathroom radio to jazz, WJJZ, and clicked off the light, eased into my darkened bath to escape this world. So damn hot was the water—so damn hot. I clinched my teeth to counter the stinging of my skin being scalded.

Besides the slit of light at the door's bottom and the smooth sound of Boney James, nothing invaded my peace. I sank deeper into my bath, allowed the water to touch the tip of my chin when I rested my head back. I leveled my breaths and encouraged my fingers to trace the crease between my breast and wander to my manicured bush. Toys were the tangled hairs my fingers had wandered to. So damn hot was my bath. So damn hot.

My mind was elsewhere as my fingers drew circles around my abdomen, not on James, the kids, or Langston. I was in a dwelling of my own, a place where I was needed, wanted, not abused, or taken for granted. "Why is life so hard?" I asked myself, as I wiped a bit of sweat from my brow and allowed my hand to return to its resting place, inched my fingers a bit further down. I allowed my bath to send me to a grander place where all that matters is me.

I felt myself stir.

The singe from my bath had begun creeping into overdue places and creating in me a new burning sensation. So hot was it that I shuddered from its pleasurable heat. I didn't register why my body was trembling, but it was.

I became lost in my world. I was alone in a canyon of sandy rocks and rivers. I shivered again, this one lasting longer than the others, sending me plunging deeper into the canyon. I heard echoes from my muffled screams, heard myself moan—not once but many times. Again, and again. I reached for that boulder of strength I thought would pull me over a cliff, only to find the boulder soft and pleasurable. I pinched a nipple's worth of earth, tested it, found it formidable to my world. Suddenly, my body arched and my insides poured out into my bath. I had to fight against swears to not let my world end. Slowly, very slowly, I returned to the singe of my "real" world. My bath had suddenly become cold, and the remains of my frustration had passed.

My bed rocked at 2:47a.m. when James eased in behind me. I surprised myself by not wondering where he'd been. I thought I already knew. That assumption made it easier to understand what was happening between us, as well as fuel my anger. But I saw no point in wasting energy on an argument that would be stapled by lies.

I wanted proof.

When James' arm fell onto my hip, I stiffened to the core. I'd already decided, in a partisan way, that if he tries anything this morning, I'd have a trick for his ass. Not only will the children be awakened by my Banshee cry, but our neighbors, too, only they'd be wakened by the ambulances' sirens, because I was amped up to cut his ass if he touched me. I let my arm rest over the side of the bed where I'd hidden the kitchen knife. I closed my eyes and held my breath until I was sure James had passed out.

Morning arrived without incident. I had to force James out of bed so that he'd make it to work on time. Needless to say, he bitched the entire time. I didn't care, though. Never bothered me a bit. I only knew that he was taking his adulterous ass somewhere today. I was sick of his shit and walked the house with the kitchen knife on my hip to prove it.

James left without me having to get too indignant. For the life of me, I couldn't understand what had happened to the man I'd grown to love during the past eight years. His bitterness and insensitivity had me completely thrown for a loop.

At seven, I woke up Kevin then went for the twins. Kia wasn't in bed. I found her downstairs, asleep on the sofa. She was outfitted in a play of colors. Her attire caused me to wonder if some Puerto Rican spirit invades her body during the night, and forces my baby to wear these outfits I'd find her in.

After the four of us smashed a box of Fruit Loops, I pulled the twins' hair into ponytails, and dressed them in cute, beige button-down short sets, smeared baby oil on their chocolate faces. Kelly sneezed and coughed the entire time. I hoped it wasn't the start of a household epidemic. The last one had been a tri case of chicken pox that had me war-painting the kids with a pink medicated lotion that Janice had given me.

I dropped the girls off and hustled Kevin to the van stop.

"You ready for school today?"

"I wanna stay home with you."

"That's not gonna happen, sweetheart, unless the van doesn't show up today."

"Oh, it's coming."

I smiled. He was right. The van always shows up. Rain, sleet, or snow. "I thought you liked going to school?"

"I do sometimes. I don't like some 'a the teachers."

"What's wrong with the teachers?"

"They always touching on me, tryna help me with stupid stuff like puzzles and drawings, stuff that don't got nothing to do with me not walking."

"Baby, they just want to help."

"Uh-uh. They be talking to me like I'm slow or something."

"Did you ask them not to?"

"No."

"Why not?"

"'Cause, I ain't crazy. Then I'll get harder homework."

"You ain't nothing but a scammer. Wait til' I talk to your teachers."

"Aw, Mom!"

"Aw, Mom nothing. You got those people thinking you stupid."

"Uh-uh," he cried. I pass everything they give me."

"So, what."

"See…that's why I don't like telling you nothing." He poked his lips out.

I playfully popped him upside the head. "Fix your face, boy."

He ducked into a shell. "Okay, dag. Why you always doing that?"

"I'm getting you back for kicking me for nine months."

A pack of schoolgirls walked by. One waved and smiled to Kevin. He shyly waved back before cutting his eyes to see if I'd seen him.

"Yeah, I saw you," I teased. I smiled and said, "You go boy!" Although I believe Kevin's too young for girls, I felt a surge of pride knowing that he's at least interested. It proves that he's becoming more settled with his misfortune and not dwelling on it.

Pedestrian traffic was light on Ridge Avenue, just the way I like it. The morning sky was a dark, bluish gray, as if it would pour down raining at any minute. With a five-block walk back to the house, I hurried my shopping.

I stopped first at a fish store to pick up seven silver trout. I had the grocer debone them while I watched. A few blocks down, I wound up spending more than I wanted on a pair of skirts for the twins. I even splurged and bought Kevin a pair of Iverson sneakers. A while back, he'd bugged me about them. I promised him that when the price fell from $80 to around $45, he'd get a pair. So, I was feeling good about keeping my word to Kevin when I made it back home just before the rain began to fall. I was cooking dinner when Tonya called. "Hey, girl."

"You musta been out this morning when I called." She sounded depressed.

I situated myself in the kitchen. I knew it would be a long talk.

"Is everything okay?" I asked.

"Not hardly."

"Man troubles?"

"What else? I just got back from New York. Chile, let me tell you what this cheap ass man did."

"Who do you know in New York?"

"Some guy I met at the dub-And before you start trippin', no I wasn't by myself."

"Mm-hm."

"I wasn't," she said defensively. "Missy was with me. I only went because he was her man's friend."

"Whatever. I ain't hatin'." I filled a frying pan with Crisco and began drenching the silver trout in cornmeal. "What was the guy's name?"

"Basil."

"A Muslim?"

"No."

"Was he cute?"

"He was alright, I guess. Too short to be permanent, and like I said, too cheap to dip the puddin'."

"You probably gave him some."

"Uh-uh, honey. This man was cheap—and you know it don't take much to please me-a little wine and dine. After that, a dance and a fat-ass spliff will do just fine."

She wasn't lying either. Tonya has what I've been told is a white liver, meaning she loves to have sex, needs it in a bad way. 'What did he do, take you to McDonalds?"

"Ha! I wish. He fed us school lunches and hugs."

I started laughing.

"Carol, he had a whole box of 'em at his house."

"No, he didn't."

"I tell you no lie."

"Did you eat?" I asked as I eased three pieces of fish into the frying pan.

"You damn right, ho gotta eat."

"Tonya, that's bad."

"Was I supposed to starve?"

"Mm…better you than me."

I listened as Tonya broke down her date from hell. I wondered why she puts herself through it. She could've been married not once, but twice. I can only assume that it was the white liver thing that prevents her from committing to one man.

We spoke for another hour while we watched Young & Restless. Before hanging up, she reminded me that tomorrow she'd have the $50.00 she'd borrowed from me.

The rain had stopped, and the sun was hidden behind a paucity of glowing clouds. It was muggy out. That "after-it-rain" moistness combined with high humidity, a slight breeze tugged some heat from my skin as I click-docked, in my favorite clogs, to pick up the children from school.

Kelly was first to emerge from the exit. She looked disheveled, tilted, as if her book bag needed to be rolled. She let loose a fit of coughs. "Hi, Mommy." She sounded pitiful.

"Hey, boo. You feeling okay?"

She shook her head and leaned into my body.

I stroked her head. "What's wrong?"

"I can't breathe."

"Did you go to the nurse?"

"No."

I touched her forehead with a backhand. She was burning up.

I scanned the mass of schoolchildren for Kia so that we could hurry home.

Kia came through the doors and skipped over to us. I was relieved she wasn't ill, too. One sick child was enough. We were a half a block away from the van stop when Kia asked, "Mommy, who that Kevin talkin' to."

I had to scan the area to find out. He wasn't where we'd normally meet. He was across the street. An alarm clicked on in my head. "I don't know who that is, sweety," I answered while quickening my pace. So not to alarm the twins, I tried to remain calm. Inside, I heard myself screaming Kevin's name. My wooden clogs click-docked across the sidewalk with a growing purpose. I had gone deaf, capable only of focusing on the man standing next to my son at a spot where my son wasn't supposed to be. My mind unfiled all sorts of scenarios that could possibly justify the two of them together. Only the evilest of the files lay open, lumped on my brain, pushing my legs to higher speeds. "Mommy, what's the matter," I thought I heard behind me. I hadn't realized it, but I'd been dragging Kelly by the hand. Kelly's cheeks bounced with every step that closed the distance between us, the man, and my son. The closer we got, the more I recalled the man's face. I grabbed the back of Kevin's chair when we'd reached them and collected my breath. "Can I help you with something?" I asked.

Nervousness covered the man's face.

# CHAPTER 6

# WESLEY

Monday afternoons were always busy at the garage. Magic was running around like a headless chicken, earning every penny he'd ever tilted from the business. All kinds of whips were stopping in for service. Benzes. Caddies. Maxima's. It was like someone had run around breaking shit all weekend. It was that busy. I was pleased when closing time snuck up on me like a bus station con man.

I pulled the garage gates, checked the rear door and windows, then left. I had just started the car and lit a smoke when my thoughts drifted back to my earlier encounter with Carol.

I'd sat and watched from my spot. Kevin had

been alone; the first time I can recall that occurring. Usually, Carol would be there when the van arrives, but this afternoon, things didn't go down that way. Even Kevin's smile had been absent. He'd looked vulnerable, sitting there unaccompanied, made me shift uncomfortably and stop blowing Os into the windshield. I'd flipped down the sun visor and studied my image in its mirror, tried to dissect my soul for a hint of whom I used to be. My heart wasn't capable of deceiving my essence. I knew that the healing of a soul could take a lifetime, so many memories I was running from, skeletons with their own skeletons in closets.

I slapped the visor up and dragged from my cancer stick, looked on as Kevin wheeled his chair to the curb. His head went from the curb to Last Chance Groceries, located at the farthest comer. Although afternoon traffic flowed moderately, trepidation guided my hand to the door handle just in case. I crushed my smoke in the ashtray, cracked open the car door, and sat with one foot dangling into the street, watching.

The curb was a foot high. Kevin eased the front wheels of the chair into the street, made it appear as if he were doing a reverse wheelie. Another two pushes and the chair leveled into the street. I reexamined why I sat and watched him struggle to cross the street, then remembered how safe it feels to steal hope from afar and not have to share my emotions or risk the let downs others endure when grasping for inspiration.

Kevin peeked east then west for cars. The streetlight was green. Where Kevin waited, the street was sloping, causing the chair to roll backward and him to push forward as if he were about to drag race and when the light changed to red, he wheeled to the other side and out of my view. I stepped from the Volvo, anticipating his emergence from behind some cars. I stretched my neck to its limit, trying to see if he'd run into trouble. I moved in closer and closer. Then I saw him. He was trying to pop a wheelie onto a curb that was at least half a foot higher than the one he'd entered the street from. He was going at it hard, spinning the chair in every direction. Frustration covered his young face.

"Need some help?" I asked.

His face had been beaten to determination. "I can do it."

I watched and waited for him to tire. "You sure you don't need a hand?"

"No."

"No, you're not sure, or no you don't need a hand?"

"I can do it."

I surveyed a group of schoolchildren passing by. They eyed me like I was making the boy go at it alone.

He'd gotten the front wheels onto the sidewalk and rested like he was in a recliner.

I quickly stepped to the chair, before he could protest, and pushed the back wheels onto the pavement.

"Hey!" he cried. He spun the chair around expertly and scowled.

"I coulda did it."

"I know, but I was there, so…"

He looked the chair's wheels over. "I would'a made it, you know. Thanks anyway, sir."

"You're welcome." I turned to leave then stopped. "Do I look that old?" I asked, smiling.

"Huh?"

"You called me, 'sir'. Do I look that old?"

He shook his head. "My mom say I should call guys over twenty-one, sir."

I twisted one of my dreads and smiled. "How old are you?" I asked, already knowing his age, birthday, and home address. "Twelve."

"I guess you have a while before you start getting called sir, huh?" His eyes were flirting with the math.

"I got twelve years to go."

"Eleven."

"No, twelve. My birthday is in December."

"Okay, Mr. Mathematician, I feel you."

A few cars passed by. An old woman pulling a

shopping cart gripped her purse on the way by. I waved at her sceptic stare. "Where you headed, shorty?"

He pointed to Last Chance Groceries and its four cement steps.

"You going to make it up those stairs okay?"

He touched his chin like he hadn't considered it.

"I could run in for you, if you need me to?"

He thought about it before nodding. A frown covered his face.

I got the impression that he didn't like to be waited on. "Whassup with the long face?"

He shook his head and handed me a dollar. "I'd like a Welch's grape soda or an orange Franks."

"Anything else?"

"No, thank you."

Before I could turn to leave, she was there, panting like she'd sprinted a 400-relay-and so were the twins. Her cropped hair was matted against her forehead and the soft, hazel eyes I'd enjoyed from a distance, were fiery pits. When she spoke, I'd lost concept of the English language. I froze, wanted to haul-ass. Instead, I fumbled through my memory while her lips moved in a mute, slow motion. While I read them, sound returned. "Can I help you with something?"

I stumbled through a response. "I'm…uh…seeing that…uh…shorty is okay."

"We're fine," she spat then spun the chair in the opposite direction.

"Wait, Mom!" Kevin hollered.

She stopped. "What?"

"He got my dollar."

I looked down at the crumbled bill in my hand then at the what- the-hell-you-doing-with-my-son's-money look on Carol's face. I raised my hands in protest. "Whoa! Hold up! I was going to run in the store for him."

She held out her hand.

When I handed her the buck, her eyes narrowed. "Didn't I see you here last week?"

I shrugged. "Probably. I live around here." A twin was glued to her side. The child gave me a blank stare before reeling off several wicked coughs. "Is she all right?"

"She'll be fine."

We stood studying the other's face for an awkward few seconds. If I didn't break from her spell, I knew I'd regret it later. "Are you going to get the soda for him?"

A cop car whizzed by with its siren screaming. We ail watched until it was out of sight, then they all focused on me.

"Mom, you gonna get the soda for me?" Kevin

asked.

"I want one, too," the healthy twin demanded. Carol's hesitance to leave her children outside was obvious.

"I can help you lift the chair up the steps," I offered.

"You're mighty helpful, aren't you?"

"Not usually."

We were at the glass display case at the store's rear, where tiny, price tags protruded from meat samples. Carol was just looking. A plastic basket hung from the crook of her arm like a purse. In it, Children's Tylenol, a dozen eggs, milk, orange juice and Dove soap.

The sick twin was still glued around her mother's legs while the other made racing noises while wheeling Kevin up and down the aisles. Carol had to almost shove her daughter away to take a step. "You sure she'll be all right? She looks like she's about to faint."

"I'm sure. Won't you, boo?"

The child gave a feeble nod.

Although I secretly knew Carol's name, I asked anyway.

"Why do you want to know my name?"

"It's not like we're strangers anymore."

"Oh, we're still strangers," she said pointedly. "Come on, boo, Mommy's all done." She turned and walked away.

The child peered up at what must've been dejection on my face. "Her name Carol," she squeaked.

Carol stopped and eyed her daughter, strolled by a sale on wheat bread and canned pineapples.

I smiled appreciatively and tagged behind.

Kevin and his sister had beat us to the front counter. Both had sodas in their hands, Kevin, his Welch's grape, his sister, a Pepsi. I took the basket from Carol's arm and began unloading it. Her staring at my dreads made me nervous. I tipped over the carton of orange juice.

"Butterfingers," Kevin said.

"My fingers are bad from boxing."

Kevin tsked. "You can't box."

"How do you know what I can do?"

"Where you train at?"

"Joe Frazier's. Why? You like boxing?"

"Not more than basketball."

"All yall guys think about is sports," Carol jumped in.

"I think about other things, too."

She looked at me with a "yeah right" face. "Like what, women?"

"Yeah, well, women too, but mostly school, my future—some other things, too." My voice trailed off on the "other things." I wasn't about to go into depth about what they were.

"You ain't in school," the healthy twin challenged.

"I sure am."

"Where?"

Carol's eyes were speed reading my face.

"Temple. I'm in college."

Carol rolled her eyes in that excuse-the-fuck-outta-me way. She collected her change, and we headed for the door. Trying to be the gentleman, I took the bag from her hand. She surprised me with a smile. I thought she'd put up a fuss.

"So, how long you been a college man?" Carol asked.

"Two years. I'm a Junior."

"I never had a college guy carry my bags before."

We both smiled. Hers was soft and inviting. I put the bag—well, Kevin took the bag and sat it on his lap while Carol and I lifted him in the chair down the stairs. Although she was petite, she maneuvered the chair easily, and now that the sun had emerged from behind the rain clouds, her caramel skin seemed like it would melt into a puddle of sweetness. I picked the bag up from Kevin's lap while Carol pushed the chair.

"You ever knock somebody out?" Kevin asked.

"I don't fight in the ring."

"See, I knew you wasn't a boxer."

"I never said I was. I said I box, train, you know—like workout."

Kevin flagged me. "Aw, man, that's not boxing."

"Sure, it is. Most of boxing is training." I thought about the charity event coming up. "You can come see for yourself if you want. Joe Frazier's gym is having a charity thing, if you wanna come check it out?"

He turned to Carol. "Ooh, can I go, Mom."

"No." Carol's answer was automatic. She spoke to him while eyeing me. "I know you don't think I'ma let you go somewhere with a stranger?"

"I thought we were past that?"

"Ha! No, you didn't," she trilled.

"Okay, then bring the whole family. Your husband…"

"Not married," she cut in.

"Well, your boyfriend."

"What makes you think I have a boyfriend?"

I ravished her with a stare from her open-toe dogs to her shiny hair. "I'd be a fool to think otherwise."

She looked me up and down. "Well, I'll think about letting Kevin come, but the twins don't like that kind of stuff."

We were crossing the street that leads into the

projects, directly into the row homes. Schoolchildren lingered around with notebooks and book bags, letting loose pinned up energy with screams and sprints. In a small, parking area, a group of boys was playing karate. The healthy twin joined in what children do and chased after five or so pigeons.

"Kia, get your behind back here," Carol called to her. "They got this thing for birds," she said, for my benefit I guess, so that I'd not think her children were crazy.

Kia walked backward to us, continued to shoo the birds.

"And what's her name?" I asked, pointing to the sick twin.

"Kelly. And this peanut head is Kevin." She popped Kevin upside the head, as usual.

"Ow!" he hollered.

I'd walked Carol and her children to the mouth of the projects and slipped her my digits just in case she changed her mind about the charity event. I wouldn't have mind escorting her the entire way home but she made it clear that she was having none of that.

My inviting Carol to the charity event had slipped out quicker than I could pull it back. Now I'll have to call Clyde and make sure he'll have seats for me. She'd said she'd think about bringing Kevin, but not the twins. My hope is that she'd show up—then, reality hit like an angry linebacker.

A long-term relationship between us would be impossible. Too much drama already tainted us, and Kevin my muse, was at the center of it all. I had to check myself for allowing Carol's friendliness to draw me into false hopes. But it was too late. I was hooked, needing to grasp onto her differently than before. Now that we'd finally met, that I've brushed against her, savored her scent, and had experienced the glint of her eyes. Reality could go to hell for all I care. Something would have to be done to change our fate.

I pulled the Volvo up in front of my home and noticed my neighbor had painted her door a bright red, bright enough to ruin the retina. I live in a two-story home in the Strawberry Mansion section of the city, across the street from a nest home. There are forty-two homes on the street, nine of them abandoned, four smoke houses, and two speakeasies. It was the kind of block where anything could occur-good or bad.

I had an hour to shower, dress, and be ready for Pam when she arrives to be taken to dinner. She'd been raving about a new Jamaican restaurant's grand opening on South Street.

At a quarter past eight, Pam arrived, late as usual and a wee- bit tipsy. She was high-fashioned in an above-the-knee, hip hugging maroon skirt and a matching button-down blouse with black lace sleeves. She kicked off three-inch, open-toe pumps as soon as she entered the living room. Her calves were powerful, accentuating stunning legs. Her legs had been what attracted me to her first, and she never needing to wear stockings was a bonus. She headed straight to the kitchen.

"There's no food in the place," I called to her.

The refrigerator opened.

"I'm not looking for food. Don't you have some wine or something?"

"Nope. We drank it."

The fridge closed.

"How do you entertain your lady friends?" She was back in the living room, flopped down on the sofa next to me.

"I know you joking, right?"

She rolled her eyes and crossed her legs. "Should I be?"

Yep. She was definitely tipsy. I reached on the coffee table for my smokes, but she got to the pack before me.

"Nope. You don't need to smoke."

"Why you trippin'?"

She gave me a drunken giggle and hid them behind her back.

"You want 'em, come and get 'em," she teased.

Her brown eyes were luring. Her deep chocolate lipstick made me crave for a sweet treat. I leaned in and pecked her lips, smelled the rum on her breath. "If you wanna make the restaurant, then you better straighten up."

She tsked, poked her bottom lip out and frowned.

"The opening was cancelled."

My eyebrows dipped. "Then why didn't you call and say something?"

"Because."

"Because what?"

"I figured we'd go somewhere else."

"Like where?"

She scooted across the sofa and squeezed the crotch of my pants. "Like heaven," she cooed then attacked me with an assault of sloppy kisses.

At first, I thought about pushing her away, sprinting from the sofa and locking myself in the bathroom. She was that rough. "Whoa, slow down," I managed to muster.

Her kissing ceased, but she was still moaning and grinding against me. She pushed me onto my back, and I felt her slim fingers unbuttoning my shirt then squeeze my nipples. A jolt of pleasure, mixed with a tinge of pain, shot through me. She maneuvered herself to where she could straddle me, had my head pinned against the sofa's arm. Her eyes never left mine while she undid her blouse and exposed her small firm mounds. I tried to read her mind, wondered if I should be afraid of the passion her eyes showed or her aggressiveness. Our lovemaking has always been give and receive, but now, the rules seem to have changed. Pam was almost wicked with her foreplay.

We were both topless. Her small breast bounced as she humped atop of me, our eyes were still locked. I reached down to remove my slacks, but she grabbed my wrist.

"No. Leave 'em." Seriousness covered her face.

I didn't argue, just obeyed. It was here I realized she had a plan.

We kissed. Grinded. Kissed some more. Grinded some more. Her moans were loud and arousing. At one point, her eyes rolled into her head to reveal white slits. If not for my own pleasure, I would've deemed her possessed, but for the waves of ecstasy that had captured my being, I'd have to certify myself along with her.

Slow and hard she humped. As slow and deliberate as a belly-dance meant to please us both. I was nearing that magical moment where I'd lose all sense of my surrounding. "Ooohh, oooh, baby," she was moaning. I tried to piece together just what I'd done to please her. She was doing all the work. I curled my toes and pushed my pelvis up as hard as I could, mashed so hard I thought I'd break my bone.

Then I was there.

Only for a second did I give thought to my slacks being on. At this point, I didn't care. I welcomed the flow of warm fluid to escape. Gradually, our bodies slowed, and our breathing eased to smooth rhythms. Pam collapsed onto my chest and laid there, lightly tracing her nails against my skin and rubbing her face against me. I felt her heart beating and understood each beat. They told of her aggression, her intensity, and her tenderness. It was almost time for her to leave me, to return back to Atlanta. She'd miss me, her heartbeat declared.

I closed my eyes and held onto her tightly, only it wasn't Pam's image on my mind.

It was Carol's.

# CHAPTER 7

# WESLEY

All day I've been lounging around the apartment, spent three much needed hours with my head buried in my Business Applications text, preparing for a pop quiz my professor had been hinting around. I needed more hours of studying, but math, especially weird word problems about double-decline methods and depreciations, makes it really easy to welcome any distractions.

I was in sweats and had my lips around a Newport when the phone rang. I let the answering machine earn its keep. It was Stacks wanting me to go clubbing. I could hear Benny's silly ass in the background, hollering about how much poo-tang we were going to pick up because Ben Diggity would be in the hizouse. "Get back with me before nine, 'cause we gonna be Audi," Starks's message concluded.

We were tight, my brothers and I. Stacks' pop was the only parent of any of ours who was still alive, but he was serving forty to life for a string of armed robberies that had stretched through six counties. He would be around forty-eight now, with thirty-three years of jailing to do. Looking out for one another is, what's kept us tight.

I dragged from my smoke and remembered the father Benny and I had shared. He'd been a drunk, died of cirrhosis of the liver, the doctors had explained to my mother the night we'd camped in the emergency room lobby. I was just seven then but remember it well.

I still remember my mother leaving her own sickbed to be by his side. That's just the kind of woman she was before a brain tumor ended her life a year later. It's hard to forget the pain and suffering of those days. Having been a child helps, but occasionally, Stacks and Benny would use our tattered past as justification for their drug business, a business I'd quit two years ago. So many things had happened then to force me to recognize the destruction I'd been contributing to. I'd already put away plenty of cash to change the outcome of my life and had known from the drama beaconing my reform, that life is too precious to waste and too knowing to be cheated.

My wall clock read 8:10 p.m. Stacks said to get back with him by nine if I wanted to link up. I hadn't planned on doing much of anything, not even calling Pam. In fact, Pam's the main reason that I've been screening my calls. Lately, all she wants to do is fuck-- not make love, cuddle, or even converse-just good ol' southern fucking before she returns to Atlanta. I haven't the slightest idea where we are as a couple, but I know for sure that: if she leaves for Hotlanta, our relationship is doomed. Our foundation seems to have been built on ground as brittle as a Saltine cracker.

I dropped the "For Men" mag I'd been thumbing through on the carpet and sifted through the stack: Jet, Essence, Source, Vibe, Black Enterprise, Code. I subscribe to a variety of black publications to heighten my social consciousness. Magic calls himself schooling me there.

My eyes wandered back to the clock. 8:18p.m. To choke off thoughts of going clubbing, I began scanning a "Source" article about a hip-hop artist under fire because of his past. I slowed my reading and dove into the story, was angered because a vast majority of the hip-hop community declared the artist a "fake niggah" because he'd crossed over, had turned from thug to golden boy when white people began loving his music.

Hip-hop is my generation and although I'm only twenty-four, the article made me want to distance myself even more from the perception of needing to exist in a similar Black cocoon for acceptance. Exactly what I've been running from for the past couple of years. I've cut loose practically all of my past associates, mostly those who'd been holding me down. If Stacks and Benny weren't my brothers, I would've long ago ditched them as well but I guess there's no changing that. I put the magazine to the side and reached for the phone. There was no use fighting the inevitable, besides, my brothers both think I've been frontin' on them lately.

We were at a circular table on a slight platform, in a line of seven other tables with the same dressings. As always, JB Winchell's was packed during happy hours. Mostly corporate types, sistahs dressed ripely for the pickings in halters clinging tight to thighs, showing much cleavage. The fellahs were decked out in Armani suits or silk slacks with reptile belts and shoes. Hugo, Dolce & Gabbana colognes clashed with one another, and a plethora of scents kept me swiping at my nose. Shaggy's "It wasn't me" pumped through the system's speakers. My brothers' tongues hung damn near on the table. I had to give my sistahs their props, they had every male head pivoting like he was at a U.S. Opening, and Venus and Serena were the principals. I'd give the club's vibe a B minus. The music wasn't ear- bursting, but just loud enough that you didn't have to scream at the top of your lungs. I think that's what I was feeling most. A heavyset dude was on the dance floor, in what looked to be a waiter uniform. He had the attention of a small crowd with a flashback of the "Pop." Several executives were cheering him on. Stacks, Benny, and I were cracking up.

"That niggah crazy as shit!" Benny kept hollering. "Yo-Yo, check this fool out!" Benny wasn't talking to anyone in particular, just hollering, laughing, and pointing. When ol' boy finished to claps and pats on the back, we curved our laughter, ordered fresh drinks, then sat back and enjoyed the eye candy.

"I never knew this joint was here," Benny said. He looked amazed.

"If you come outta the jets for a minute, you might have," I said. The club was my choice. He and Stacks had wanted to go to the "After Midnight" or "Lazorro's," raunchy hip-hop clubs although, Lazorro's is a step up from the Midnight.

"Is this where all you college brothers hang out?" asked Stacks.

"This is only my third time here. A white boy put me down at that."

Benny had his eye on a caramel complexion sister with a brown weave down to her booty.

"Cut it out! You tellin' me that white boys be all up in here checking out the sistahs."

"Yep." I sipped my Coke on the rocks and lit a smoke. Stacks joined me. Lately, we've been at odds. I'd been pressuring him to get out of the biz he loves. "How's business?" I asked him.

"Shit kinda slow right now. It'll pick up when Bush opens up more trades with Mexico."

"Trade? Mexico?" I sucked my teeth. "Fool, what do you know about trade?"

"Oh, you think 'cause a brotha thugged out, he can't know shit 'bout foreign policy?"

"That's exactly what I think."

"It's my business to know this kinda shit. You gettin' your PHD in business, and I'm getting mine in streetology."

A pretty, brown-skinned honey with a Cleopatra hairstyle sauntered by us and captured our stares. It looked like she had two midgets hidden beneath her blouse.

"Gotdamn!" Stacks hollered, loud enough for her to hear.

She tsked and kept on stepping. Benny and I shot Stacks a "you're-an-idiot" look.

"What?" he asked.

I shook my head. Stacks has no concept of

women's needs and desires. He's become so accustomed to hoochies and strippers that to him, understanding the differences in female ideologies somehow makes a man soft. I don't know whom, not me—I'm not up to the task—but someone will have to open Stacks' eyes to the strength and independence of the modern female.

I surveyed the ocean of sistahs displaying elegance from head to toe. I was certain that, with the time it'd probably taken these women to prepare themselves for their night out, they expect a brother to overwhelm them with appreciation of their womanhood, with more comforting lines than "Gotdamn! What big titties you have!"- because that's actually what Stacks had said. I didn't feel like debating with Stacks about his streetology degree. We know full well where the other stands. I dragged my smoke. "So, how's big girl treating you?" I asked Stacks.

"Like a king."

"Oh, yeah?"

"Damn Skippy. She be cookin' all kinds a shit, like my skinny ass pushing four-hundred pounds or somethin'."

I grinned, remembering the feast she'd set out for us my first visit over to the crib. I'd been Thanksgiving in June.

"Maybe she tryna give your skinny ass a hint?"

said Benny.

"Uh-uh, my brother. She loves this body just the way it is."

"Or all the gold you wrap around her big ass," Benny added.

We all laughed, swigged our drinks. Stacks was drinking a Rum & Coke, Benny a Heineken.

The DJ switched the vibe. Brian McKnight filtered a stream of "I love you's" throughout the club. Benny had grabbed hold of the caramel complexion sistah with the extensions that he'd been checking out. She'd been teasing men all night with her second skin of spandex. I had to give Benny his props. He and Stacks may have some archaic views on women, but Benny does have good taste. The women he dates are always fine as hell. It was hard figuring out what he brought to the relationship other than misery.

I wasn't much for dancing, and neither was Stacks. Actually, I prefer doing my macking from the sidelines, and Stacks prefers to watch and talk about everybody else. I had left the table for drinks and was on the return when I saw her. I stopped dead in my tracks.

Her hair was finger waved with tan highlights to match her bronze skin and hazel eyes. She was smiling. I tried to maintain my smoothness, but it was too late. I was sure my smile parted as wide as Moses had parted the sea.

She waved.

I pushed a toast to her with my drink and nodded.

Back at the table, the butterflies ruled my insides.

"Who was that?" Stacks asked.

"Somebody front down the end." Carol was with a heavyset sistah shaped like the liberty bell. The friend was wearing chocolate lipstick and a tight leather outfit. They sat at a table next to the club's floor to ceiling window. I sat there, gawking, giving false smiles to Stacks' stupid jokes. Her presence was magnetic. It was hard to keep my eyes off of her.

"I never seen her down the way."

Stacks was staring at me. "That's because Shelly got your ass on lock down 24-7." I pulled a cigarette from the pack and lit it. When I looked back to Carol's table, two suited brothers were taking seats across from them. I dragged hard from my smoke, gulped down some Coke and swallowed harder than normal. One brother strolled to the bar and returned with two drinks and two bottled iced teas. I thought of a hundred—well, what seemed like a hundred ways to ease my way over to Carol's table and cock block, but the Mr. Smooth in me kept me glued to my seat, fuming, and puffing tight jawed from my Newport. I was staring so hard that

Stacks had to push my arm to get my attention.

"Whassup, dawg, you cool?"

I nodded and sipped my drink. "Yeah, I'm straight. Why?"

"You actin' like sis got you sprung. You hit that?"

"It ain't like that. We just cool."

The DJ changed the vibe. Jay-Z's "Jigga" hit lifted people from their seats and had dancers on the floor hollering, "Jiggaaaa. My Niggaaaah!" I don't know if the soft sounds of Brian McKnight had me tripping, but Jay-Z's upbeat rhythms, had pulled me from my sombemess. Although my gators tapped the floor and my head bobbed in unison with the music, my eyes continually roamed, taking long hard looks at Carol. Having watched her for two years, I could tell she was bored. Occasionally, I'd catch her look up in my direction. Unlike the first time we'd made eye contact, I didn't drop my eyes, but I met her smile and felt a connection between us.

Stacks tapped my arm. "Oh, snaps! Check Benny out!"

I looked where Stacks pointed to. The woman in spandex was damn near touching her toes. Behind her, Benny was grinding on her rump shaker, shooting down my theory on the class stages of women. I turned back to Carol just as her and her friend was heading toward the restrooms and the men at their table began huddling.

The DJ changed the vibe with a DMX hit. I wasn't sure of its name, but it had a hard baseline and the entire club on their feet-even me-but I wasn't up to dance. I wasn't about to let no IBM geek bump me out of contention. I made my way through the crowd to where the restrooms were and posted up.

The girlfriend came out first. Carol followed. She saw me standing there with a Kool-Aid smile and stopped.

Mr. Smooth was gone.

# CHAPTER 8

# CAROL

It was my first night out since Kevin's accident. Two years, six months, and eight days. "Girls' Night Out" is what Tonya kept referring it to, during the cab ride downtown. Tonya had shown up on my doorstep early this morning before any hint of a sun's existence. As soon as I saw her, I knew she was in the midst of one of her three day party binges and that my place would be just a stopover til she rested, taken care of some hygiene issues, and eaten. She'd helped me dress the twins for school, prepare Kevin, cooked eggs and sausages for breakfast, and surprisingly, walked with me to drop the twins off at school and waited with me at the van stop. Suspicions peeked when I realized that the entire morning she'd run her mouth, had me so ready for her to shut up, that I'd agreed to venture out with her on this "Girls' Night Out" thing. I'd thought the obstacle would be convincing James to babysit the kids. Surprisingly, he'd said yes without me having to use my head—literally. He'd said that my recent attitude signals my need for some R&R. He'd only agreed because Tonya was with us when I'd mentioned it. He didn't want to reveal how much of an asshole he's been lately.

Tonya was more excited about tonight than I. I know she has very few female friends to hang out with, but I was shocked at the pampering I received just for agreeing to join her. She'd provided everything possible to make my "Girls' Night Out" incredibly special. She'd even gotten our hair and nails done up really nice, charged it to a credit card I never knew she owned-especially since she collects welfare just as I do. She laughed when I pointed that out, then had the nerve to flash two others she'd recently received through the mail. I play strangled her for not putting me down with the hookup. She agreed to do just that-only if I didn't act too stuck up tonight.

We exited the cab in front of what appeared to be a bar, an elegant exterior, painted creme with a coloring of brass trimming. Huge smoke glass windows ran across its front. The script brass sign above the establishment read: JB Winchell's.

It was warm out. A starless night. The downtown lights provided enough illumination to see as clearly as if it were daylight. I'd taken great care dressing, from my single carat studs to my open toe Anne Klein's. I was wearing my silk, blue pants suit with the wide collar, and for this occasion only, Tonya let me borrow her beloved platinum herringbone and diamond pendant. Any skepticism I had about the night ended when we entered the club to Brian McKnight's soothing voice.

It took some seconds for me to adjust my eyes to the club's dimness. When I did, I saw the club was larger than I'd thought, and nicer than its outside. We hadn't even cleared the doorway and Tonya was shaking her big booty. I had to laugh. "Girl, you crazy," I giggled.

She put on her boogie down face, the puckered lips, get- down-and-dirty look. She bounced a few steps doing the "Wop."

I was rolling. As children, she'd made me laugh by doing the exact thing. Nobody makes that face the way she does.

Nobody.

My laughter settled into a smile when I looked toward the bar and saw Wesley's Cheeto's grin. I wiggled my fingers' hello, and a warmth cloaked my body, a sensation that kept me smiling longer than I should've, up until Tonya and I slid into window seats.

"This place is the bomb, girl," Tonya said excitedly.

"It better be. You dragged me down here."

"Oh, be quiet, Carol. Nobody dragged you. You needed to get your old-maid ass outta the house anyway. Treat yourself sometime. Let that sorry ass man work for a change."

I pointed a finger at her. "Don't start."

"Okay, I won't. Listen. She began rolling her hips in her seat and singing bars of Brian McKnight's "Anytime".

I could tell she was ready to get her groove on.

I scrunched my face up. "I'll stop it, Tonya. You don't need to make that face."

We both laughed.

"Ladies."

We looked up to see two suited men. They both looked and smelled of corporate America. One was bearded. The other wore a thin mustache. I turned to Tonya to see her reaction because I was out of practice.

"Hello," Tonya sang, just the way white women did when they were acting all friendly.

"How are you ladies tonight?" the beard one asked.

"Good," I answered.

"May we join you?" the mustache one asked.

Again, I turned to Tonya questioning.

Dumb mistake.

I should have known her fast ass would invite them to sit with us. She was already thinking about free drinks. I had a reason for wanting to be available. I looked up and saw the disappointment on Wesley's face. I felt cheated then flattered although I shouldn't have.

I consider myself a one-man kind of woman, and right now, James is that man.

"Are you ladies enjoying the evening so far?" the beard one asked. He sat across from Tonya and the mustache one parked across from me. I was guessing they'd staked their claims from across the room, before even arriving at our table.

"We just got here," Tonya answered.

"My name's Aaron and this is Malcolm." He thumbed toward my golden skinned prize.

The guy with the mustache clasped his hands beneath his chin like he was praying. "Since you've just arrived, I guess I'll have the pleasure of being the first to ask you to the dance floor…uhm—" He tilted his head.

"Karen. My name's Karen," I lied.

Tonya looked at me funky, knowing I don't give my name to strangers.

"I'm Tonya," she answered.

"Pleased to meet you ladies," said Aaron. He lifted a ringless finger to Tonya and gave her a limp handshake. We all followed suit, laughing and shaking hands. I noticed that both of their hands were soft as velvet Clearly, they worked with their minds, had soft, cushy jobs. I recalled James' callous touch.

"Would you ladies like a drink?" asked Malcolm.

"A Mystic iced tea would be nice."

"Rum and Coke for me," Tonya added.

I looked at Tonya. "You can make that two Mystics-in a bottle- -with the tops on," I told Malcolm.

He left mumbling under his breath. I was sure he didn't appreciate me suggesting that he'd slip mickies into our drinks, but I didn't care. He wasn't my type anyway. I could tell these things immediately. Most women can, unlike men, whose interests never seem to rise above the neck when first introduced to women.

While Malcolm was gone, I found time to look in Wesley's direction. A couple of times I caught him eyeing me, too, and felt the thrill I felt back when James and I had begun courting. I ignored Tonya and Aaron so that I could enjoy the sensation of once again being desired. I also wondered who Wesley's partner was-then a heavyset guy joined them.

Malcolm returned to the table with two Mystics-with their tops' intact-and two drinks, one he gave to

Aaron.

"So, what do you do during the day?" Tonya asked. It's just her way to go straight for the pockets.

"You mean what kinda work do I do?" Aaron asked.

She shrugged.

Aaron smiled. "I sell real estate."

"What kind?"

"All kinds. You name it. I sell it."

She looked at Malcolm.

"I'm a loan consultant."

"Well, don't we mix-n-match well? I need a loan to buy a house. I guess I hit jackpot tonight, huh?" Tonya joked. We all got a good chuckle out of that.

"Girl, you crazy like that glue," I said.

For the better part of an hour, I did much of nothing but listen to Aaron and Tonya chat it up. Tonya was using her phony laugh, the high-pitched "he-he" with the "Oh-my-God" drag on the end of it. I've heard her use it a hundred times, and each time the man gobbled it up. Sporadically, Malcolm would ask a question, but mostly, he was doing what I'd been doing. If I could read Malcolm's thoughts, I'm certain the words "stuck up bitch" were somewhere in there.

Aaron and Tonya were clicking. Laughing. Flirting. and touching. Tonya's such a whore. I finally became bored with it all and pulled my sister to the restroom. Three other women were inside. I let her have it anyway. "I did not get all dressed up to watch you flirt with some old man."

"He's not old."

"Honey. I see gray in his beard."

"I like a little salt on my pie, plus, that's a sign of wisdom."

"And old age."

Neither of us carries much makeup, just lipstick and lip balm. We shared the balm, and I went first because Tonya was wearing that ugly, chocolate lipstick that she knows I hate. We picked hair from each other's face, then Tonya stuffed herself down into her button-down shirt and pushed her D cups to expose more cleavage. "Why aren't you talking to that cutie pie, Carol?"

I picked some imaginary lint from my blouse. "Chile, please. We are from totally different planets, plus you know I like my cake black, not yellow."

"Girl, James got your ass trained. You scared to have fun. Ain't nobody say that you gotta fuck 'em. Shit loosen up. You know you might not be able to get out again no time soon."

My thoughts went to my babies. I wondered if James knew to give Kelly her cough medicine and to put

Kia's eardrops in. I had a sudden urge to call and remind him. Later, maybe, when Tonya's not around, and I won't have to look into the "you're whipped face" I know she'd give.

It had been quiet in the bathroom. A muffled thumping.

Now, back in the mix, the music reawakened my senses and sent a high-voltage seething straight through me. "Pain is Love" by Ja Rule is what the DJ was spinning. I was mouthing the words and on Tonya's heels when I looked up and saw Wesley.

Tonya stopped when I did. She looked baffled when I gave Wesley a smile, and her, my go-ahead-and-do-your-thing look. Without a word, she turned and sliced through the crowd.

"You clean up real nice," Wesley teased.

I looked down my nose at him. "Oh, no you didn't."

"Oh, yes I did," he mimicked. He reached for my hand.

"Come on, let's dance."

Before I could protest, he was pulling me toward the dance floor, right past the company I'd been keeping. I felt Malcolm's eyes cling to me as I zipped by. I felt guilty, but at the same time relieved that he'd rescued me from what would've been more of Malcolm's boring company.

I've never been a great dancer, but compared to Wesley, I was Debbie Alien and Janet Jackson in one package. We danced the last of Ja Rule's "Pain is Love," then kept to the floor as the DJ went into a Bob Marley cut I'd heard several times before. I was doing all I could to keep from cracking up at the serious faces Wesley was making while going through a series of corny dance moves. The brother couldn't dance a lick, and I think he knew it. I was impressed that he was willing to embarrass himself by dancing with me. He did, however, manage one smooth move, a slide to the side, a dip, with a twist at the end of it. It looked a little like the old dance "the Flintstones".

I looked toward the table where Tonya was. She and Aaron were there, but Malcolm wasn't. My eyes swept the place. I spotted him at the bar-alone. It was probably best not to feel obliged to keep company because Tonya and Aaron had bonded.

Without pause, the DJ mixed into Sysco's "Thong Song."

A smile surfaced on Wesley's face.

I grabbed him by the hand. "Uh-uh. I don't think so, buddy," I said, leading him off of the dance floor.

He faked confused. "You don't think so what?"

"This ain't nothing but a hump song."

"Oh, I see. You don't do the butt songs, huh?"

"Not unless it's with my man."

"I can respect that."

"Thank you." I led Wesley to the bar, unsure if it would be disrespectful to take him back to my table-after all, I hadn't even excused myself to Aaron's friend who was now peeking at me from the other end of the bar. "Order me a wine cooler?" I asked Wesley.

I pointed a chastising finger at him. "And don't open it. I'll be right back." I shuffled to where Malcolm sat, fingering a drink.

He looked up and gave me a weak smile. "I guess somebody beat me to that first dance, huh?"

I bit the inside of my lip and scratched the side of my head with a forefinger. I was speechless. I'd never dissed anyone quite this way. "Uh…I'm sorry about that, Malcolm."

He held up a palm to stop me. "You don't owe me any excuses."

"I know, but I want to-"

"Don't worry yourself," he interrupted. "I'm not good company right now anyway. I'm going through a tough divorce."

"Oh, I'm sorry to hear that."

"Thanks, but the divorce is my fault. Like I said, I'm not very good company."

"That's not it at all," I said. "He's my…my…" The lie just wouldn't come.

"Your ex?"

"Yeah-my ex. I don't like to call guys ex's."

"I'm cool with that."

"Thanks."

He nodded.

I looked back at Wesley who was watching us. An awkward moment fell between Malcolm and me. I rocked on my heels a few times. "Well, Malcolm, I better go."

He popped up from his stool. "Oh, yeah, okay then. Well, uh…if you ever need loan advice let me know." He offered me a business card.

"Thanks. That's sweet of you. I will." I palmed the card all the way to where Wesley stood with an unopened cooler. His smile was lovely. Welcoming. Assuring. He definitely looked delicious standing there waiting. I fought so hard not to blush, that I never noticed the crumbled card fall from my hand until it hit the floor. For a second, I thought about picking it up, then decided the only loan I'd need, I was looking at it.

"Brothas kinda pissed, huh?"

"No. He's too nice for that."

"Is that why you weren't feeling him?"

"And what makes you think that?"

"I figure, you with me now, so…"

"I'm not with anybody. I'm already spoken for."

"Spoken for? You mean have a man."

"Have a man, spoken for, married. What difference does it make?"

Wesley shifted, changed the subject. "So, what brings you to the club?" He drank from the glass, giving me a great look at his chiseled profile. His dreads sparkled in the club's lighting, made it appear he'd put silver glitter in his hair. I hoped not. It would be a shame to find out that he's gay.

I pointed to his table. "Who are they?"

"My brothers."

"Is there just the three of you?"

"Yep. Moe, Larry, and Curly."

"And which is you?"

"Definitely Moe."

"The head stooge, huh?"

"Sadly. How about you?"

"What about me?"

"Are you the only gorgeous child?"

"Kinda." I pointed to Tonya. "That's my foster sister there, so, you be the judge."

He nodded like he understood. "Do you two hang out a lot?"

"Nope. She's been trying to get me to come for

the longest. I finally caved. Three kids will do that. But you understand, college man and all."

He nodded. "Yeah, I follow you. Things sometimes get complicated, right?"

"Mm-hm."

"Can I ask you something, though?"

"No, you can't have my phone number."

He smiled. "No. That's not it."

"What then?"

I passed him my cooler to open.

He did, filled my glass to the rim and sat it next to me on the bar top. "Why do you keep saying that college guy thing?"

"Because that's who you are."

"But that's not all of who I am-and that's not the answer I'm looking for."

"What would you like me to say?" I sipped my drink.

A crowd was filtering from the dance floor to the bar. We moved closer to make room. I was close enough to get a good whiff of his cologne. A fresh, leafy scent.

"It's like you're trying to separate me from something or somebody."

I squinted, considered his words. I knew exactly what he meant, knew the answer, but because I liked him, I held back. I was already committed to James and acting other than sarcastic to Wesley won't prevent me from doing something I might regret later.

"I'm not separating you from anybody although, you are different from a lot of guys from the projects."

"Well, I am from the hood, you know?"

"I know. You told me."

"So, how am I so different?"

"It's not that you're so different. It's just that it's rare to find a young Black man willing to sacrifice the hood, his friends and all for college. I only say it to compliment your decision." Wesley took a gulp of his drink, nodded in thought, then turned back to me. "Bull."

"Excuse me?"

"That's bull. I don't think that's the reason you say it at all. I think you say it for the same reason other females from the jets say it: for self-security."

"Self-security? And what do that supposed to mean?"

"I think you believe that a brother might look down on a sistah from the hood because he may be better educated or live a different lifestyle."

"That's not it at all."

"You sure?"

"I'm positive."

"Then it could only be one other reason."

"What?"

"You love me."

We broke into laughter.

I sipped my wine cooler and enjoyed a wonderful thought of us as a couple.

An hour later, Wesley and I were acting like old friends, talking, laughing, touching-on the hands and knees only. Once I'd purposely laid a palm on his biceps to see if the package was better than the wrapping. We'd connected on more issues than I could've imagined. It was refreshing to know a young brother who seems to sympathize with the struggles us young, Black mothers go through. I've become so accustomed to the thugged out mentalities of neighborhood black youth, that my heart and mind skeptically accepted Wesley's views. His words were comforting, but my insecurities forced me to keep circling the niggahs-ain't-shit band wagon, waiting to pounce on the first hint of contradiction. I may not have been feeling Malcolm, but I was definitely feeling Wesley.

He even listened while I rambled on about Kevin and the twins, wanted to know the little things about them like; their favorite cartoons, colors, and singers. Little things that someone who plans on being around them would want to know. While I'm talking, he doesn't just nod at what I say like James does. Wesley looks me in the eyes as if he's trying to picture my words in them. I had surprisingly melted in his easiness and released out a pouring of words like he'd injected me with a truth serum.

The seductive voice of Tyrese coining from the club's speakers and my third wine cooler, had me feeling it. 'Would you like to dance?" I asked, trusting Wesley to behave. It was a slow song, and I was curious. It's said that you can tell how a man makes love by the way he dances-not that I was contemplating sleeping with him. I just had a sudden urge to dance.

"Sure," he answered. He held my hand all the way to the dance floor, held my waist while I draped my arms over his shoulders. The fit was nice.

I looked over at Tonya. Aaron was now beside her. They were just as occupied with one another as Wesley and I have been. When the song ended, we joined them at the table. Tonya was smiling as if I were a Def Comedy Jam comedian. I wondered if she knew my thoughts were on the heat and hardness I'd felt against my leg only seconds ago.

"And who are you?" Tonya asked.

"How are you doing? I'm Wes."

"His name's Wesley," I said, showing my preference.

"Well, Wesley, I'm Tonya and this is Aaron."

The men shook hands. Wesley sat across from Aaron, I faced Tonya.

"I saw you two out there slow dragging," Tonya teased.

I held up a hand like I was taking an oath. "Don't even go there, Tonya," I warned.

"Go where?"

"You know where."

"Mmmmmm." She rolled her eyes.

I noticed the wall clock behind the bar read 1:15a.m. I tried to remember the last time I'd stayed out so late. I couldn't. Sometime back when James and I had been dating. I thought about James' reaction to me staying out so late. "I think it's about time for us to go," I said to Tonya.

She looked at me with unbelieving eyes. "Go? Tell me that's not what you just said."

"I got things to do tomorrow."

"Like what?"

Aaron came to my rescue. "I think Karen has a point. It is kind of late. I have things to do in the morning also."

I watched Wesley catch his tongue from asking whom Karen is. Instead of embarrassing me, he offered me a ride home.

Aaron extended the same courtesy to Tonya.

We both accepted.

Outside of the club, the dawn sky, downtown lights and empty streets seemed surreal. Tonya and I exchanged good-byes and be carefuls, then Wesley and I took to the sidewalk.

"It's not a far walk to the car."

"I don't mind," I said. "It was getting claustrophobic up in there anyway."

"I know."

We walked 8th, 9th, and 10th & Market Streets, past the Gallery, a beauty salon, Kids R Us, jewelry stores, Woolworths, and a mixture of other stores in between. The lights of Market Street pivoted onto storefronts, and traffic was sparse with plenty of taxis. We'd stopped at stores displaying clothing, jewelry, and furniture. I was surprised at how knowledgeable he was about interior decorating. I wondered what other surprises there were besides the ticket he snatched from a Volvo's windshield wiper. "I hope this is your car?"

He swore at the ticket while reading the red and white street sign fastened to a pole. "WEEKEND PARKING-7pm-2am." He looked at his watch. "It's not even two yet."

"Yeah, but Friday's not considered the weekend."

He tilted his dreads and reread the sign. "Nah, I

don't see it"

"Well, it is."

He opened the passenger's door first, ushered me in.

I pulled the lock up on the other side.

"Thanks," he said when he was in. "I'm telling you, Carol, Friday starts the weekend."

"If you say so."

We drove in silence fora while, until we'd cleared the downtown area and were heading north on Broad Street. "Have you thought about coming to the fund-raiser?"

"No. Not really."

"I guess Kevin's not interested, huh?"

"Oh, he's interested," I said matter of factly. "I just haven't decided."

"Why?"

"Too many other things, I guess."

"I'd like you to come—you and Kevin I mean."

We made small talk until I had him stop a block from my row home. We didn't have to speak. We both felt it. I hurried from the car before he'd try and kiss me. I certainly wanted him to, but I also didn't want James' crazy ass popping up and jumping to conclusions-even if I'd already explored them mentally. I kneeled down to the window. "I guess I'll see you around, huh?"

"You always call me."

"Good. I hope you don't let my number go to waste." I smiled, wished I'd let him kiss me just to see if I'd have melted. "Bye, crazy legs."

I watched the Volvo's tail lights until they'd faded into tiny, red dots in the night. Once again, I felt cheated, but this time because of my own doing. I turned into the walkway, ready to return to my lowly slice of Earth. Halfway up the walkway, I backtracked and scanned the street for James' van.

It was gone.

"I know this fool did not leave my kids home alone," I mumbled while I dug in my pocket for house keys. "He can't be this sorry-then again…"

I rushed up the ramp mumbling a host of obscenities.

# CHAPTER 9

# CAROL

My alarm clock read: 10:23 a.m. I awoke from my pitiful night's sleep with burning eyes from the morning's glare that had flooded my bedroom. I was on my back, with heavy, unopened eyelids, listening to life filtering in through the window. Broken glass, a crying child, shouts, an Usher song, "U Remind Me," each sound blending with familiarity, assuring me that I'd not been cheated of life during the night.

I stretched my nakedness a full five seconds then ran my hand the length of my torso. I stopped at the soft mound, remembering that it was where Wesley had pressed against last night while we'd danced. I opened my eyes and grinned, rolled onto my stomach and buried my face into the pillow. I adjusted the knot on my do-rag, pressing against the base of my skull, then recalled my return home from "Girls' Night Out."

I'd sped up the stairs at breakneck speed to check on the children. They all had been asleep. I checked to see if James were home. He was. He, too, was out cold, and beside our bed was a near empty fifth of vodka. The sight had been pitiful, James in a drunken stupor with his mouth gaped open, snoring. I'd been relieved that he'd not left the kids home alone, felt guilty for the obscenities I'd thrown his way.

Hours ago, I'd heard James stumbling around the bedroom, had heard him trip over something and felt the bed tilt when he'd caught his balance. I'd also winced at the sound of a steady stream of pee, breaking the morning's quietness. I was relieved that he, along with the scent of alcohol, hadn't returned to bed. But that had been earlier. Now, I wondered why he hadn't returned.

I sat up and surveyed the room. I looked on the dresser for his house keys. They were gone. There's been times when James has been so predictable. Then there's lately, where it's been damn near an impossible thing to do. I tired quickly even trying to figure out where he'd gone. The absence of his keys became sufficient enough for me.

I slipped into my XXL Tweedy-Bird nightshirt,

went to the twins' room first, curious why the house was so quiet. They weren't there. I checked Kevin's room. He was gone, too. I hurried downstairs, barefooted and beginning to worry, trying to remember if today is a day we'd planned a family outing and I'd forgotten.

It wasn't.

The living room, dining room, and kitchen were all empty, and the question, "Where the hell are my babies?" kept repeating itself in my mind. I opened the front door and stepped outside. I surveyed the area, down the block's walkway, then at and into neighbors' windows, as if someone were watching, pointing, and laughing at a nasty prank being pulled on me. It was uncharacteristic of my children not to wake me up for something. I stormed back into the house, dialed James' mother's number. On the third ring, a child answered. My child. Kia. Confusion tapped me on my shoulder, and fury began replacing my fears. I wanted to speak to her father.

"Whassup, babe?" James answered.

"You, what's up. Why didn't you wake me up and let me know that you were taking the kids?"

He laughed.

I didn't find a damn thing funny.

"Carol, you was knocked out. I shook you, but you told me to get away from you."

"I don't remember that."

"You was sleep."

"Well, you shoulda shook me harder!" I yelled.

"Damn. Whassup with you, girl? You act like I kidnapped 'em or somethin'."

"You did!"

"C'mon, Carol, you said they wanted to visit their Grandmom, so, I brought 'em over. What's the problem now?"

"James, that was a week ago." I felt my fear diminish, but I was still spitting pepper.

"Alright, so I'm a little late. You cornin' over or what?"

I plopped down on the sofa and pulled the receiver from my ear. I breathed deep to calm myself before replacing it. "Keep 'em the fuck with you!" I slammed the receiver back in its cradle then stomped upstairs. I didn't appreciate him taking my babies the way he did, and wanted him to know it, just in case he entertains the thought of doing it again-father or not.

I ran a hot bath, soaked for a half hour, lotioned, pressed, put on old jeans, a thin rugby shirt, and soft, white leather Reeboks. It was 1:30p.m. when I left the house, heading nowhere.

I wound up at Liz's.

Her front door was open for me, the flies, and

whoever chose to enter. The place was muddled with new debris, but the mildew smell was gone. I headed straight upstairs to Liz's bedroom, where I found her doing her norm.

She raised a plump finger for me to hold on a second. "Yeah, okay. Uh-huh. Bye-bye." She hung up. "Girrrl, let me tell you what this fool across the street did."

"Hi to you, too."

"Honey, forget that. Listen to what this fool done did."

I sat in the same cloth-cluttered chair I'd sat in before. Her hair sprouted out like she'd been electrocuted.

"You know Perry across the street, right?"

"Yeah. The crazy guy with the bug eyes."

"Mm-hm."

I knew exactly what Perry she meant. He was a wild eyed seventeen-year-old, who'd wash every neighborhood car for three bucks, if he could.

Liz pointed a stubby finger at the window toward Perry's house. "Him and Pookey, Clara's boy, called they self shootin in. That's what they call it when they snatch the money outta somebody pocket wit'out touchin' em. Anyway, some old man caught Perry's arm cornin' outta his pocket."

Liz had her damn fool face on. "Chile, the hack didn't let go the boy's arm, and Pookey got to hittin the damn man upside the head. Every damn hack up on Ridge and Colombia Avenue started putting foot in both they asses. Now Clara's old rickety ass, call herself tryna press charges on the hacks, talkin 'bout they ain't have nothin' to do wit it. I could kick her old ass, Carol. Whew! I tell you, girl-people today." She paused, squinted, and tilted her head. "What James done did now?" she asked. The semblance of a third chin appeared out of the rolling mound of neck fat that she carries.

"Everything." My voice sounded defeated. "It seems like everything he does aggravates the hell out of me."

She rolled her eyes. "Mmmmmm. You the one stayed with his ass. I told you a long time ago that his ass was throwed."

I had to admit that she had. "I remember," I mumbled.

She cupped an ear at me. "What? Huh? I didn't hear that," she joked.

I smiled.

So, did she. "Ya'll probably just need a break from each other. Hell, you been chasing behind that man and those kids way too fuckin' long for me. How long yall been together now?"

"Twelve years."

"Honeyyy, you need to take your ass out somewhere. You probably need a change' a dick."

My mouth fell open.

"I'm serious, Carol."

"Liz, you need to cut it out," I laughed. Wesley immediately came to mind.

"I'm serious, Carol. What you been doin can't be healthy for somebody your age. You need to go out and have some fun."

"I go out."

"James mother's house don't count, girl."

I hadn't planned on telling anyone about last night, but I needed to defend myself. "For your information, I went out last night."

"Stop lying."

"If I'm lying, may one tit go flat."

"Well, shit, we ain't gotta worry 'bout that, those itty-bitty things you got."

"You call these little?" I looked down at my boobs. We joked this way so I wasn't offended. She still had that I-don't-believe-a-word- of-your-bullshit face. "I did go out," I insisted.

"Okay, where'd you go?"

"JB Winchell's."

"Downtown's JB Winchell's?"

"Is it another one?"

"Who'd you go there wit?"

"Tonya."

She tsked. "Oh, Lawd, not that hoe."

I leaned over and playfully slapped her beefy leg. "Don't be talking about my sister like that."

"I call 'em like I see 'em."

I slid back in my seat, felt the comfortableness of the mess of clothing behind me. Liz's tightening her bedspread around herself presented the print of a nipple, made me look elsewhere.

"Where was James?" she asked.

A sly smile escaped me. "Watching the kids."

"And he just let you roam the streets all night with Tonya?" Her tone was disbelieving.

"He didn't *let* me do anything. I went because I wanted to. If he wouldn't have babysat, then I would have found somebody else."

"Mm-hm. If you say so."

Her wise ass smirk irritated me. Now I'd have to tell the rest to keep face. "And I met somebody, too."

"A guy?"

I twisted my lips. Because Liz swings both ways, she assumes all women share her desire. "Of course, a guy."

"Was he cute?"

"Kind of-yeah, I guess so. I already knew him, though-well not really. We met last week when I was picking up Kevin."

"So he's from around here," she stated.

I nodded.

"Carol, the last thing you need is another project niggah."

"He don't live in the project."

"Do I know 'em?"

"I don't know. He goes to Temple."

"Temple college?"

"Yup."

"You better call his ass, hard as it is to find a brotha that's about somethin'."

"I don't even do that."

"What, have friends? Keep 'em on a leash, just in case. At least you'll be givin that thing to somebody well deserving of some sistah-love."

I shook my head, disbelieving. Liz is a trip. One thing I can count on with her is brutal honesty. I guess that's why I continue to traipse up to her dank bedroom. "I don't think I can do that, Liz. I'm not slimy like these two-faced skeezers running around the projects."

"You're not like 'em. They don't have agendas. They fuck just to be fuckin, stupid, broke ass niggahs at that. Not a lot of people look at the future like you do,

Carol. And if this guy could be somethin in your future, then keep the door open is all I'm sayin'."

I chewed my bottom lip while I listened to Liz go on about how brothas this, and how brothas that. She seems to have all the answers to how to get a man-and a woman if need be.

It was after 4:00p.m. when I left therapy with Liz, confused and brittle, ready to phone Wesley and hint for him to rescue me from my one-mans-woman mentality. From how we'd connected last night, I was confident he'd not hesitate for a second to rush to my aid.

I was heading home, slow poking through the heart of Raymond Rosen projects. Heat waves could be seen smothering the neighborhood buildings ahead of me. The eight skyscraper buildings standing like concrete guardians, seemed a mirage surrounding two large courtyards. Plenty of residents occupy worn, wooden benches, and children ran the lots, tossing bottles and sticks. High above me, someone had a stereo speaker pumping Ja Rule's "Holler-Holler" from their window.

I crossed the street, headed toward a pathway that leads to my block. Six teenage girls crowded the sidewalk, all of them cute. One I paid special attention to. She was the same girl who'd spoken to Kevin while we'd waited at the van stop.

She waved to me.

I waved back. I noticed that all of their clothing revealed plenty of skin, from miniskirts to shorts, sleeveless and belly shirts, made me wonder if they were out to tempt teenage boys or grown men. At twenty-six, my motherly instincts wanted to stop and tell them to put some clothes on, but then again, fashion has changed, and with the softening of societies' restrictions, and women's independence, I seriously doubted if anything I'd say would make a difference to the girls. I wondered what life might be for me if I hadn't had children, if my Baptist upbringing had clung to me during my teens. More often than ever I ask myself, why am I not more spiritual, more faith driven with a lot of the decisions I make to guide and motivate my own children's lives. I just kept walking and smiled at all of them.

I turned into my block and welcomed the sight of my front door. I had begun to sweat, was dry mouthed from inhaling stale air during my walk.

Inside, I stripped to my bare essentials then showered in cool water until I'd been revived from my lull. After I'd lotioned and poured baby powder on myself, I phoned Janice, wanted to know if the children would be eating there, or should I prepare something here for them.

She met my question with laughter. "You think I

would send my grands home without feeding them? What kinda Grand momma would do that?"

"I just asked because I ain't fix a thing."

"Well, there's no need to. They'll be eating here."

"Thanks."

The line was silent, quiet enough for me to hear the phone line humming.

"James told me you hung up on him."

"Not really. We were through talking."

"Uh-huh, I bet. I called earlier, but you were out. The girls want to know if they could spend the night."

"What about Kevin?"

"Kevin is Kevin. I'll find some way to convince him to stay, too."

I was in my bedroom sprawled across the bed. I sat up.

"Thanks, Janice."

"Whatever I can do to help. Maybe you and James could use this time to talk?"

I didn't respond.

"It's a thought," she added.

I hung up from Janice with a calmness. I'd been uptight all day, and not having to deal with the children, could prove therapeutic. Already, I was planning to put on my Luther CD, dive into his antidotes for love, then I remembered Kia had broken the stereo system, so I settled for a cold, turkey and cheese sandwich, and poured two cherry hugs into a tall glass of ice. I put on a VCR tape of "Romeo Must Die" and curled into bed. It was a bootleg version of the movie, but I admired Aaliyah enough to overlook the tape's discoloration.

James staggered into the bedroom well after nine, shortly after the movie had ended. I didn't bother looking up at him, just kept thumbing through the pages of the "Essence" magazine I was reading.

He spoke first. "Why'd you hang up on me?"

Without looking up, I answered, "I was upset." I turned a page.

"You still mad?"

"I was upset, not mad. Dogs get mad. I'm not a dog."

"I know that. But you know what I'm sayin'."

"Mm-hm," I hummed. I cut my eyes at him, not wanting to make eye contact out of fear that he'd see my hurt and try and make it up to me. Oddly, I wanted to stay angry at him for as long as we've been together. I snapped back another page and let my fingers scroll the words. I wasn't reading, just pacing myself. I wanted answers to questions that would change both our lives as well as our children's.

James laid down next to me in jeans and a red "Just Do It" T- shirt. He laid his keys on his chest and closed his eyes like he'd not relaxed all day.

"Did you give Kelly her cold medicine?" I asked.

He nodded. "I took all that stuff to my mom's."

"And Kia's ear medicine?"

"All of it."

"I'm surprised you even knew about the medicine."

He laid quietly in his stench of alcohol.

I studied his chocolate skin. His string sized beard and goatee needed shaping up, and his cheeks were thinner, compared to a month ago. He looked worn. "Why'd you go to your mom's without me?"

He shrugged. "I told you why. I hope you ain't gonna take me through the ringer again?"

"And again, and again, till you give me a better answer than that. You must've told the girls not to wake me up or they would've."

"Is that why you rammin'?" He opened red eyes.

"No," I lied, not wanting my selfishness on display, but instead his inconsiderableness. "I was worried. I thought something happened to them. How'd you get to your mom's anyway? The van wasn't there last night."

He closed his eyes back and licked his lips. "I lent it to somebody."

I slammed shut the magazine and stalked to the

dresser. I didn't need a thing from the dresser, just didn't want to be in the same bed with him. I kept my back to him. "Since when did you start loaning out the van? You won't even let me drive it."

"That's 'cause you can't drive."

I peered over my shoulder and rolled my eyes. I was wearing my favorite Tweedy-Bird nightshirt and had my head wrapped in a scarf. I spun 180-degrees, and before I knew it, the question flew out. "Are you cheating on me, James?"

"Cheatin!?" He propped up on his elbows.

"That's what I asked."

"Huh-ell, no!"

I stood there, staring daggers, strumming my fingers on the dresser's top like the ticking of a time bomb. His defense broke my trance.

"Baby. I would never do that to you."

"Then where the hell you been going every night?" I didn't want to reveal what Kevin's friend, Jay, had said. I was saving that for another time, when I have a name and address to throw in his face. This was just a trial run, a chance for him to come clean.

He sat up. "I be out driving. Sometimes I might hang out with Greg, Spence, Ronnie, people from the job." He approached me smiling, like he was enjoying my insecurities. "Sweety, I'd never cheat on you. For what?

You're all I need, plus, I would never risk losing what we share." A slight smile was still there. His words became buttery, smooth enough to ease me into tranquility and settle my anger some. They were what I wanted, what I needed to hear. The closer he came to me, the more I returned to the putty he'd molded many years ago. He clasped my face between his calloused hands.

I shoved him away. "Uh-uh, James. It's not that easy anymore. I'm not buying it."

He let his arms fall to his sides and huffed. "C'mon, Carol. I'm not cheatin' on you. I'm goin through some things about where I am in life. Shit like that. Things that got me doin' and sayin stuff that's unlike me."

I folded my arms and listened to his spiel.

His words were a baritone molasses. Words dripping from his thick, brown lips like the Luther antidotes, I'd wanted to hear earlier. He was piling it on about how he wants the girls to go to college, how he'd like to move us out of the projects and into a safer neighborhood, away from the drugs and violence. He stretched it about wanting to give me the fairytale wedding I deserve. Talked and talked and talked until I wished I'd never brought up the question that had started his mouth moving. It's been a while since we've communicated, so I listened. I was waiting for clues to whether his ideologies have changed. There were none. I sat on the bed and watched him pace before me. In the twelve years we've been together, he's never spoken so much at one time. Normally, he's laid back. Soft spoken.

I accounted some of what he was saying to alcohol. The rest, I believed, came from the heart, things he's been wanting to say to me for a long time, maybe. It was after midnight when James finally stopped talking. Relief settled in me when he left the room to shower.

I climbed into bed, listening to the shower's beat, allowed my mind to shuffle through all of what James had said to me. Like a card trick, I picked a card, any card, and chose that to ponder on. I'd chosen the children's futures, the card which I care about the most.

Neither James nor I'd gone to college-neither had our parents, mine who'd abandoned me or his who'd accepted me while I carried Kevin to term. Recalling those years, brings to mind the struggles James and I had gone through to reach this point. College would be a great thing for our children. A chance at a better life than I'd given myself.

I was dosing off when James came to bed. An alarm beeped in my head, and my legs slammed shut. I crossed my ankles.

"Are you sleep?" James asked. His arm snaked around my waist and tugged me-not nearly as aggressively as he'd been before, more like, prodding, asking, needing me.

I turned to face him and made the mistake of looking into pools of onyx. His eyes were a wealth of sadness that pierced the wall I'd been building to resist him. We both had grown over the years, and now, more than ever, I felt it. I was lost in the eyes of a stranger, trying to rediscover the man I'd fallen in love with. I felt my body go to him for comfort, felt our lips touch to a kiss and heard me moan when my eyelids eased shut. I didn't want them to shut, but they did. I didn't want to taste the alcohol on his lips, but needed to do that, too. I at least owed James the chance to prove that all he'd said was real, and not just the rambling of a man donning big wishes. I opened my eyes to see he'd been watching us kiss. I wanted him to read my mind. To know what I need is for him to tell me that everything's going to be all right, to be patient.

As our tongues danced, I felt my T-shirt lift and my panties slip down around my ankles. I allowed him to roll me on my back and taste from my nectar, sending me to a celestial place where even Venus: The Goddess of Love, couldn't have possibly visited.

I ran my fingers across his wavy hair, moaned, then tried to pull his face inside of me as my hips rotated with the rhythm of a well-oiled machine. For a long time,

I'd been frustrated. Angry. Allowed myself not to need or want anything for me. I groaned, bucked, and dug my nails deep into James' skull.

He yelled.

I apologized then pulled his face up to mine and could taste my own juices on his lips.

He entered me quickly, grabbed my lust at its core and shook it. I fainted into a perfect world, where pleasure is all to be remembered. I cried out while he sucked the spot just below my earlobe. Like always, I rocked back and forth with forceful swirls of my hips. My squeals earned through until our body wrestling ended and the last spasms shook through me.

James had a concerned look on his face when he asked me what was wrong.

I hadn't even realized that I'd been crying, but knew I needed a way to tell James that I was no longer in love with him.

# CHAPTER 10

# WESLEY

I closed my Business Communication text, my notebooks, then recited part of an oral presentation that Professor P.T. Bingle said will account for one-third of my final grade. When I felt it was fair, I walked to the shower mouthing it some more. Even while I crushed a bowl of Fruit & Fiber, I went about memorizing it until the words flowed as naturally as a Tupac rhyme. I dropped my cereal bowl in the sink, snatched my keys from the coffee table and skedaddled. I had to work this morning, open up the place really.

Last night, after I'd dropped Carol off at her place, I'd gone straight home. There were three messages on my answering machine--Pam, Benny, and Magic.

Magic needed me to open the shop this morning, Pam was Pam, and Benny phoned to find out if I'd scored with Carol. It'd been late, and there had been no point in returning Pam's call, she'd have complained anyhow.

The perfect morning it was. Cool. Sunny. Scattered clouds and barely any traffic. Not many people in North Philly leave their beds at 7:00 a.m. on Saturday. If Magic hadn't asked for a favor, I'd have been afforded that luxury as well.

I drove the long way to the shop, followed a light 33rd Street traffic through Fairmount Park, turned left onto Baltimore Avenue until I came up on 17th Street, where I hung another left to get to Parrish. City traffic was sparse. Even with me taking the long route, I'd made it to the garage in less than thirty minutes.

Across the street from the garage was a junkyard, fenced by fifteen feet of mixed woods tied together with hanger and rope. A comer-bent parade of the homeless, lugging last night's collections of aluminum cans lined the fence, awaiting the yard's opening so that they could cash in.

I stumped my cigarette in the ashtray and went to open the garage for business. I had just flicked the light switch on when my beeper went off. It was Pam.

I settled at Magic's desk, propped up my feet like I owned the joint, and lit a smoke before dialing Pam's number. As soon as I heard her voice, I regretted calling.

"Where are you?" she snapped.

"At work."

"This time 'a day?"

"Magic has something to do. He'll be in late." Her panting indicated that she was in the middle of her daily aerobic workout.

"Who was she?" Pam spat.

"Who?"

"The slut my girlfriends saw you with last night."

I pulled the phone away from my ear and my feet to the floor.

"Shit," I mumbled, then replaced the receiver.

"Well?" she was saying.

"A friend, that's all."

"That's not what I heard."

"Well, it's the truth."

"If it's so much the truth, then why not say her name instead of calling her a friend?"

"Huh?"

"Don't play dumb, Wes. You know what I mean. I heard about your little slow dance."

"Oh, yeah?" My mind rewound to the dance that Carol and I had shared. I touched where she'd pressed against and adjusted myself, crushed my cigarette in a ceramic ashtray shaped like a Bentley. 'What, you got your girls spying on me now?"

"You damn Skippy. It's a good thing, too."

"It was just a dance, Pam. If it makes you feel better to know, she already has a man and three kids. We just cool and that's it."

"Mm-hm. Just a dance, huh? Cool, huh?"

"Yep. Just a dance." Even as I said it, I wished it'd been more. Carol does have a man, and my lie to Pam was a necessary one. Her jealousy could easily become rage coated with obsession and overprotectiveness. I didn't need her going psycho on me. I tried sounding as level-headed as possible. "Pam what's the point in going out to have a good time if you don't socialize? All your little posse saw was a dance, okay?"

"Yeah, well, I know I better not find out that you're fooling around on me."

I laughed. "Check you out, fooling around. You sound like some MTV chick."

"Don't play with me, Wes. I'm serious."

"Alright, I'm sorry if I fed your girls ammo to come at you with, but why worry about what your girls think, when you should concern yourself with how I feel about you not trusting me?"

"I never said I didn't trust you."

"Then what's this conversation all about? Your girls watching me?"

"I can't help it if they know we're together and want to look out for me."

Two *bings* rang in the shop.

"Look, Pam, somebody just pulled in. I gotta go."

"Am I going to see you later?" she asked.

"You know it."

"At your place?"

I stood up, ready to serve the customer. If I say no, like I wanted to, she'd never let me off of the phone, so I agreed.

"I love you, boo."

"Love you back," I said then hung up. I wasn't particularly looking forward to the rendezvous with Pam. I was instead hoping to hear from Carol and pick up where we'd left off last night. I hurried out to the lot where a brown Oldsmobile sat with its motor running.

Inside, was a gray-haired woman with a large German Shepherd in the backseat. I approached the car from its rear like a state trooper, felt better knowing the windows were up. "Can I help you?" I asked.

The woman balled up her face at me and tucked something between her thighs. "Where's Mr. Coffee?" she grumbled.

Ervin Coffee is Magic's real, jacked up name. Family and friends had started calling him Magic back when the LA Lakers were "Showtime."

"He'll be in later. Is there something that I can do for you?"

"I…I don't think so. It's important to see Mr. Coffee. I have something for him."

"You can leave it with me. I'll make sure he gets it."

Her thin eyebrows dipped on her weathered, brown face. She wet her thin lips and scanned the lot like I was lying about Magic not being around. "No. I think I'll wait." She suddenly sped off, left skid marks in the asphalt.

I watched the car speed into traffic, tilting on two wheels. I went back inside and crawled beneath a Plymouth propped on two cement bricks.

While wrestling with the car's broken axle, I thought about Carol and how wrong I've been for even considering a relationship with her. She deserves much better than someone carrying so much baggage. It was obvious we'd vibed last night that we view life so similar. Carol allowed me to see just how shallow my relationship with Pam really is, did so without even knowing that I was involved. The issue just never came up. It was as if no one else had mattered last night, just us.

I reached down to my side for a monkey wrench. As I clamped down on a bolt and twisted, my mind wandered back to last night.

I've never been sprung on a woman in my life, but somehow, Carol had managed to stranglehold my machismo in one night of words. Talking to her was so easy, much easier than with Pam, who only rambles about her needs and my faults. That's where Pam and I falter.

Pam and I had never established our relationship based on anything other than sex. Our relationship began as a college fling and has evolved some, but not much. Already, Carol and I have traveled far deeper than sexuality, regardless of the obvious physical attraction between us. Carol was cute, average, but sexy enough that a brotha would still have to fend off the hounds from sniffing around her. She accentuates her personality being well grounded, propelling her unreachable by most other females. Her personality makes her whom men enjoy-a homey-lover-friend.

However, I worry where Carol's concerned. I worry she'll discover my past and possibly never forgive me for having lived so foul; for the poison I'd pushed; the people I'd hurt; the secrets I keep, so tightly wrapped, that my dreams may never be dulled, always an abstract vision of good against evil. To pursue Carol would mean constant worriment over whether I'll be capable of sacrificing as much as myself as she seems to. I've always been selfish—until recently. Uncertain if I'm ready to commit myself totally. Carol would need, want, and expect total commitment from her man. Her words and eyes had told me so. Eyes I've studied for years from "my spot." And where will Kevin fit into my life? I'll no longer be able to witness my muse quite the same ever again. Yes, I have a lot of questions where Carol's concerned, questions I'd rather not find answers to, because I was sure the answers would prevent me from pursuing what I want so badly.

At 11:18, I was back behind Magic's desk, searching through drawers, just to be nosy. Two "bings" rang in the shop the moment I stumbled across Magic's pom collection. "Shit," I cursed, closed the desk drawer and hustled from the shop.

The brown Oldsmobile with the gray-haired woman and the German Shepherd was back. "Where's Mr. Coffee?" the woman insisted.

"He's not here yet."

She looked tired. Angry. The dog looked bored, the two seemed compatible. I stooped at the window until we were eye to eye.

"Ma'am, you can leave whatever you have for my uncle with me," I offered.

"I'd rather leave it with Mr. Coffee." Her eyes roamed the area, looked everywhere but at me. "I ain't got all day to be waiting on Mr. Coffee, so, if you says yall can, then I 'imagine you just as deserving as he is." She slid a hand in a purse at her side and smiled at me really grandmotherly.

I should've been watching her hand and not her smile. I never saw it coming, only felt the warm liquid douse my forehead and eyes, flow across my cheeks and lips. I stumbled backward.

"What the hell…"

"Give that to your two-timing uncle! And tell him don't call me again!" With that said, the woman sped off. Her tires screamed above all my obscenities.

Through clinched eyes, I watched the Oldsmobile turn into traffic—until the burning began.

My face was on fire. Hot-hot. A kind of hot that made me think that my mug was being stung by a thousand wasps.

The old woman had mace me.

"Aw, shit!" I shouted. I went to wipe my face with my shirt, but realized I had on overalls. I used my sleeve, squinted, and ran toward the shop, blind and cursing. I tripped on a concrete step and stumbled inside, fighting to keep myself balanced. It began burning so badly that my breaths were short gasps through my nostrils that set my sinuses ablaze and had me coughing up organs. I reached up and touched my skin, just to see if it was melting. "SHIT! SHIT! SHIT!" I yelled, all the way to the shop's sink, stuck my head beneath the spigot and opened the cold-water valve. I cupped handfuls of water onto my face and sighed while the burning subsided. I still couldn't breathe, though-especially from my nose. I huffed and puffed beneath the faucet and wondered why the woman had mace me. Who was she? What did Magic do? Will she be coming back so that I could strangle her old ass?

After ten minutes of running water over my face, I stepped from the sink and found a clean towel nearby. I patted dry what felt like raw skin, then the heat from the pepper spray returned. I rushed back to the sink.

The burning had just become tolerable when Magic strolled in the shop, lugging two suitcases. I grabbed the towel and tried not to rub my skin while patting it dry. "What's up with your peoples?" I asked.

He dropped the suitcases and walked to his office door. "My peoples?" he asked evenly.

My soaked collar cooled my neck. "Yeah. The old lady that mace my ass?"

"Mace you? Who?"

"Some lady in a brown Old's that called you a two-timing Mr. Coffee."

His eyes widened. "Blanche was here?"

"Is that her name? I should get her ancient ass

locked up."

"How long ago was she here?"

"Man, forget that!" My arms flailed wildly. "What's up with you and this psycho chick?"

Magic flopped into his desk chair and let loose an exasperated breath. "Damn. I'm fucked."

I was still patting my face with the towel. "What's going on, Magic?"

"Gloria found out about Blanche and threw me outta the house. That's probably why Blanche showed up here."

"Gloria threw you out?" I asked, surprised. She was usually super nice.

"Don't believe a big butt and a smile, Wesley. Gloria ain't as easy going as you think."

I sat in the worn leather chair across from his desk. "How'd she find out?"

"A damn cleaning bill. You know, one of those receipts they give you when you turn your clothes in to 'em?"

"I know what a cleaning bill is."

"Yeah, one of those things. It had Blanche's address and phone number on it. I left it in the pocket of a shirt Blanche gave to me sometime last year."

I shook my head unbelievingly. "You've been cheating on Gloria for a year?"

"Not a year."

"What, two?"

He looked away from me. "Longer than that."

"Longer? You lying?" Surprise laced my words. I knew Magic did a lot of flirting, but never knew he was cheating.

"Hell, I been seein Blanche before me and Gloria got married."

I felt a bit of the respect for my uncle slipping away. I thought skimming profits from the business-their business-was lame, but him cheating on Gloria, his bread and butter, lowered the bar. I sat quietly, watched Magic stare off into space for a moment, then I got up. I remembered the suitcases he'd brought into the shop. "You plan on sleeping here?"

"Til' she put me outta here, too."

"I guess, shacking up with the psycho broad is suicide, huh?"

He didn't answer, just sat there, brooding.

I walked out into the shop area and wondered how long I'll have a gig. Gloria and I were pretty tight, but I couldn't see myself working at the garage unless Magic would be around. It would be really tacky to work for the woman who'd fired the family member who'd hooked me up with the gig.

A couple of hours later, I left Magic sulking at his

desk, cursing his stupidity. I did assure him, however, if he needs a place to crash, then my door is always open to him.

On the way home, I stopped for groceries and toiletries. It was well after five when I pulled up in front of the crib. I was surprised to find Pam perched on my porch. When I exited the car, I expected her to leap up and drill me with questions, considering how fucked up my day had gone already. I touched my face and remembered getting Maced. "Hey you," I grinned.

Her smile seemed forced. She jumped up. "Hurry, hurry, hurry. I gotta pee."

I jiggled my house key from the ring and opened the door.

She wiggled by me, straight to the John, did a Marion Jones over my gym bag beside the sofa.

I set my keys and the grocery bag on the coffee table and dove, face first, onto the sofa, thankful to be home.

Pam didn't bother shutting the bathroom door. I heard the toilet seat drop then the steady sound of water breaking water. "What took you so long to get home?" she asked over the sounds.

"Magic and Gloria are going through something. I stayed for awhile to kick it with Magic."

"What happened?"

"They had a fight." I heard the toilet flush, then running water.

I rolled onto my back just as Pam was entering the room. The top button of her slacks was undone, and she had a hand on her flat belly and one on her forehead.

"Whew! I thought I was gonna pee my pants waiting on you."

"Why do women do that anyway?"

"Do what?"

"Wait til' the last minute to go to the baurrrgg!"

Pam sat on my stomach and peeked in the bag. "Chips, cookies, sardines. Yuck. I didn't know you like those nasty things?"

"They're good for you. People say they help your sex drive."

"You mean oysters, don't you?" she asked seductively, making herself comfortable by straddling me.

"What's the difference? Seafood is seafood. All that aphrodisiac shit is myth anyway."

"Maybe not." She rubbed her bottom against me, caused my member to stir.

I twisted from beneath her. I wasn't about to allow her to hump me dry again. She'd raked skin from my piece the last time.

"Where you going?" she whined.

I laughed and snatched up the grocery bag. "Away from your kinky butt."

We met again at the kitchen. Her shoes had been left behind and her lips were poked way out. She whined like a child. "Come back in the living room."

"Nope."

She sucked her teeth and opened the fridge, studied its contents. "You never have anything to eat."

"I got chips," I declared.

She scowled at me. "Don't nobody want no chips. Where's the real food? I know, let's order a pizza."

"You know ain't no pizza getting delivered around 32nd Street.

She slammed close the refrigerator door. The pouting resumed. "I'm hungrrryyy!"

"Poor, babbbyyy," I teased. I kissed her poked out lips and felt the hum of her protest.

We held hands on the way back into the living room.

"Feeeed Me!" she yelled.

"Okay, okay. Put your shoes on."

I was impressed. Amazed. Surprised that Pam could or would wolf down a He-Man's plate of grub the way that she was. Baby back ribs, buttered noodles, greens, biscuits coated in cranberry sauce- piled high was her goal. I wasn't at all as hungry as she apparently was, so I'd settled on a rib sandwich.

We were at Ida's, a soul food joint, on Ridge Avenue, a landmark known to Philadelphians for its Spicy Ribs and spirited desserts. Ida's was small, fifteen linen-topped tables lined against one wall, on the opposite side, where the food was prepared-the kitchen area, and a line of dessert displays in floor-to-ceiling refrigerators. Several other customers were enjoying meals as well—particularly a family of seven, who'd pushed three tables together. A mountain of food was on their table. I wondered what their bill would look like.

Pam's waving brought my attention back to her. She needed a napkin.

I handed her one of mine. "Have you thought about lifting your head out of your plate to breathe while you eat?" I asked.

She giggled and wiped barbecue sauce away from her mouth and cheek. "Very funny. Ha, ha."

I bit my sandwich and watched her go at it. "You ready for graduation?"

She nodded.

"I hope you and your sorority sisters don't do something crazy like a streak across the stage."

She finished chewing most of what was in her mouth. "Don't you wish?"

I smiled. "Not with the crowd you hang out

with.”

She gave me her you-know-you-wrong look. “You need to stop hatin on my girls. If not for them, we wouldn’t have met.”

“So true, so true.” I sipped my iced tea.

“While I’m back in Atlanta, I hope you know they’ll be my eyes and ears?”

I shifted some.

I think she noticed. Her tone became matter of fact. “Wes, you know my dad’s offer for the sales position still stands, right?”

“Yeah, I know. Transferring might not be good for me, though.”

“Why? Ain’t we country folk smart ‘nough for ya?” She put on her best Southern accent.

“Pam, I don’t know why you think your butt is country. Ain’t nothing country about you but your appetite. Plus, Atlanta’s a big ass city. South don’t always mean country.”

“Then why not transfer?”

An obese couple entered the restaurant. Their faces were determined, like they were about to throw down some serious grub.

Pam was staring at me when I turned back around. “What?”

I asked.

"I'm waiting for an answer."

"Come on, Pam, I've lived in Philly all my life. I just don't know if I'm ready to pick up and roll."

She leaned back, snapped the top button open on her slacks and rubbed her belly. She began making that tsking noise with her mouth, the noise people make while trying to clear food from between their teeth. Pam's eating habits are disgusting, just the way that I prefer. I can't stand the neat and always-trying-to-be-cute types. The type Pam was seventy percent of the time. "It's not like you'll be picking up and leaving, Wes. I'll be there. A job. A home."

I looked away like I was considering it. She'd smack me if she knew my primary regret would be having to leave Kevin and Carol. I turned back to her and frowned. "I thought we'd talked about this already?"

"We have." She looked grim. "Wes, we both know that if I move back to Atlanta without you, our relationship won't stand a chance."

"You don't know that."

"I do know that. It's a fact. Long distance relationships fail eighty-seven percent of the time."

"Who told you that?"

"I read it."

"Where?"

She shifted in her seat. "Today's woman."

I laughed.

She joined me, right after she tossed a biscuit at me.

We were back at my place. Anita Baker's "Rapture" made good on its effort to release a love virus throughout the room. Pam and I were enjoying a game of "Strip Scrabble," a game that she was winning. She was kicking my butt so bad that, a couple of times, I thought about throwing her out of my crib. She was that bad a winner. "I'm burnt out," I lied, needing an excuse to quit.

"You're only tired because I'm close to getting my prize." She eyed my crotch.

"You trippin'. It ain't over. What's the score anyway?"

"My kicking your butt to your butt whipping."

We'd moved the coffee table and had taken our game to the carpet. Pam was down to her floral, lace bra and slacks, and I had on only striped boxers. We'd changed the Scrabble rules a bit. If one of us challenges a word that proves to be correct, the challenger has to lose an article of clothing. I was near naked, so I'd lost a lot or won, depending on the way you look at it.

Pam pushed the game aside and crawled over to me. "Do you really want to quit, baby?" Before I could protest, she was on me, reaching.

"Is this all you want from me?" I managed between kisses.

"Maybe." Her aggression found me with a cool palm and massaged me until I was ready. Her kisses soon became seductive vacuums that sent my insides through a whirlpool. I knew we'd wound up here. Kissing. Tasting. Enjoying. She was on her knees coaxing my lips to her small breast.

I rewarded her with small, circular lickings, intended to send her to an orgasmic atmosphere. I slid her pants below her slim hips and traced her belly's peach-fuzzed hairline, leading to her nest of treasures with my tongue. I tickled her belly with my dreads. A turn on for her, she'd said. I paused to inhale her almond like scent. "Let's go to the bed, baby," I moaned.

My body danced as Pam did her trick with the condom. And when I entered her softness, I drifted into a palace of riches that I wanted to possess forever. I felt her fingers cup me from behind and pull me deeper inside of her. It hadn't taken long for her warm flood to engulf me and her passion to begin to clutch and grab at me with every rotation our bodies encountered. I slipped into an abyss. If this is how good it feels to be used for her purpose, then I wanted her to use me up.

Finally, when I was unable to hold myself any longer, I spun myself, laid rigid inside of her and thought all of my insides would wound up as hers. Afterwards, as we lay catching our breaths, my mind began to clear. Pam had coiled herself around my body, and I wondered if this would be our last time making love.

# CHAPTER 11

## CAROL

At 6:40 am, the sky was as dark as an El tunnel, dark enough for streetlights to cast shadows across the bedroom, and early enough for James to have started his shit.

I was in my Tweedy-Bird T-shirt, leaned against the bathroom door, watching his filthy mouth flap a mile a minute. He'd pushed major buttons this morning, causing my nostrils to flare and my lips to purse tightly.

"I do what I can. Not a lot of guys will put up with your bullshit, Carol!"

He had to be joking. "My bullshit? You the one running the streets all hours of the night, coming in here smelling like booze."

He stalked by me, damn near knocked my shoulder out of socket. "I know you better watch where you walking!" I spat.

"Then get out the doorway then."

We'd been going at it since 6:00 am, since James woke up with a chip on his shoulder. We'd made love only hours ago. And now, when we should be in bed cuddling, asleep in a common-law-marital state, we were up and at each other's throat, for a reason I couldn't fathom, other than he'd started it. "I wish you just hurry up and go to work, James, because you're just a miserable ass man."

"Oh, I'm going alright! I'm gettin outta here! You should be grateful you got a man that works and provides for you and those kids."

"They're your kids, too. And the kids ain't got a damn thing to do with your attitude."

"Oh, no? Ha, that's what you think."

"And what do that supposed to mean, James?"

"You heard me."

"No, I didn't. Did you say you don't want to take care of your kids anymore? Huh, is that it, James?"

He dressed like a fire was ablaze in the room, fought the room's dimness for his work boots. His facial features were hidden because of his charcoal skin. I was tired of arguing, so I stood at the bathroom door and watched him jump around the room, talking to himself. He trashed the closet for his jacket and snatched his tool belt from behind the door.

I wished I'd closed the bedroom door. I was sure the children were listening. Our eyes locked when he stormed out of the bedroom.

I held my place until I heard the front door shut and screen door bang behind it. I fell across the bed and sighed, "What the hell was that all about?" I felt drained.

Kia and Kelly were in my room almost immediately. Both wore long faces. Kia was crying.

"What's wrong, boo?" I asked. I sat up and stretched my arms out for her.

Kia fell into them.

"She cryin' 'cause you and Daddy was fightin'," Kelly informed me.

I rubbed Kia's back and hushed the most emotional of my three children. "Aw, boo, don't cry. Mommy and Daddy gonna be fine. We were just talking loud. That's all."

Kelly had moved to the window to look for her father. I could see her grief as well, but she'd never tell you the things that bother her. She's the one who keeps me guessing.

I wiped a streaking tear from Kia's face and kissed her forehead, just the sniffling of her crying was left. "Are you ready for school?" I asked.

She shook a head of wild hair.

"Why not?"

She shrugged.

"'Cause she was being nosy," Kelly said.

"Was not," Kia countered.

"Uh-huh."

"Was not."

"Uh-huh."

Their arguing signaled that the morning had returned to normal, and as soon as William Dick's doors open, their little asses would be gone. I turned to Kelly. "I guess you weren't being nosy, too?"

Kelly sauntered before me; each child leaned on a leg. My two babies. Twins. It's still difficult believing that I'd given birth to two children only minutes apart. Kelly was older by seven minutes, and her personality shows it. She believes she has all the answers to the world's problems stored in her seven-year-old mind.

"I need the two of you to do me a big favor, okay?"

They nodded.

"I don't want yall worrying about me and your daddy. As long as we have you, we'll be together, alright?"

Again, they nodded.

"Good. Now take your nosy behinds in the bathroom, wash the white stuff out the comer of your eyes and from around your lips. And when yall come downstairs to eat, bring the big jar of blue hair grease and the cookie can of barrettes." The girls scurried from the bedroom, assured that Mom and Dad will never separate. I wasn't so sure of that, but for the girls' sakes, I said what I had. The reality is the frustration stemming from my relationship with James is beginning to stress me out. I was unsure, how much more of the arguing and fighting I could take. On my way to Kevin's room, I bit at my lie. I'd hoped to forget an already plagued morning and start my day from the moment on.

Kevin's door was shut. I knocked twice before walking in, and had to eye surf heaps of clothing to register which pile was actually Kevin. He was in bed tucked into a ball, facing the wall. I kicked through the piles and sat on the bed next to him. His eyes were open.

"The whole block heard yall." He didn't bother turning around.

"It's not as bad as you think, Kevin. We've been through rough times before."

Kevin sat up. His boyish features were hard. "I told you he don't care nothing about us no more. I been said you should kick him out. Look how he been treating us, Mom. He don't even wanna be around us."

"Of course, he does."

"No, he don't. All he care about now is K.K."

K. K. is Kevin and James' way of referring to Kia and Kelly. When James is upset with all the children, he'd use the acronym, only he'd add a K, making it K. K. K. I didn't find it cute at all.

"I'm serious, Mom."

"I know you are, sweetheart. But it's not that cut and dry." Kevin's eyes were pleading.

I held his hand in mine, wanted to reason with him so that he'd understand my dilemma. "Should I give up on your sisters' daddy just because we argue? They need him around them, too."

He lowered his eyes to our hands.

"Believe me, Kevin, I'm looking for answers' also-for what's best for all of us, not just for me."

I tilted his head up so that our eyes could meet. "Sweetheart, just give me some time to work things out, okay?"

Kevin nodded then gave me a weak attempt at a smile.

We walked the project's edge, enjoying the morning sun and the slight breezes that were disappearing just as suddenly as they would arrive. Lisa and her daughter, Mira, had joined my clan for the walk this morning. It was the first time since the school year began that we'd walked to school together. We usually meet while picking the children up, but this morning, her company was welcomed. Talking with Lisa kept my mind off of my hectic morning.

"I'm not going to tell you about those shoes no more, Mira!" Lisa yelled.

Mira and Kia were pretending to jump double-dutch while Kelly pushed Kevin's chair. Mira was having too much fun to pay her mother any mind, let alone, worry about scuffing her new shoes.

"You should try Germantown Avenue instead of Ridge, Carol. They got the hookups for kids. Discounts out the ass."

"I need more than discounts. I need some free shit. My money has to go to bills this check."

"Uh-uh, girl. Those bills would have to wait, 'cause a heifer like me ain't tryna be no broke bitch for two whole weeks."

"Tell me about it."

Lisa rolled her two gray eyes. "Carol, you ain't never broke. You need to stop frontin'."

"Oh, I be broke," I assured her. "I just keep my broke ass in the house til I get some money."

We crossed Diamond Street as a group then the children broke off again, leaving us moms lagging.

Both of us wore clogs, thigh shorts and sleeveless

tees. Lisa's body was slim, firmer than mine, and I thought she was prettier, too. When she dresses up, she'd easily catch the eye of any man she chooses to-including mine. But if I didn't want James' sorry ass anymore, then I couldn't see how she possibly would.

Lisa and I separated shortly after the van headed to Roxborough with Kevin aboard. To clear my head, I decided to hike the two miles to the check place on Lehigh Avenue, and was pleasantly surprised that the atrium held only eight people, lined at two open windows. Unlike my last check day, there was no camping out of the homeless. The air was stale from the weekend closure, but at least the stench of molded clothes was gone.

It was my turn at the window. I gave the teller my ID and waited while she went through the routine of counting and shoving the bills through the slot. Her disinterest didn't move me a bit, and I showed it by stuffing the bills into my pockets with a gigantic smile.

Outside, I stopped at the sidewalk vendor to re-up on incense.

I bought two packs, Cinnamon and Blue Nile. The balls of my feet were sizzling from walking the two miles in clogs, so I decided to catch a hack.

I chose a Jamaican woman with a boyish haircut, wearing a Kente. She happily led me to a burgundy something that resembles a Mazda. Every time she'd jolt the stick shift to drive faster, her conversation would pick up, too. She was talking nonstop, as if we were home girls.

"Dis' ting 'as gotta change, see?" She was talking about the streetlight. "C'mon, c'mon. People's got tings ta do, places to go. Do ya not, laydee?"

I nodded and smiled, not wanting to seem bored with her talking. The truth was that I could barely understand what she was saying, her accent was so thick. I was sure the lady was a nice woman and all, but my mind was busy trying to decipher James' recent behavior change. I definitely wanted to know how twelve years of happiness-well, not complete happiness, could dissolve in only a few months' time.

"Ya know, laydee, tis a crayzee world we in today. Mon try an' take women's independence for granted. We need to stand up on our own two feet an' be da queens, as our ancestor-mothers were. We…"

My mind drifted to a better possible life for my children and me. I needed a good paying job to accomplish such a goal, and I've been considering going back to school, especially now that the children are older and Kevin's situation is more stable. Before having the twins, my plans had definitely not revolved around DPA checks or dependence on a man. I think leaving open the possibility of returning to school could be good for me. The way things look, my days with James may be numbered, and I'll have to provide for my babies on my own.

I had the hack drop me off at Diamond Medical Center so I could renew Kia's ear medication. I was surprised when she walked me to the clinic's door, hugged me and said, "Queen. Sistah. Be strong." It was spooky, like she'd been reading my thoughts. It also made me feel selfish and insensitive for ignoring her gossip during the ride.

I left Diamond Medical Center pissed off and rundown. "Two damn hours!" I cursed under my breath. That's how long it had taken to get a prescription filled, something that should've taken just five minutes to do. I had wanted to run a few more errands before heading home, but after experiencing the clinic half of the morning, I put everything else on hold and headed home to clean. And that's what I did.

I started from the living room, straight through to Kevin's room. My three hours of work left me sweaty, funky, and with thirty minutes until the girls' school let out. I spent twenty of it in the shower, then hustled up to William Dick. I did a double-take when I saw James' van parked outside of the school. Whatever emotion makes a mother turn an easy stride into a hurried gate, that's what I was feeling, because James has never picked the girls up from school, and after our argument, I would never have guessed that today would be the day. I tried masking my concern when I reached the passenger's side window.

James was smiling.

"What's wrong with you?" He asked.

I forgot I chew my bottom lip when I'm nervous.

"Nothing. I'm just surprised you're here."

He nodded that he concurred.

"Well, it was a slow day, and the boss gave us the afternoon off. I thought I'd do you a favor."

"Thanks. That was sweet of you to think about me-especially after the way you stormed out of the house this morning." My tone was more accusing than appreciative. I wanted to imply that I hadn't forgotten. I'd succeeded.

His smile disappeared. "Baby, I'm sorry. I was trippin'. All day long that shit's been on my mind. I damn near fell offa the scaffold thinking about ways to make it up to you."

The thought of him fallen from a twenty-foot scaffold made me smile. He must've misunderstood my smile for forgiveness, because he exited the SUV and stood next to me, all tall and broad, and pressed his lips against mine in reconciliation.

I pulled away mid-kiss, just as a pack of schoolchildren broke through the elementary school's door.

James' sleight of hand was confusing, the change too dramatic. How someone could turn 360-degrees in one morning was beyond me. I decided to keep the shield raised.

The twins emerged from the sea of children more surprised to see their daddy standing there than I'd been. It was evident, their small, curious eyes were searching for clues of this morning's argument.

I'd dressed them in jeans and pink blouses with different color ribbons to hold steady what had been bushy ponytails. Kelly's ribbon was gone, and her hair hung wild across her cheeks. She looked like a baby Cleopatra with a blowout. I gawked at the red juice stain covering Kia's front and shook my head.

"Look at yall, looking like the homeless."

They eyed each other's look of confusion.

"Uh-uh, Mommy," Kia began.

I held up a finger to quiet her excuse. "I don't wanna hear anything you have to say, little girl. It's time for your little butts to learn how to do laundry."

Kia hung onto her father's waist.

Kelly stood next to me.

"You gonna pick up Kevin now?" James asked

me.

I nodded while finger combing Kelly's hair.

"Then I'ma run the girls on home."

"Why can't we wait for Kevin together?" I asked.

"I got somewhere to be in a few, and I still gotta change my gear."

I looked over his work clothes and stained Timberlands. I could've pressed the issue but was in no mood to argue. Besides, it made no difference to me if he came or went. "Yall go ahead and get in the van," I said to the twins. "Your father taking you home."

"How long you gonna be?" James asked.

"Not long. The van'll be here in a little while."

"I'll see you at the house then." He turned to leave then spun back around. "Oh, that's right, I'm on E. You got a few dollars on you, for the tank?"

I peeled a five-dollar bill from the twelve I'd brought with me and handed it to him.

The van dropped Kevin off a half hour later than usual. The driver, an aged, overweight White Woman, with a huge mole on her cheek apologized. She'd blamed her tardiness on a traffic accident. Kevin was pumped.

"It was awesome, Mom! You shoulda seen all the fire trucks and police cars that showed up!"

"Kevin, somebody could've been seriously hurt."

"But they wasn't. Ow!"

I popped him upside the head like I usually do when he says something stupid. "There's nothing good about accidents, Kevin." He rubbed the spot where I'd popped him. "I know. I was talking about the fire trucks and cop cars." He wiped some dirt from the Iverson's I'd bought him.

"I know you was at school frontin' with your new kicks."

"Nah. They know what time it is. Thanks."

"You're welcome."

We were silent until we reached the edge of the projects, where I let him roll himself. We were side by side, passing 2309 building. Beside the building, steam pipes needed to be repaired and several areas of grass had to be dug up, leaving huge dirt mountains. Large slabs of plywood covered the gaping holes, and plumes of steam poured out from around the woods' edges. Children had taken to the dirt mounds as if they were playgrounds, hurling rocks, and mud packs at each other.

"My friend, Jay, said that his aunt's name is Rhonda. She live in Johnson Homes." He was watching me closely, searching for a reaction.

"Rhonda, huh?"

"That's what he say her name is. Now what, Mom?"

"I'll ask James about her."

"Why not just leave him?"

"I can't. I thought we'd talked about this, Kevin?"

"I know."

I went behind Kevin's chair to push. I refused to let him see the fury or the hurt in my eyes. My mind unlocked the image of every Rhonda I've ever known. There weren't many, and I wondered if Rhonda is that "somewhere" James had said he needed to be.

I'd expected to see the van parked down the ramp, in front of the block where we live. It wasn't there.

"Mom, I thought you said James drove K. K. home?"

"He did. He had to get gas first."

I pulled Kevin into the house, and was surprised the television was on, so was the dining room light. The twins sat Indian style on the floor and were watching cartoons.

"Where's your father?" I asked.

"He left," they answered in unison.

"And left yall by yourselves?" I helped Kevin from his chair to the sofa. "Did he say where he was going?"

"Nope," Kelly answered without batting an eye from the TV.

I felt the hairs curl at the back of my neck,

wondered what could have been so important to James that he'd leave my babies alone.

It was after six when I sat the children down for dinner. Lamb chops, Rice-A-Roni, and peas. Although I was upset with James, I'd put away a plate of food for him in the microwave. During our twelve years together, I've found it more productive to interrogate James after lovemaking or while he chews away at the love I'd put into his meals. It was difficult to watch Kevin pick at his food, peek at the empty chair, at me, then to his sisters, who were happily demolishing their meals with slurps and wet fingers. Kevin wears his emotions like diamond cufflinks. I caught his eye and smiled, even though I knew he was anticipating the upcoming explosion between James and me. He was worried. I wanted to run his mind away from his grief. "You know that boxing thing is this weekend, if you still want to go?"

He shrugged and shifted in his seat. "It's probably gonna be corny anyway."

"Maybe not."

"I wanna go," Kia chimed.

"No, this is for Kevin. Just like when you and Kelly went to Chucky Cheeses."

"Aw, Mommy."

"Don't 'aw, mommy me." I turned back to Kevin. "Let me know if you change your mind, but not at the last minute, okay."

He nodded. His worriment had not left, but the gleam in his eyes showed that he was mentally reviewing the possible events that would make up the benefit.

After dinner, I took on the task of washing the girls' hair. One at a time, I parked them on the floor, between my legs, and greased their scalps. I was talking on the phone to Janice when I twisted the last of Kelly's braids. "Now, go upstairs and bring me down the scarf and my big brown pocketbook," I said to Kelly. I stretched my bare legs out and leaned back on the sofa.

"-and all you need is a little bit of sugar in the greens, with smoked turkey, not that processed stuff, and they'll keep running back for more."

"Janice, I'm not even tryna pick no whole bunch of greens, let alone wash 'em."

"Well, chile, that's the only way to cook 'em. Put those girls to work. They old enough now."

"You ain't never lied about that."

Kelly shoved my pocketbook and a handkerchief in my lap and flopped back between my legs.

"Ow, girl! Watch it!" I cried. "Get your narrow behind offa my foot."

"Well, I'ma let you go," Janice said. "I see you got your hands full."

"Mm-hm. This child nearly broke my leg just

now."

"I'll call you tomorrow."

"Alright then." I hung up the phone and went about wrapping Kelly's braids. "Don't be sleeping all wild on it," I warned, just as I'd warned Kia earlier.

Tomorrow there would be clothes shopping to do, a cable bill to pay, and finally, I plan to put a down payment on a new washer, because the eighty-dollar hunk of metal we own, keeps breaking down every other wash. We've already paid twice its worth.

I rummaged through my pocketbook for my purse. I couldn't find it. I searched again to be sure before having to make the trip upstairs to look for it.

"You kids been in my bag?" I asked the twins.

They were always messing in my things, playing dress up. "No," they hollered with unity.

I tried recalling if I'd put my money somewhere besides my purse.

I hadn't.

I leaped from the sofa, hoping what I feared hadn't happened, took the stairs with my mind nearly made up, and wound up tearing my bedroom apart. Doused drawers ransacked the closet, overturned the bed. I even checked the bathroom and started searching places I knew I hadn't gone. I became so upset that my entire body shook like I suffered from malaria.

"Oh, no the hell he didn't!" I yelled over and over. How could he steal from me and his children?

My pulse carried the pace of a wild stallion, and I tried to calm myself before I developed a nosebleed or something. I picked up the bedroom phone and speed dialed Janice. As soon as she picked up the telephone I barked, "Your son stole my money!"

"He did what?"

"Stole my kids' money!"

She was silent, probably on the other end shaking her head, thinking what I was thinking. "That's a damn shame!"

"Why would he do something like that?" Janice asked.

"I don't have the faintest idea, but when you see his sorry ass, tell him he might as well not bring his ass here." I slammed the receiver back in its cradle.

Seconds later, the phone rang. I let it ring and ring. I yelled to the kids not to pick it up. I didn't want to speak to a soul, let alone one of James' family members. I sat on the bed and palmed my face, tried not to cry, but I couldn't help it. I was fed up with James' bullshit. It was over.

# CHAPTER 12

# WESLEY

Rows of spectators encircled a 20x20 sq. ft. ring-not only from floor level, but from the balcony, too. Joe Frazier's gym was packed.

"Whoop. There it is! Whoop. There it is!" Spectators were shouting while a midget, costumed as a circus clown, danced around the ring, avoiding a giant of a man in silver wrestling tights. A pint- sized referee joined the two.

Today, many great fighters packed the historical building.

If they weren't present physically, their photos graced the walls' wood paneling, a mixture of modem greatness with classic: Ali, Dempsey, Marciano, Meldric,

Holmes, Spinks, Leonard, Duran, Hagler, Louis, and of the course the man, himself. Smokin' Joe. "Whoop. There it is!" The crowd chanted with the music. Laughter has been bouncing from wall to wall ever since the charity event had begun.

I was sitting ringside, three rows back. Every time someone slammed to the mat, a thunderous "Blam" a nerve inside of me popped. That's how close to the action I was. I sat among a few notable celebrities: Bill Cosby, Will Smith, and Cris Byrd just to name a few who've intensified my delight.

Mr. Cosby and Will Smith were seated together and had twice stood to goof on one another as if they were part of the show.

The benefit's objective is to raise funds and awareness for sickle-cell anemia, a disease which accounts for many deaths among African Americans. Although the cause for which so many have come together in support of is a morbid one, the atmosphere has remained quite festive. There was no place I'd rather be.

My head swung toward the entrance for the umpteenth time.

I was again hoping. Waiting. An outburst of laughter forced my attention back to the ring where the giant was staggering around hurt, and the midget had taken to the top rope, despite the referee's protest.

When the dwarf slipped from the top rope and banged his privates, pure anguish covered his face, giving warrant to another outburst of laughter from the crowd.

Tickets for the benefit had not been easy to come by. I had to pull a favor from Clarence for the three seats I'd reserved, two which are empty beside me. I spied the entrance again and sighed. The main event would be starting soon.

Circus music filled the gym while the giant chased the midget in circles until becoming dizzy and slumping to the canvas. The midget raised his arms victoriously, leaped onto the giant's belly and pinned him to the referee's three count. Applause erupted for the midget while he flexed his imitation of a world class bodybuilder.

When the ring cleared, an emcee, a white-haired gent with burnt brown skin, sporting a tuxedo, spoke a heartfelt message about the cause.

I was nearly ready to concede to having been stood up when Carol and Kevin entered the gym. I restrained myself from yelling at them like an enthusiastic child. Too many slips in my Mr. Smooth image and Carol would almost surely, in my opinion, be turned off. I excused myself through the row until I'd shuffled to the center aisle where they were.

Both looked lost-more nervous than anything else. For all of the anguish I'd put myself through during my wait for them, the smiles on their faces when they saw me approaching made it all worthwhile.

I greeted Kevin with a handshake and Carol with a wide grin.

"I'm glad you're here. I didn't think you'd make it."

"We were sidetracked."

"We wouldn't have if you and Aunt Tonya didn't take so long at Grand mom's," said Kevin.

"Boy, hush." She playfully plucked the back of Kevin's head.

I escorted them to the third row then realized there was a problem. Kevin's wheelchair wouldn't fit through to our seats.

We shared now-what looks.

"Give me a minute." I cleared my throat and bent to the ear of an older man. He and two teen girls occupied the three seats from the aisle inward. "Excuse me, sir. Would you mind if we switched seats, my brother's chair can't fit through to ours?" I pointed to the three empties.

The three of them eyed Kevin then the seats. The women were quick to nod "yes."

"Why can't you go 'round?" asked the man.

"Like I said, the chair won't fit."

Displeasure ruled his stare. "Oh, okay," he grumbled.

I believe the unflinching cooperation of the females he sat with influenced his decision. I helped Kevin into the aisle seat and folded his chair beside him. Carol sat beside me.

"I don't think he wanted to move," Carol said.

"Too bad." I reached behind Carol to tap Kevin and caught wind of her vanilla scent. "Do you recognize them?"

Kevin's eyes followed to where I was pointing then grew large as marbles. His mouth fell open, but it was Carol who gushed, "Oh, my god! Tell me that's not Will Smith sitting there!"

"That's him, mom! Him and Bill Cosby!"

"Oooh, he is soooo phine!" Carol added.

"So, you think Mr. Cosby's phine, huh?" I asked.

"Not him-Will."

"I could let him know you think he's cute."

"And? He's still not my type. Too light."

"Can I get their autographs?" Kevin asked.

"I'll see if I can work it out," I answered as if I were their managers.

We were all smiling-and kept on smiling—all the way until the benefit ended with former, heavyweight champs, Larry Holmes and Joe Frazier, playfully sparring followed by a song of unity, sung by Philly's own, Pattie Labelle.

It'd been the first time I've heard Pattie sing-live. I've heard her many times on wax, but in person, her voice had been so much more electrifying. She'd had us all holding hands and swaying our heads back and forth.

Because of Pattie, I'd been given the perfect opportunity to do what I'd been wanting to do since Carol had shown up. Touch her. Carol's hand had been small in mine…soft as baby skin.

When the benefit had ended, Carol had clapped and whistled as loud as anyone. She'd thoroughly enjoyed herself and so had Kevin. If I hadn't been hooked on Carol before, I was hooked now.

I'd been especially impressed with Kevin. He'd been surprisingly reserved, a cool little brotha with curious eyes. Checked out everyone around him the entire time.

And when I'd noticed his look of being preoccupied with his own shortcomings, I witnessed his bravery, the courage I use as my own inspiration, rise above harboring pity. Twice we'd caught each other's stare. Each time, his smile assured me that I'd been accepted and slowly erased some of the sorrow I'd felt for him.

It was after five. We were at Milano's Pizza, just off of Delaware Avenue, in Kensington. The only fault I could raise about the benefit would be there had been no food there to eat, just popcorn and hotdogs, none of which I'd had an appetite for. It was Kevin's idea that we have pizza. I was cool with whatever. So far, Carol was, too.

The pizza parlor was near empty, the few other customers were Caucasian. The decor was of Old Country Italian. Huge, oak tabled booths lined the walls. The blinds had been pulled to block out most of the sunlight. Just the yellowish glow from the candle shaped bulbs lit the parlor, but the air conditioning set the tone for Milano's comfortableness.

I felt bad about Carol's uncomfortableness with eating in public. Nevertheless, Kevin and I dug into the large mushroom pizza like two hungry cavemen.

Carol was shaking her head, wearing that look that women give when they're disgusted. "Yall eat like pigs."

We giggled and kept at it, exaggerated our ferociousness.

"Eat your pizza, Mom," Kevin said around a mouthful.

"Yeah, eat your pizza, Mom," I echoed.

Carol sipped her large Coke and continued her

head shaking. She bit into her slice as if it had feelings.

"I hate that."

"What?"

"Women who front when they eat."

"Oh, you tryna say I'm frontin'?"

"I'm not trying to say nothing. I'm saying it. You know if you were home, that slice 'a be history."

"He right, Mom."

She aimed a glare at Kevin. "Boy, hush. The pizza is hot."

I glanced around us. "Nobody else seems to be having a problem."

She tsked, picked the slice up from the paper plate and snatched a huge bite from it.

"Happy?" was her muffled reply.

"Yep."

A mother with three children was in the booth beside us. The children were stretching the cheese from their pizza like gum. Pizza sauce covered their tiny, pale faces, and their mother continuously begged for them to get off of their knees and stop playing with their food.

They'd sit for a hot minute then climb back up to stare at us like they've never seen Black folk before.

"How's school?" Carol asked me.

"It's cool, I guess."

Carol wiped sauce from the sleeve of her beige

blouse with printed angels. The blouse complemented her hazel eyes. And for the first time, I noticed the small scar, glistening above her top lip. "What's up with the, "'I guess'?"

"I'm still getting used to school."

"Is the work hard?"

"Not really…at times, I guess. When it piles up, I think the stress of having to get it done is what makes it hard."

"You seem to have your thing together."

I laughed. "Me? I don't think so. I still have a ton of issues I'm working with."

Kevin reached across Carol for another slice from the pan.

"All hidden deep?" she asked.

"Not all of them."

"Just the juicy ones, huh?"

"It depends on what you consider juicy."

She rested an elbow on the table, laid her head in her palm. Her eyes searched my face. "Who are you?"

I half smiled, leaned back, and revealed just how perplexing her question was. I blew out some air. "Who am I?" I let the words linger.

Kevin was watching.

"I'm the kinda person who used to dodge that question."

"So, that makes you what…?"

"Trying to grow-morally. I'm a guy trying to redeem himself for making some bad decisions." My eyes were on Kevin.

"How old are you?" asked Kevin.

"Twenty-four."

Carol folded her slice in half and took a large bite. She wiped her mouth with a napkin.

"I can't wait til' I'm twenty-four," Kevin said.

Carol finished chewing. "You're still young. How many mistakes could you have made?"

"Believe me. A lot."

"You ever killed somebody?" That was Kevin. His eyes were wide and excited.

I smiled away his question, but a twinge of remorse charged through me.

"My friend, Danny, was killed. He got hit by a car, didn't he, Mom?"

Carol nodded then picked some unseeable thing from Kevin's face. "He sure did, honey."

Kevin kept on talking. "The car didn't stop or nothin'. Whoever did it had to be a coward. Would you had stopped, Wes?"

I looked at him surprised, scratched the edge of my mustache before answering, "I would now. But I'm not sure if I would've in the past."

Carol stopped chewing and stared at me.

Kevin glanced away then turned back. "Well, at least you're honest about it. A lotta people say they would, but I know they be lyin'. They only say it 'cause they think they supposed to." Kevin returned to his slice while Carol and I shared an awkward moment.

My appetite was lost. The parlor had become as stuffy as a broom closet. My past had bum-rushed me like a gang initiation. My palms were moist when I snapped back from my daydreaming.

Carol had noticed. "You okay?"

"Yeah, yeah. I'm cool."

"You didn't look cool."

"I was thinking about some things."

"I saw you. Was it your lady friend?"

I smiled without an answer and flipped the script.

"How's everything with you and your man? You happy?"

Kevin eyed his mother. I assumed he wanted an answer, too.

"What?" she laughed. "Why yall looking at me like that?"

"Answer the question," Kevin pushed.

Right then, I knew there was turmoil in her relationship. Her hesitation spoke volumes.

"It's under review."

"Under review?"

"Yep. That's all I'm saying." She smiled and waved to the hyperactive children in the next booth.

Kevin shook his head and sipped his drink.

We ordered a pizza to go and left Milano's with large Styrofoam cups of sodas in our hands. There was still daylight left "Where to, partner?" I asked Kevin as we settled inside of the Volvo.

"Let's ride around for a while."

"Huh-ell no! This ain't no hooptie," Carol told him.

He sank into his seat with a hmph.

"I know the perfect place, if you have time that is?"

"Some," said Carol.

"Good.

I pulled the car into city traffic and clicked on the radio. Yolanda Adams' "Open Up My Heart" filled the interior. Carol was trying her best to keep up with the song's lyrics. She was impressive with the parts she knew. Then again, I was a bias audience, unlike Kevin, who was covering his ears and wailing werewolf calls and laughing.

All hell broke loose when I joined in with my best baritone.

Kevin's howling rose several notches, then, when the song ended, we all began cracking up. It was an all-out comedy feast.

I turned off of Allegheny Avenue and five minutes later was swerving the smooth asphalt road of Fairmount Park.

"Where are you taking us?" Carol asked.

"To my castle," I remarked in my best Dracula imitation, my Mr. Smooth, semi-thug demeanor turned off.

We were occupied with our own thoughts as we past the Reservoir amidst the thicket of evergreens. I don't believe it was anyone's intention not to converse, but the park's scenery was breathtaking, one to behold during a quiet drive.

I turned out of the picnic grounds onto East River Drive and headed west for ten more minutes, pulled the Volvo onto a narrow, dirt road leading to a gray mansion.

A huge white sign, bolted to a black, iron-spiked gate read: SMITH PLAYGROUND. I turned to Kevin. "There's about two hours of daylight left. What do you think, partner?"

Kevin was sitting up straight. His eyes were dancing.

Carol turned to the backseat with a grin. "Well? Do you wanna go in or what?"

He nodded with his focus on the park's entrance.

We emerged from the parking area with Carol pushing Kevin's chair. I went to purchase our entrance tickets, and on the way in, stole an eyeful of Carol's booty.

The sway of her hips caused her rump to jiggle in her tight, beige cotton slacks. I licked my lips and enjoyed the view, wished I could've stayed behind her longer, but she stopped, forcing me to stand side by side with her.

"So, where should we start?" I asked of either of them. There were several rides for us to choose from.

The Up & Under roller coaster, the Saltshaker, and Bumper cars, to me, are must rides-especially for newcomers. Benny and Stacks used to grind me up so bad for punking out on the rides that I now force myself to ride them every time I visit the park. I'm still learning to enjoy riding them.

"What's over there?" Kevin asked, he was pointing to a group of visitors who were huddling with their necks stretched upward.

"That's the Saltshaker."

"Why they call it that?"

"I'll show you."

We headed in the ride's direction, never taking our eyes from the huge, fiberglass ball as it slowly rose more than twelve stories. Then dropped.

Even from across the park we could hear people's screams. Not girly screams either, but the screeching of adult males as well. The huge ball stretched a massive bungee cord to a near stop, then shot back upward, half the distance it had fallen. The ball bounced five or six more times in the same manner then swung freely until it came to a complete stop.

Dizzily, riders began emerging from the ball on unstable legs. Some onlookers began pushing loved ones toward the ride, but most wouldn't budge. Carol wouldn't go near it as well.

"Come on, mom," Kevin coaxed.

"Uh-uh, I don't like heights."

"We're going to be inside," I said.

"So?"

"So, come on." I grabbed Carol's hand and tried pulling her.

She wouldn't budge.

"You tryna be the oddball?"

"Uh-uh, I'm not ridin' that thing." She yanked her hand from mine.

Kevin and I laughed at the fear covering Carol's face, and so did a few onlookers.

"Suit yourself. You ready, Kev?"

"Yup."

An instructor helped me lift Kevin into the ride

then checked the straps that formed an X across his chest.

Kevin was smiling from ear to ear.

So was I.

We returned Carol's wave as we began our twelve-story ascend over the park. The floor was clear so that we were able to watch the ground fade and the shrinkage of spectators.

Carol hadn't yet taken her eyes from the ball. She was shielding the sun from her eyes with one hand and waving with the other.

I looked to Kevin. "You, ok?"

He nodded.

The higher we climbed, the more intense his expression became, I sensed he was becoming nervous, simply because, as a frequent rider, I still experience nervousness.

The ball stopped rising along with the humming of its motor. Five seconds…ten seconds…then it happened. I closed my eyes. My body was being lifted from my seat and my feet unplanted from the floor. I peeped out of one eye to see the ground rushing upward at me. The screams and prayers inside of the ball were deafening. I twisted my head to Kevin.

His fingers were gripped around the safety bar, and his eyes were bulging. A Kool-Aid grin covered his face.

Suddenly, my insides felt as if they were being stretched. I thought the pizza I'd eaten would splatter the walls the second we were snatched upward-then bounced and bounced-then swung.

When the ride ended and the instructor was unfastening Kevin's seatbelt, Kevin was still smiling.

I felt nauseated exiting the ride, and my insides felt like Jell-O. I tried hiding the effects of the ride when I saw Carol standing there, laughing.

"I told you not to ride that thing," she giggled.

Several minutes past before the nausea subsided. Usually, the ride wouldn't have affected me. I contributed my motion sickness to the pizza.

We were headed for the roller coaster.

I have to admit that I wasn't looking forward to another episode of tosses and turns. I couldn't punk out now, though. Kevin kept smiling at me like everything was all good.

I smiled back at him with forced enthusiasm, and Carol, she just kept laughing at me. She reached for my hand and squeezed it in an expression of gratitude.

I knew that Mr. Smooth would be joining Kevin on the Up & Under roller coaster.

# CHAPTER 13

## CAROL

Existing a phone booth, I blushed just thinking about my actions over the past two weeks. I'd added voice mail to my telephone service and couldn't seem to stop checking it for Wesley's messages.

For me, Wesley's voice has become enough to enlighten every dark mood my mind wanders into. Maybe it's because most of our conversations have revolved around what we desire in an ideal mate, qualities we've seem to have already found in one another.

I haven't been this giddy in years, not since Langston and I began experimenting with sex in his grandmother's basement. The smile on my face could've been surgically planted there two weeks ago, and still not have expressed my joy.

I joined Tonya on the comer of Susquehanna & Dauphin Streets.

"Who'd you call?"

"Nobody. I checked my messages."

Tonya scrunched up her face. 'You don't have a machine."

"I added voice mail." A sly smile escaped me, enough to rouse Tonya's suspicion and get her started. She pointed a manicured finger at my grill. "Oooh, bitch, you got another man!"

I tsked. "What? You trippin', girl. Don't nobody have no other man."

"Bitch, don't play me, ok. I know all the little tricks we women do, alright?"

"Stop being so damn nosey."

"I will-just as soon as you tell me what messages your homebody ass got to check."

I blushed enough to foil my deception.

Tonya jumped up and down. Her miniskirt was so short, it damn near exposed her panties. "I told you! I knew it! I knew it!"

She was always getting overly excited about nothing. "Calm down, Tonya. Dang. People looking at us like you crazy." I grabbed her arm to calm her. "Girl, would you walk?"

Again, her face balled up. "I don't care about these people lookin' at me."

"Well, I do. I live around here."

We were coming from the check place. It was Tonya's check day, and I finally needed to borrow fifty-dollars from her-with James stealing my money and ail. Tonya had treated me to getting my nails and eyebrows done, and herself to an expensive one-piece, leather tiger-striped jumpsuit.

A family on the stoop of their home, eyed us like we were crazies.

"How yall doin?" Tonya asked them sarcastically.

They offered smiles and waves. In the ghetto, recognizing crazies was as easy as recognizing the police.

"Tell me who he is," Tonya demanded.

I smiled at my sister. "If I do will you act like you have some sense and promise not to say anything?"

"Cross my heart, hope my weave catch fire." She blessed herself.

"His name's Wesley."

"Snipes I hope."

"Nope."

"Well, do he look like the brother?"

"Tonya, this guy is so-phine. I'm talking good-goodity-moo phine. He has those thingies in his hair."

"What thingies?"

"You know…those things Jamaicans be wearing…"

"Dreadlocks?"

"Yeah. Those things."

"Oh, god, Carol. Those things look nasty."

"No, they don't-plus, his are short. They're cute."

"All of 'em ugly to me." Her eyes widened. "Wait a minute, girl. I know this ain't the same guy from the club?"

I smiled.

She rolled her eyes at me. "I thought you said that he's phine?"

We were turning into Raymond Rosen when her head snapped toward me. "You gave him some poo-tang, didn't you?"

One of my dogs slipped from one foot. I hopped around on the other foot to retrieve the other clog. "No. For your information, we're just friends, talk on the phone, emotional uplifting that's all."

"Mm-hmm. What's next, emotional back rubs?" She looked upset. "I don't believe you, Carol. You been seeing this guy all this time and ain't tell me nothin'. Tell me this…Do this friend have a J.O.B.?"

"Yeah. He's a mechanic."

"That's good, 'cause your ass needs fixing."

"He also goes to Temple."

"Temple where? College?"

"Yep."

"Honeyyy, you better pull out those Kama Sutra books and snag you a piece of his future."

"I'm with James already." I regretted allowing James' name to curse my lips, especially since Tonya and James hate each other's guts. I'd also made the mistake of telling her about James stealing my check. I braced myself for her criticisms, but none came. All she gave me was a don't-be-no-fool look.

Tonya walked with me to the Big Field where she slipped two Trojans in my short's pocket and said, "Get your freak on, girl." She laughed herself to tears while walking away.

The two of us are so different that I wondered how we get along so well. We're much like Jekyll and Hyde, and sometimes, I believe that I live my darker side through her.

From two-hundred yards, across the huge tar field, I could see the back of my row home. My mind drifted back to two weeks ago, the night James and I had clashed. The night I'd confronted him for stealing my children's money.

I sent the children to Tonya's for the night and sleep had been just a memory of mine. It'd been late when I heard the front door close, and still, I hadn't come up with how I'd confront James. But just in case of any domestic violence, I'd taken the liberty of strategically stashing kitchen knives all around the house.

I was already in jeans, so I slipped on my Reeboks, breathed deeply, and headed downstairs for war.

James was lying on the sofa with a faraway look in his eyes. He greeted me with the gull to smile. "Hey, babe."

"Don't the fuck 'Hey, babe' me, James. Where's the money?"

"Don't start trippin', Carol."

"Trippin? James, where's my kids' money?"

He licked his lips and snorted loudly. "It's in my pocket."

"Give it to me." I held out my hand, palm up. I knew damn well there was no money, but I did it anyway. It was an alternative to attacking him.

He sat up. "I got you—chill. Damn."

"Uh-uh, James. I don't wanna hear shit. You had no business taking it in the first place!" My anger was about to boil over. All day, I'd waited to confront his sorry ass, and through my anger, my mind couldn't register all that I wanted to say, because words weren't first on my agenda. Kicking his ass was.

He tried to stand up, but I pushed him back down. He sneered up at me like I was crazy, and I just may have been because something inside of me had snapped.

"You don't have to stand up to give it to me!"

His eyes were menacing and his face broke, serious. "I told you I had it. Now back the fuck up off me!"

"I'm not going nowhere till you give me my kids' money!"

He laughed at me, tried to again lift from the sofa.

Without thinking, I punched him square in the nose.

He fell back down and grabbed his face. "What the…why the hell…you…"

That was all I heard. I was on him. Hurling blows against his head.

He curled into a ball when he realized he couldn't grab my flailing arms without catching punches to his face.

When my flurry tired me out some, my hearing returned.

"Calm down, Carol. I got it, baby. I got it."

I finally heard my own voice. "I'm tired of your shit! I'm sick of it!" I was huffing and puffing when I backed away, tried desperately to catch my breath. "Where's my kids' money, James?" I begged. "How could you do this to us?"

Slowly, James emerged from his shell, my barrage of punches seemingly not having left a mark on him. "I'm sorry, baby. I swear I am. Just calm down a minute and I'll tell you."

I pointed to the front door. "Get the fuck out, James! You don't give a shit about us! Just get your shit and get the hell out of our lives! All you care about is you!"

"Come on, Carol, don't do this to me."

"I don't wanna hear it, James. Please, just get your shit and get out!"

Hesitantly, he lifted from the sofa.

I stepped back some to allow him past while hurrying to recall if I'd stashed any kitchen knives around the living room. I felt confident I wouldn't need them. I felt indestructible, especially when I noticed the trickle of blood at the tip of his nostril.

James faked like he was passing me, then grabbed me, pulled me to his broad chest in a bear hug. My arms were pinned at my sides, and I thought he'd throw me to the floor, but he didn't. He merely held onto me, smothered his face into my shoulder. "I'm sorry, Carol."

"No, get off me, James!" I was helpless in his

grasp, hating to have to listen to his lies and feel his tears against my skin. I didn't even bother trying to free myself. I just stood there, fuming, hating him for what he'd done to me, for his arrogance, his selfishness, and his ability to have manipulated me into believing that he loves and respects us as a family. I stood rigid with hatred for how I've trusted him; allowed him to string me along with a belief that one day we'd marry and make the struggles we've gone through well worth it. Yes, there was hatred for James-but there was also a love for him that was just as raw, a love mostly for whom he represents: my children's father. I love him so because my children love him and trust him completely. I love him for the care and effort he'd given them over the years. I was certain that I was no longer in love with James, but loved him only as someone would, a dear friend. It was this love that allowed a calmness to settle in my voice. "Let me go, James," I asked, still upset, but no longer angry. My anger was replaced with curiosity. I wanted to know what had possessed him to do this to us.

"If I let go, will you let me explain?"

"Just let me go."

"Will you, baby? Please."

"Yeah. We can talk," I agreed, mostly because my arms were becoming numb, and I just wanted him off of me. When I felt his grip, loosened, I quickly pushed him away. I folded my arms, Jeanie-like, and eyed him impatiently. "Well?"

He sniffed back what appeared to be remorse and wiped his face with a palm. I'd never seen James cry before and was glad I hadn't.

The sight wasn't pretty.

"Can I sit down?" he asked.

"Go 'head, but don't get comfortable."

"I hear you, Carol—believe me, and I don't blame you. You deserve a lot better than what I been givin' you." He sat on the sofa and eyed the black tile floor. He began rubbing his palms together like his confession would be deep.

My antenna went up. Regardless of how much I wanted to hear this, I wasn't about to allow him to go into one of his hour long speeches.

"It's like this, Carol." He paused. "I don't even know where to start."

"I wish you say something."

He nodded. "Okay, I'm just gonna say it. I been uh…uhm…I been…uh, using cocaine for the past six months. I'm sorry, baby. I swear. It's got nothing to do with you and the kids."

Okay-there was the confession out of his own mouth. It dangled in front of my face like a plague that needed destroying, I stared at James and huffed, unbelievingly. "You joking?"

He shook his head. "I wish I was."

"James, I know damn well you ain't spent my children's money on no drugs."

Again, he shook his head, kept his eyes on the floor.

"Then where's the money?"

"I used it to pay a debt."

"You telling me that a debt is more important than your kids eating? Who'd you give our money to, James?"

Embarrassed, he looked away. "I had pawned the van and had to borrow the money to get it back." He rushed his words as if they'd slip by me.

"What!?" I exploded. "How the hell do somebody pawn a damn van?"

He shrugged, had that l-don't-know-l-just-did look.

"Is that where the van was the night it was missing?"

He nodded.

"Get your kids' money, James. I don't care how you do it, just do it."

"Where am I supposed to get it from, Carol?"

"That's your problem. And so is finding a place

to live."

That argument had happened two weeks ago, and things have settled between James and me since, only after he'd agreed to go into a drug rehabilitation center, and came to terms surrounding our relationship.

We were officially separated. And only after his drug recovery would I even consider reconciliation.

I hadn't been the ruthless bitch I'd wanted to be. I've allowed James to stay at the house until a bed at the rehabilitation center opens up for him. I did it not for my conscience, but for the girls' sakes of having their daddy around.

I crossed the Big Field to my row home and wondered if showing James so much leniency will backfire on me. For the past two weeks, he's hardly been at home or at his mother's. I've checked. But to question him or try to restrict his movements would probably only complicate our living arrangement and send him the wrong message.

When I entered the house, I headed for the shower and rejoiced about Janice having the children for a couple of days. I ran the shower cold to suppress the excitement that had built over the thought of meeting up with Wesley. A dose of Wesley, I feel, that will be good for my soul.

The message he'd left on my voice mail was short

and sweet, his voice, a sensual baritone. *"Hey, Carol, this is Wesley. I haven't stopped mv heart from beating over your vet. I hope it never does. I can't wait till dinner. Dress nice. The night is yours."*

I don't think I'll ever forget those words or the lunch date we'd shared two days ago, at the Mont Serrate, on South Street. He'd also taken me shopping at some of Society Hill's plush boutiques, treated me to a feast of perfumes, flowers, and balloons. His appreciation of me had been endless, exactly what I'd needed during a time when I was feeling so unappreciated.

I dried off with a towel then babied myself in Jergens lotion, gave my special places a bit more attention-just in case. I shimmied into my red halter dress that accentuated my body's curves. It falls six inches above the knees and displays enough cleavage to set fire in any male's mind. I added three-inch pumps to push my booty out when I walk. With Black men, a sistah could never have enough booty, and tonight, I was determined to give Wesley an eye full.

I checked myself in the bathroom mirror, selected hoop earrings and a thin, gold necklace with a Nefertiti piece. I also settled for a little lip liner and sprinkled a pinch of golden glitter on my shoulders and chest. I smiled when I thought of Wesley possibly finding specks of glitter on himself in the morning and thinking about me all over again.

Just as I raised the phone to call Janice to check on the children, James walked in the house. I placed the receiver down and began fidgeting with items in my purse.

"Where you goin'?" He questioned with eyes that scolded me from head to toe.

"Out with Tonya."

"Again?"

I slammed my purse shut, without extracting a thing. "Yep. Again."

"Where you goin' that you gotta dress like that?"

I surveyed my outfit. "Like what?"

"Like a hoochie."

"I'm not for it, James. We settled this weeks ago."

He puckered his lips and set down the bag he'd carried in.

"I don't clock your whereabouts, do I?"

He was swallowing his complaint. I could see his fury over the agreement we'd made.

"Is this why you wanted my mom to babysit, so that you can run the streets with your hoe-ass sister?"

"James, don't start your shit. I'm going out. I deserve it."

He turned his back to me and palmed his

forehead like he had a headache. He stood silent for a few seconds until I tried to walk past. He grabbed my arm. "You ain't goin' out tonight. You might as well go and take that shit off."

I gave him a stem stare, as if he'd lost his fucking mind. "Get your hands off me."

"No. Uh-uh, fuck that. You my woman. You not gonna be out there hoeing."

I snatched my arm away. "I'm my own damn woman first of all, in case you don't remember, we broke up. Second, if you put your fuckin' hands on me again, I swear, I'm calling the cops on your ass. You don't own me. Now try me." With that, I strolled by him and out the front door. I heard a crash behind me and hurried my pace. I didn't feel like testing James' sanity.

Daylight had begun fading to evening and a half moon appeared to be in walking distance. I wasn't keen on walking through the project's plaza alone, in heels, with my assets luring the wolves, so I took the back route, around Glenwood Avenue to meet Wesley.

It'd been my idea for us to meet away from the projects. I didn't want to risk Wesley and James bumping heads or nosy neighbors spotting us together. Where the van picks up Kevin, is where we'd agreed to meet. And every few seconds, I'd peep behind me as I walked, just in case James was ignorant enough to follow me.

Wesley's Volvo was already there waiting. A chariot to my rescue, it seemed. The closer I got to his car, the stronger I sensed that his eyes were raping me. It was hard enough to strut my stuff without blushing, so, when he trotted around to the passenger's side and opened the door for me, I allowed myself to smile til he was back inside, beside me.

He was decked out in black slacks, a white cotton shirt, and a silk black vest. He even wore cufflinks, I noticed, when he grabbed hold of the steering wheel. Very few twenty-four-year-old brothers from the hood wear cufflinks on a date. I thought, either he's trying to impress me, which he'd already done weeks ago, or he really is different from the average brotha, which in itself is impressive and refreshing.

"I'm glad you're early," he said.

"I'd never keep you waiting," I signified.

He caught on quickly and smiled. "Good, because I have something planned. A surprise."

"What kind of surprise?"

"Damn, you look mmm-mmm good!"

I smiled. "Thank you. You look rather dapper yourself, but don't try and dodge my question. What kinda surprise?" I asked, raising my tiny fist at him.

"Okay, you don't have to beat me down. How about I show you?"

We rode Diamond to Broad Street, where we headed southbound into Center City. I thought we would have dinner at a downtown restaurant: Bookbinders, La Bee Fin, Little Italy, but Wesley kept traveling until we'd reached the Ben Franklin bridge. I didn't want to show my concern about leaving the city, so I swallowed my inquiry and fingered the CD case.

"Oh, my bad. You wanna hear something?"

"That depends on whether you have more than hip-hop." He pulled a CD from the case. "Here, check this one out."

I lifted D'Angelo's "Voodoo" from his fingers and smiled. "Mr. Preparation, huh?"

"I don't look at like that. The brother's just smooth. I like his style."

"Mm-hmmm." I put the CD in and pressed "play." Hypnotic tones of D'Angelo's "Naked on My Video" filled the car.

I slipped into the music and allowed the lights of the Camden skyline and the darkness of the Delaware River soothe my thoughts and render me into a state of tranquility. I let my head fall back on the headrest and closed my eyes. "I love this song," I crooned.

"I don't blame you. I have to give the brotha his props. He's cold."

We slowed through a toll and skidded onto the

Jersey expressway. I had no idea which one we were on. They all seemed alike to me.

"How's Kevin?"

"Oh, God, that boy's a trip. He asked about you yesterday, but I told him we haven't spoken since the benefit."

He nodded. "You know I have mad love for shorty, right? I know not being able to walk has to be hard on him."

"He'll never let you know that, though. He always tryna act all brave. I don't know where he gets the strength, certainly not from me."

"Yeah, right, cut it out, Carol. I haven't run across many young sistahs as strong as you."

I laughed. "Mm-hmm. Yeah, ok."

"Seriously. Look at yourself. Your beautiful, dependable, loving. You're raising three beautiful children in this world despite the setbacks you've had to face. You're a survivor. I probably would've broke down long ago. Sisters today are strong as hell. It's us brothers. We need to step up to the plate and claim our responsibilities."

I melted right in my seat, just deep enough to prevent me from leaning over and sucking Wesley's lips from his face. I smiled instead. "It's not easy getting men to face truth nowadays."

"I know. I'm only saying it because Black men are failing, filling up prisons and morgues. That's why when you look around and all our Black women occupy the jobs that Black men had once occupied, you wonder. I know I do."

I looked away from him knowing that I wasn't among the workforce he spoke of. My financing is welfare. A choice I'd been forced to make, two years ago, in order to be able to stay at home and care for Kevin after he'd gotten shot. Now that Kevin's situation was more stable, and the twins are older, I've been thinking about taking some vocation courses.

"Are you ok?"

"Yeah, I'm fine."

"You all of a sudden got quite on a brother."

"I'm ok." I leafed through the CD's. Tribe Called Quest. Kenny Latimore. Babyface. Macy Gray. Jay-Z. Tupac. Alicia Keyes. "Have you lived in Philly your whole life?" I asked.

He clicked on a turn signal and switched lanes. "Bom and raised."

"You ever get tired of it?"

"Of Philly?"

"Yeah."

"Sometimes, I guess. Don't think about it much. My days are too full. Between work and school, I don't even get enough time to hang out. I've been slipping lately, though."

"I hope I've had something to do with that."

He didn't answer, just smiled, a smile that told me that it wasn't just my thought, occupied with "us."

"WELCOME TO ATLANTIC CITY" the green and white sign above the highway read. We'd been driving for forty-five minutes and it only seemed like twenty.

I smiled. "Atlantic City. Is this my surprise?"

"See, If I'd have told you, then you wouldn't be surprised." We turned to the off ramp doing at least 75 mph. "Do you drive a lot?"

"I used to. Not anymore."

"Why not?"

"I'm not the same person I used to be, so there's no need to do the same things, hang out at the same places."

"You keep saying that. What kinda person were you?" Wesley's expression became somber, like the question really bothered him.

"Oh, I'm sorry-"

"No. Ifs not you. It's just that I'm a good listener, but I hate having to talk about myself."

"I'm feeling that. I'm the same way."

I'd keep everything bottled up inside of me until

I'd explode. It's a miracle I've already shared so much of myself with Wesley. "Hopefully, over dinner, all of that will change," I said. Dinner was outside, aboard a dock that had been converted into a tourist attraction. We were on the ship's deck along with a host of couples with so much tonguing going on, I thought, they'd spiked the food. After an hour under the stars and inhaling the cool ocean's air, I found that it wasn't the food that had set fire in the couples, but the night's salty breezes and candlelight created the mood. It was perfect.

Wesley and I had the shrimp with lobster tail and a bottle of Zinfandel. We laughed and talked as if we've been friends since birth. He was extremely easy to talk with. While the water rose against the beach and my shield was slowly being lowered, I blabbed to him about everything, from me losing my virginity to my live-in relationship with James.

Occasionally, he'd sip his wine, comment, or nod. But mostly, he allowed me to vent.

After dinner, we strolled barefoot under the stars and I admitted my guilt.

"I'm sorry for boring you with this baggage."

"You could never bore me."

"Don't be so sure. I sometimes talk too much."

"Not tonight you didn't." He grinned and reached for my hand. I was glad he did. It's been a long time since I've felt so admired and protected. He'd taken me a million miles away from "my world."

We were back on the highway by 11:00 p.m. and Kenny Latimore's soothing voice was drifting through me, massaging my mind.

At 12:20 am, Wesley was rousing me from my sleep. It took a moment for the familiar, North Philly surroundings to settle in. I yarned and stretched. "I'm sorry. I fell asleep," I mumbled. I took another look around. "Why'd we stop here?"

He smiled. "I live here. I also need to use the bathroom, bad." He reached for the doorhandle. "You staying or coming in? I'll only be a sec."

It felt as if my bladder might burst if I didn't empty it soon.

"You promise not to attack me?"

"Don't worry, I won't bite unless you ask."

I couldn't get to the bathroom fast enough.

He pointed me upstairs, in its direction.

"You want something to drink?" he called up to me.

"I'm fine. Thanks." I found the bathroom, dropped the toilet seat and let loose. I checked out my surroundings.

Nothing I saw indicated I was on another woman's turf, although, there were two toothbrushes and two brands of toothpastes on the sink's counter.

I cleaned myself, flushed, then snooped in the medicine cabinet. Bayer. Cologne. Men stuff. Things that made me smile and reassured my confidence. I searched a hairbrush for hairs other than Wesley's-female hairs in particular. The brush was clean.

I rinsed my mouth and finger brushed my teeth with Aim until my mouth was refreshed. I checked my face in the mirror once more before returning downstairs.

Wesley's living room was dull. Simple. Manly is how Janice would describe it, no plants, no curtains, just shades and cream- colored walls. The sofa and love chair was a rust color matching the thick, burgundy carpet. A clock, stereo, and computer were the only other furnishings.

The kitchen is where Wesley emerged from, palming a pager. He gave me a smile on his way upstairs.

I heard the toilet seat lift then the splashing of water. I began wandering around downstairs-just looking.

When Wesley returned, I was deep in his icebox. I closed the fridge and entered the living room just as he was flopping on the sofa.

"What were you doing, raiding my food?" He was slipping on a pair of Nikes.

"Just looking."

"Tryna see if a brotha eating right?"

"Something like that. I see you aren't."

"Yeah, well, just don't mess with the chips. I know where everything's at."

"Ha, ha. Martin Lawrence."

He smiled up at me. "You ready?"

"For what?" I answered, realizing I'd been lost in his eyes.

"To get home."

"Oh. No, let's stay awhile," I answered. I felt confident sauntering to the sofa. I accidentally brushed a breast against him on the way by and my nipple sprung to life. I kicked off my pumps and took a seat.

"It's kinda late, but would you like to hear some music?"

I shrugged. "Show me what you got."

He pulled a CD case from the stereo cabinet and selected one. When he bent over, I couldn't help but notice how perfect his butt was shaped. I looked elsewhere to avoid even going there, but my nipple was still acting up.

"You down with this?" he asked, forcing me to turn back toward him. It was the case for Sade's newest CD. Seconds later, softly, her sultry voice filled the room.

"I'm down with all the sistah girl hits," I

answered.

"I can tell. That's one of the things I like most about you. You're not all caught up in the hip-hop craze like other young sisters. You're versatile."

"Oh, I like hip-hop."

"I do, too. But that's not what I mean. I mean you're well grounded. Smooth."

"Smooth? Me?"

Yeah, you. You don't even dig it, do you? That's just what I'm talking about. You're always being who you are."

"That's what having children will do for you."

His eyes focused away from me. I'd lost him somewhere.

"Do me having kids scare you?"

"It depends."

"On what?"

"Whether they're Children of the Com or Children of the Hood."

"Which do you prefer?"

"Definitely, Children of the Com. They carry knives. The other's carry guns. Ouch!"

I popped him upside the head. "Stop talking stupid, Wesley."

"How about if we stop talking period?"

"Then what would we do?"

"I'm sure we'll think of something."

Our faces inched closer as we spoke. "Are you sure about this?" He whispered.

"Mm-hm. You?"

"I'm sure."

His breaths lingered at my lips for a brief moment before our bodies melted against one another's. He pulled away and searched my face for something. "What about James?"

Our tongues danced a slow drag that stirred a fire throughout my body, a heat that lingered just below my pelvis. I used Sade's lyrics as inspiration to continue. "*Is it a crime for me to want you and for you- to want-me too*". I was definitely feeling my girl at the moment and allowed myself to become raptured by Wesley's kisses. I reached for him and moaned at the feel of him pulsating, begging to be freed. I unzipped his slacks and squeezed him.

He moaned into my mouth.

"Do you have something?" I gasped, trying to catch my breath.

"Mm-hm."

I hated the moment we'd separated but smiled when he returned with two condoms.

"This one's for later," he said, smiling. "Come on."

We were undressed before we reached the bed.

I'd known for weeks that I'd wanted him but was now surprised at how my body needed him.

His body was toned the way I like, a shade lighter than his hands and face, but still dark and sexy. The way his eyes devoured my nakedness turned me on more. I pushed him onto his back and kissed his bare chest. I circled his nipple with my tongue and licked him across the belly. Just the feel of his arms caressing my arms and back had my skin tingling.

I kissed him-there-for a while.

From his navel to his neck I rose with more licks and nibbles.

I smothered myself in him, not caring about this being our first experience. This was something I needed, something that I had desired for weeks.

In the background, Sade's voice coaxed me on, so I reached for him when he was ready. My insides were already wet and on fire. And when I lifted over and onto him, the sensation of him entering me damn near made me cry. I shuddered.

I was lost.

Pleasure forced my head to fall back and I gasped, slithered atop of him like a rattlesnake. "Ssssss." Oh, God, we were a perfect fit. I slowly rolled my hips to Sade's rhythm. I took my time so that I could enjoy the loving attention Wesley was giving to my breast.

He pinched them, turning on a faucet of titillation, then rolled me onto my back without leaving my nest.

He remained on his knees, and I lifted my bottom up to him, crushed two handfuls of the bedspread and bucked as hard as I'd ever done before as joy ripped through me. I lifted up and trapped him there while I buried my screams into the crook of his neck and exploded.

I bit my lip as I slowly began regaining some composure, rode the wave of pleasure while stroking his back and contracting my muscles around him. "It's ok, baby, go ahead," I whispered in his ear. "Ssssss. You can do it, baby. Come on. Oooh."

As I'd hoped, his strokes became more precise, more intense, had a fulfilling purpose to achieve. I felt my own pleasure begin to bubble again and met each of his strokes with a soft hum. I squeezed him deeper into me, then cried out when I felt him erupt along with me.

Silent and fulfilled, we settled into each other's arms and caught our breaths. Minutes later, I felt him slip from inside of me just before I dozed off.

In the morning, I awoke in Wesley's bed-alone. I wrapped myself in a sheet and tiptoed down to the kitchen. Wesley was nowhere in sight. I returned upstairs to find a sheet of loose leaf taped to the bathroom mirror: "Gone for food," it read.

I showered then dressed, stripped the sheets from the bed and replaced them with clean ones I found folded on a hamper in the hall. I sat down to phone Janice.

Before I could lift the phone from its cradle, I heard the front door close and headed downstairs.

"Did you get anything good?" I asked.

Wesley was pulling groceries from a brown paper bag and placing them on the table.

We met with a kiss.

"No good morning, huh?"

"I'm sorry. Good morning. Now, did you get anything good?"

"Hungry?"

"Yep. Starved."

"I thought you would be here." He pulled a bag of Lays onion rings from the bag, like a magician, and handed them to me.

I snatched the bag like an excited child. "How'd you know I love these?"

"I have my sources."

"Kevin told you, didn't he?"

"Wouldn't you like to know?"

"Aw, be quiet."

After a bacon & egg breakfast-that Wesley

cooked, he dropped me off at home. He had to work the afternoon, so we made plans to hook up afterward. Truthfully, I wasn't ready to see the Volvo pull from the curb without me, and if I could've, I would've stayed the entire week with him.

I waved to a neighbor, who was all up in my business, and took to the walkway smiling. My smile stayed frozen until I saw the white envelope on the floor of my home.

Again, only Kevin's name, written in black ink, was on it. And like always, my hands trembled as I fumbled with the money inside.

# CHAPTER 14

## WESLEY

Lying used to come easy to me, used to fly from my tongue habitually, leaving behind a trace of a smile as a chaser. Now, all it does is leave my mouth bitter with a sandy film that turns my stomach and pierces the armor I've been covered with for the past two years.

I should be happy expected to be. But instead, my head-the one with the brain-and my heart was in battle over the mess I'd gotten myself into. Maybe Stacks and Benny were right. Could I be more gutless and hypocritical? Maybe doing crooked and conniving shit is the only instincts I know how to use to get by. And near the top-not that deep down inside bullshit—I know Carol deserves better than my selfishness.

I pushed the machine's blue "start" button and watched the Buick's tires rotate at 85 mph. My mind drifting back to the worst day of my life—the day that had sparked what I had hoped would be a transformation of my soul.

The three of us had been partners-Stacks, Benny, and me. We thought we'd had it all figured out, knew the inside scoop on where he would be, who he'd be with and when.

Bittles had been a nemesis for our business as well as to twenty or so other drug dealers, who had hustled in the hood. A loose cannon. Someone who would show up under the Yum-Yum tree and clock cocaine for hours, without any regard for whose comer it was. There are rules to every game, even the "Coke Game," and Bittles had broken them all in the short time he'd hustled on the strip.

For many dealers, the worst part had been having to sit and watch Bittles pockets get fatter from cocaine sales he'd robbed another dealer of. Many hustled closed mouthed about it and put up with the big man's growing network. But when Bittles began surrounding himself with a crew from outside of the neighborhood while shooting local dealers for hustling under the Yum-Yum tree, too, word began floating about how somebody needs to slow his roll.

Shit hit the fan when other dealers discovered that Bittles had the neighborhood 5-0 on lock and was systematically eliminating all competition in order to maintain his stranglehold on his fast-growing network. After several months into his coup, Bittles ambition reached me and my brothers-Stack especially.

For three years, my brothers and I had been dealing weight. Benny and I were at the house bagging up when one of our workers rushed in with the news. "Stacks got hit!" He yelled, four times, three unnecessarily, because after the first, he had our attention. "Stacks didn't stand a chance," he said, sadly.

It had been four against one-in an alley-them with guns, Stacks with the common sense of a mule, three thousand dollars, and seven ounces of cocaine he'd stupidly refused to give up.

Stacks had caught it badly. Shattered jaw, two swollen eyes, twelve butterfly stitches in the back of his head. At the hospital, he looked sickening, all wrapped in white gauze.

Benny had been hyper ever since getting word that Bittles was responsible. "I'ma kill 'em! I swear to God, I'ma kill 'em!"

"Chill. He gonna get everything he got coming, but we have to do it the right way." I said.

We left Jefferson Hospital's emergency ward at

four in the morning, filled Stacks in on our intentions, and headed to a row home, behind the projects, a hideaway we used for cutting and bagging cocaine.

For three frustrating days, Benny and I were forced to sit and watch Stacks limp around, favoring Dark Man. We were well aware of Bittles crew waiting for us to hastily retaliate. So, we sat simmering and planned. We needed the neighborhood gossip of Stacks' beat down to tone down some, and for Bittles' crew to move on and victimize a few others. We needed a diversion. An out. It took until the end of the week for that opportunity to arrive.

Stacks' face was healing, but his ego wasn't. He was bitter. Benny was nervous. I was scared. Neither of us had ever done what we were planning to do.

Stacks had Bittles' schedule all figured out. He gave the impression that he'd been anticipating this moment for a long while, because he not only knew times and places but reasons. He wouldn't refer to Bittles by his name, only refer to him as "That Fat Mutherfucker" or "That Bitch-ass Nigger."

Bittles stood six-three, 350-pounds of roundness, and took no breaks from crazy, even on Christmas Day. Tiny craters covered Bittles burnt toast complexion, and he always wears a sneer that could easily intimidate Riddick Bowe.

Intimidation is something that will no longer happen. It wasn't until we'd loaded two nines and a dock, had I realized the true magnitude of premeditated murder. I wanted out right then, but there would have never been a day that I would be able to face my brothers if I'd backed out now. It could have easily been I hunchbacked, wrapped in white gauze, after being robbed and pistol whipped. Whether I wanted to or not, a ghetto's tradition says that I have to. As the oldest brother, it's expected of me. I wasn't about to buck tradition.

At dawn, we stole a '88 Reliant, and parked across the street from Bittles' Range Rover. Stacks had said that the house we were eyeballing was where "'That Fat Mutherfucker" bagged up his coke.

After two hours of waiting, shifts began changing. Working folk and schoolchildren started replacing the smokers and vagabonds. Daylight had begun creeping up on our plan, as did our impatience, mine in the driver's seat, Stacks' beside me, and Benny's riding shotgun. Every eyeball was fixated on the gray, spray-painted door with the black "2315" drawn high above the peephole. There was no screen door to hinder our view, and all the shades were drawn. In the car, no one spoke, just watched, and waited for the house's door to open. Ten minutes later, I could hear nervousness in our breathing when finally, it did.

Three thugs, all grinning and sporting plenty of platinum, filed outside. Bittles' six-three frame held up the rear. He was smiling the broadest of them all.

Just as we had planned, I started the engine and snatched down my ski mask. Stacks and Benny followed suit, only they stooped out of sight.

My heart was racing, pacing its own record as I whipped the car into a u turn. I had the Glock poised at the window when I eased to a stop thirty feet in front of the crew and cut loose a thundering of gunfire over the car's roof, awakening the early morning with the ghetto's alarm clock.

Benny and Stacks were firing, too. Even after Bittles had fallen, gunfire still roared.

One of the posse had been returning fire while sprinting. I'd been chasing him with bullets when the kid turned the comer a millisecond after I'd squeezed the trigger.

I saw how awkwardly the boy hit the pavement. I froze, slid back into the driver's seat and sped off.

The entire episode had taken less than twenty seconds, but what I hadn't expected was for the effects to linger years later, grip my soul, and wring away so much of what used to be me that I'm now struggling to know if I'm coming or going.

I abandoned my thoughts of whom I used to be and pressed the red "stop" button to end the Buick's tires from spinning. The hammer shaped wall clock above the tool shelf showed 4:25 p.m. I stepped outside for a smoke, trying to forget my skeletons and focus on the lifestyle I've fought two years to create. I could never forget, though. The memory of what I had done, gnawed at me like a hungry pit bull.

Bittles.

Kevin.

Each a horrible nightmare that I'm sure will forever haunt me.

I dragged from my smoke and eyed the junkyard's traffic. Any misery I was experiencing, I feel is deserving, I told myself. Forget the changes and sacrifices I've made. What's been done, has been done, and I should be more concerned with Kevin's happiness more so than my own.

"Boy, what you doin' out here? We still got two radiators and a fuel-line need fixin." Magic was carrying the porn collection I'd stumbled across. Black Tails. Players. Black Lust. Black Heat.

At least I knew his flavor.

He lifted the plastic, trash can lid, next to the "BEWARE OF OWNER—FUCK THE DOG!" sign and dumped the magazines inside.

"Why'd you do that?"

"I got a sickness that needs curin', and they ain't helpin none."

I plucked my cigarette butt damn near off the lot. It hit the asphalt and rolled another five feet. "What you need is therapy," I told him.

"Hell, if I ain't learned enough 'bout women after fifty-six years 'a dealin' with 'em, then I s'pose you right—but I'm too old for crap like that to set in my thinkin."

The owner of the junkyard wobbled outside his yard's gate. He was a huge man with the strut of a pregnant cat.

Magic and I waved.

Magic backed up and gazed over the shop. "I'm thinkin' 'bout redoing' this front, here. Paint it up real fine and add some extra things 'round the place. You know, spruce it up a bit."

I smiled at my uncle. It's amazing how losing the love of a woman can promote so much change in a man. Here it is, Magic had stolen from Gloria's business to care for his mistresses, and now, when he'd been caught, he suddenly has a conscience to repent. I still believe to know Magic well, despite being unaware of the crazy chick who'd mace me. He was simply shamefaced. If Gloria decided to take his baldheaded butt back, today, he'd probably do the exact thing a week from now. I gritted on my uncle and sighed. "You're more pitiful than I am."

"How you figure that?" He turned and walked into the shop.

I followed. "Because, you should already know better. I'm still learning."

He shot me a get-the-fuck-outta-here-with-that-dumb-shit look.

"Doin' stupid shit has no age limit," he replied. "Maybe when I go see that shrink, I'll take you with me."

I left Magic in the back room with his therapist, a full bottle of Tiger Bose. I was on 33rd Street, heading northbound with a storm cloud for a mind. I was caught between love and common sense, and throughout my life, it's been common for me to lust for love.

At a red light, I jerked to a stop behind a gray Maxima, almost bumping it across the yellow stripe. I tooted my horn and waved an apology.

The driver, a young White woman, gave me the finger for my effort.

The entire time we waited for the light to change I could see her peeking into the rearview. She probably thought that I had used the bump as a ploy to lure her from her car so that I could carjack her. Yeah right.

I beeped my horn five or six times, just to rile her

for stereotyping me.

She ran the light.

I turned onto Norris Street, laughing, thinking more clearly. I don't think I'll ever be unconcerned with whether I should become so attached to Carol. Intimate, in love possibly. It would be foolish to expect to build a relationship based on lies and deceit. I'm no relationship specialist, but I'm fairly confident that rule is high on their list of no-nos.

Then there's Pam. Where does our relationship fit on the chart? Our relationship seems to be headed straight into a danger zone. Going to Atlanta to work for her father is something I'm just not feeling. Besides, adjusting to another learning environment could be brutal.

I pulled the Volvo up in front of my crib and wondered if not telling Carol about Pam had been intentional. It's not like I would have lied to keep Pam a secret. I assumed that by not mentioning her, it could somehow indicate how insignificant she may be to my future.

I checked my messages as soon as I entered the house. The indicator flashed "3". I pushed the first. It was Benny. "Yo, bro, get wit' me. Blue Velvet got this thing goin on in a couple days. We gotta make plans. This shit's gonna be the bomb. Holler at me."

The second message was from Magic. He wanted to know if I had taken his girly mags out of the trash can. They had disappeared that quick. What did he expect doing business across from a junkyard? His garbage is another man's treasure. Being lonely must have settled on Magic fast.

The third message made me forget every trouble and nearly break an ear to not miss a word. It was from Carol. Earlier, we'd agreed to meet. "Hi, Wesley. I'm calling to say thanks…well, not thanks, but-you know. Anyway, call me when you get in. I'm waiting to hear from you. Bye."

I didn't pause to lull over what I'd been thinking about all afternoon, never even tried to rationalize the message. Her number is on speed dial.

# CHAPTER 15

# CAROL

I couldn't believe I almost slept with him, again. Here I was barely hanging onto one relationship with my fingertips, and now, another with my toes. I feel like I'm being stretched from a dock to a parting ship-praying I'll not crash into the ocean. I've fallen before.

Long ago, I had promised to give myself some in between time if James and I were to ever break up. But we hadn't and now, we're only separated. Nonetheless, I've been cursing my hormones for failing to control themselves with Wesley.

For the umpteenth time, I casually picked up the telephone and paused a shaky finger over the numbers. For a second, I wondered if I were sprung, then I realized that my emotions were all jacked up over James having been the only man in my life for the past twelve years. Again, I replaced the phone receiver in its cradle.

It was after four and Oprah's topic of the day- Welfare Moms Survive, had me twisted tighter than a sailor's knot. The guest, a thirty- four-year-old, African American mother of four, was grinning over how she overcame a lack of motivation for wanting to become more than a welfare recipient. I was feeling the sister. I mean "really" identifying with her. I knew I could walk in her footsteps if only I would apply myself.

I swigged my cherry Kool-Aid and turned the television volume up a notch.

"It was that simple," the woman was saying. "All I did Oprah was, sat my behind down and study. I'm telling you…I told the kids, my man, and my girlfriends that, between nine and 11:00 p.m. is my time, and that I didn't want to be bothered for nothing."

Oprah gave her guest a high five. "You go girl!"

I thought about how my children would react if I tried telling them not to bother me at a certain time. Hell, already today the twins have phoned four times from their grandmother's with dumb questions and complaints about nothing.

Oprah's guest had raised a hand to display her two-carats diamond, engagement ring to the audience.

The audience stood and applauded while Oprah raised her guest's arm like she'd won a prizefight. I wiped my watery eyes.

Returning to school has been something I've been wanting to do, especially now that the children are older and the stay-at-home mom thing has become played out, not just with me, but with many moms of the twentieth century—Black moms in particular. Everything begins with a dollar nowadays, and because our men are overpopulating prisons, productive Black men are scarce, and Black women carry the burdens expected of two parents. Wesley had been right. More Black women are in uniform. As a child, I recall the uniforms worn by women today were worn by men. Security guards. Police officers. Prison guards. Even the gender of Corporate America has changed. Independent women in business suits were everywhere. Honestly, the idea of returning to school and joining America's workforce has become more appealing since Wesley has entered my life.

While the credits rolled up the TV screen, I felt like I had been left behind an excursion to a better world. I wanted and needed more in my life, a reason to be thankful for something besides my children's wellbeing.

Today's not the first time I've felt cheated. Whenever my mind swivels back to my mother's absence, the feeling would surface. I have a knack to dwell on the negatives. And for me, foster care could have happened to anyone, but it didn't. It happened to me. Other than spending my childhood wondering about what would push my mother to pass me off to strangers, my days with my foster parents weren't normal ones. They were devoted Jehovah's Witnesses, and tight with a buck. I sometimes still wonder why they had wanted me there in the first place. I wondered if what I'd heard about only 144,000 Jehovah's Witnesses getting into heaven had anything to do with it. I had been eight years-old then, and thirteen when I became pregnant with Kevin. My pregnancy didn't seem like the big crime my foster parents had made it out to be. I was pregnant, not dead. I even thought about giving it away, as I'd been given away. But, with my love for Langston, that solution wasn't an option. Needless to say, my foster parents were all for giving up my child. I would overhear their whispers about how embarrassing it would be for them and their shame and their budget and their, their, their. I heard the whispers so frequently, from around the home's comers, that I finally packed up and left. Dropped them a one-page letter, assuring them that I was fine and was sorry things hadn't worked out with us. I also informed them that I was keeping my child-no need to worry themselves any longer about finances and embarrassment.

James had entered my life at this juncture, and with me needing a home, and Janice having taken a liking to me, I quickly moved in. Janice's obsession with Kevin had been scary at first. It had taken a long time for me to trust that she wouldn't try and take my son from me.

The single condition Janice had placed on me, for free room and board, was that I re-enroll in school. It had taken some adjusting, but, eventually, I began to feel like family. And James, he was simply thrilled to have live-in pussy at his convenience. Things had gone along well for everyone until I graduated from William Penn High with the twins growing in my belly.

The road has definitely been challenging for me already. From what the sister's testimony on Oprah exhibited, the road is what you make of it, and right now, my road seems to have been paved with a dusty ideology of a homebody.

Lately, I've been tired of feeling stifled into putting everyone's priorities and emotions ahead of my own. But, with me, being tired wasn't nearly enough to push my agenda ahead of my children. Now, with James about to enter a rehabilitation center, I knew that any inspiration to join the work force, will have to sit behind my need to stabilize my home.

It was after 7:00 p.m. I had broken down and left

a message on Wesley's machine for him to call me when possible. It was unlike me to act all sprung over a guy. But Wesley's intellect, sensitivity, and lovemaking had my nose wide open. I ran my tongue across the roof of my mouth, still able to recall the mint flavor he'd stained there. I was in a playful mood when he returned my call. I did something I had not done since high school. I turned off all the lights, stripped down to my Victoria's Secret, and lay on the bed, drawing itty bitty circles around my belly button with a finger.

"Yeah, I'm missing you, too," Wesley said. His voice was smoother over the phone, deeper for sure, but much, much sexier.

We had been teasing each other for almost an hour, and the crotch of my blue Victoria's had become damp. "How much do you miss me?" I asked.

"Beaucoup."

"Enough toooo…do what?"

"Why you doing this to me?"

"What?" I asked innocently.

"Teasing me like this."

"Am not."

"Are to."

"Am not."

"Then tell my Willie that."

"Let me talk to him." I heard the ruffling of the

phone during a pause, then he was back on the line.

"Did you tell him?"

We both giggled like high school teenagers.

"You didn't just put the phone down there, did you?" I asked.

"Well, you asked to talk to him."

"I'ma hurt you, watch."

"When? Soon I hope."

"You're not worried about getting tired of me?"

"Never that."

"Good." I picked at a few strands of hair forming a line to my bush. I was trying to resist the urge to say it, but it came out anyway. "I want you tonight," I rushed. Already I knew what his response would be.

We were on Wesley's sofa, illuminated by the television's light, cuddling and checking out the flick "Soul Food," my 90's favorite. We were at the part where the towel fell loose from the brother's waist and he shouts to Nia Long, "Stop looking at my dick!" I peeped over at Wesley's crotch, and he mimicked the actor.

We laughed.

It was comfortable in Wesley's arms. Quiet. Tranquil. He never talks a lot, which is something I like. I don't think many brothers realize how powerful silence can be, or the significance of cuddling up with a woman.

Sometimes a sister just wants to fall back and

relax, minus the drama that life creates. It's refreshing to not have that line crossed while your man is around. Not feel crowded, but safe. That's how I was feeling—safe.

When the credits began rolling up, neither of us bothered to move. We sat there watching a blank screen. I cleared my throat. "You gonna get that?"

"Nope." He had abandoned his T-shirt, shoes, socks and was wearing shorts. His muscular frame was that of a caramel calendar guy, and his dreads gave him the resemblance of a Jamaican god.

Both my breasts have been swollen since I had entered his house, but now, they were threatening to burst through my thin, cotton blouse, have been since the movie's sex scene, where the cousin screws Vanessa Williams' husband.

We sat in silence, except for the ticking of the wall clock. I nestled into Wesley even more, but not yet ready to jump his bones. "I'm seriously thinking about taking some community college courses."

Wesley's thick eyebrows rose. "Really? Good for you."

"Yep. I've been thinking about it all day. I think it's something I should do."

"Now, all you have to do is decide."

I climbed onto his lap and ran my finger from his chocolate temple to his thick brown lips. I played with his dreadlocks.

"Maybe I'll come to Temple and take some of the courses that you do."

"Neither of us would graduate."

"Why not?"

"We'll distract each other."

"You mean you'll be distracted. I'll be fine." I gave him a peck on the lips and felt his excitement against my tush.

We kissed.

My eyes wandered to the blinking light of his answering machine. This was my second visit to his home, and each time, he's allowed the machine to pick up his calls, with the speaker turned off.

I pecked his lips again and wondered if I was his first, second, or third option. I couldn't help pointing to the machine. "People are looking for you."

He flagged the machine. "Let 'em wait."

I put on my best I'm-not-concerned smile, but indeed I was. I wasn't about to get caught up in a serious relationship with someone who's already committed to another, regardless of my own baggage. It was also obvious that, if he was with me, then he and I were looking for something other than what our mates were offering. For me, I needed companionship. I'm still trying to figure out what Wesley could be needing.

I lifted from his lap with hardened nipples. As much as I wanted to devour his body. I feared another letdown relationship.

Too much of Wesley could be dangerous.

"I think it's time for me to leave." I straightened my thigh high skirt and blouse and held a handout to him. He grabbed my hand and lifted. "Why you leaving?"

"It's after eleven."

"I thought your kids were at their grandmother's?"

"They are."

"Then why not stay?"

"I have my reasons."

"Can I at least drive you home?"

"Sure."

Wesley slipped on a pair of Adidas and a sweat suit. In the car, he also slipped an R Kelly CD on. We vibed to "Twelve Play" as we drove Diamond Street toward Raymond Rosen.

I turned the radio down some and grabbed his hand.

"Are you upset because I didn't stay?"

"No."

"You sure?"

"Positive."

He gave my hand a squeeze and turned left on

24th Street.

I was surprised at how disappointed I was with his answer. Maybe because he was able to shrug off cuddling with me, without being able to sex me up-especially since I had propositioned him over the phone. I had forgotten all about that until now. I felt bad about having raised his hopes. "I wish you were upset," I said.

His eyes narrowed. "What?"

"I said, I wish you were upset. It'll at least show me that you want me around."

"That's crazy. Where'd you get that philosophy?"

"I don't think it's so crazy."

"Well, we all have our opinions. And for the record, I do want you around. More than you know."

I leaned over and kissed his cheek. "Thanks."

A red light halted us behind a Dairy Queen truck. Wesley pulled a Newport from his pack and lit it up.

I watched him drag from the smoke and pull away from the lighter. We were nearing the ramp that leads into the project's rear. He held the cigarette outside of the window and blew his smoke there, too. "Can I tell you something, Carol?"

"Yeah."

"I've never been in love before."

I looked at him and smiled, kept my tone even. "Why?"

"Too shy. Too insecure around women, I guess. Sometimes I don't know what to say or do, but I do know that being with you is something that's necessary for me."

I felt a warmth shoot through my body as I watched this beautiful man.

His eyes weren't on me, but on the road. The smooth sounds of R Kelly made Wesley's words sink into my soul with a subtle groove. He continued. "Carol, I don't ever want you to mistake my respect for what you want over what I want as a sign of my lack of need for you. Believe me-l do want you around."

We were quiet for the rest of the ride, both relishing in our own thoughts. We were turning the bend which leads to the block where I live, then I saw him-not Wesley, but James. He was making an exchange with a stocky, well-known drug dealer.

I felt myself slither down into my seat. Only my eyes slid in their direction as we drove by them unnoticed. I didn't want to look back to see if who I had seen was indeed James, my girls' daddy, my so-called ex, purchasing cocaine. I kept my eyes' straight and my mouth tight. I thought my heart would burst if I held my scream back any longer.

# CHAPTER 16

## CAROL

My body had been numb when I kissed Wesley good night at his car. I had gone to Wesley for comfort, but instead, had returned home even more rattled. I had believed that I understood the extent of James' addiction, but not until I actually witnessed James buying cocaine, did the truth of whom I had allowed to live around my children sink in. My children's father or not, James could no longer be trusted.

When we drove by James, my initial reaction was to scream out his name, explain to the drug dealer that he was a father and why not to destroy him, but I was too embarrassed then-plus, my friendship with Wesley would have been exposed. I had depended on James honoring our agreement to stay clean while he waited for a bed to open at the rehabilitation center.

If Wesley hadn't been there, I'd probably still be in the streets, screaming and cursing. Instead, I had come straight in the house, kicked off my flats, and stormed up to our bedroom, where I now stood, staring at James' clothes, strewn around the room. Suits. Sweats. Shoes. Sneakers. Belts. Ties. Underwear. I had dumped it all. I've never noticed the enormity of James' wardrobe until now, and no way in hell was I packing all of his shit, like I had intended to. He would have to do that himself.

I surveyed what used to be our room and saw James everywhere, all the bedroom furniture we had bought together. The bed. Dressers. Lamps. Carpet. I had been tossing James' clothes from the closet with such fury that I was now winded. I was furious over James' stupidity, at myself for giving James so much of myself, my life. Now that I'm aware of James' addition, his erratic behavior, lack of money, and reasons for running the streets, finally makes sense to me.

I shut my eyes to steady my breathing, to make the tears that streaked down my cheeks stop running. So much of me has been wrapped around James that, now, my life already seems as half empty as the closet I was staring into.

For months, I've been flirting with the idea of ending our relationship. But now that it's become more than a tease, the complications of doing so, weighed on me with guilt. It felt as if he were dead and had left me to fend for our children.

Outside my window, the wail of a siren and its red lights, ricocheting onto the bedroom walls, pulled me from my thoughts. Slowly, I began folding and hanging James' clothes back where I had snatched them from.

I couldn't do it.

I couldn't allow myself to abandon James like I had been abandoned, like he'd abandoned our children, emotionally and financially. James was sick and has been for a long while. Whether or not I was still in love with him, doesn't change the fact that my girls need their father, healthy and sober.

I refolded his T-shirts, jeans-wrapped his favorite, leather blazer around a coat hanger and smiled lightly. I sniffed back tears while remembering him freezing in the blazer all during one winter.

Up until recently, James had been good for me-- good for the children, which, for me, still remains what's important. For all the years of good he's provided, another chance is something he's earned; whether he deserves it, is something else. Of course, concessions will have to be made on his part. For all that is good in a man, the evil of drugs could wipe it away in one season.

It was after 1:00 a.m. when James' things were back in place. I snatched a pillow from the bed, a comforter, and bounced downstairs to the sofa, where I left them.

Back upstairs, I jammed the bedroom's doorknob with a chair, pulled a dresser in front of it, and climbed into bed.

Morning seemed to have come several times during the night. If I could've lounged in the bed forever, I would have, but I couldn't, so I traipsed into the bathroom, drowsy as hell.

The mirror had to be lying, because in it was a stranger with mussy hair, and red, puffy eyes and swollen cheeks. Not mustering the strength to wrap my hair before passing out had made matters worst. I sighed at the fruits of my laziness before running a cold shower. I forced myself to stand beneath the frigid water until my body shivered awake.

After showering, I spoiled my skin with Jergens lotion then dressed in a watermelon T-shirt, a black ankle length skirt and clogs. I topped it off with one of Kevin's black Sixers' caps.

It was Friday, and I wasn't supposed to pick up

the kids until Sunday. Two days without my babies had been enough rest for me. I appreciated Janice's offer to keep her grandchildren while James and I work through our problems, but after seeing James buying cocaine last night, I wanted the children home with me and James to stay with his mother. I had intended on telling this to James this morning, but he hadn't come home last night. I guzzled two glasses of orange juice before heading over to Richard Allen.

Janice's eyes were curious black pearls when she opened her front door and saw me standing there. "Hey, Carol. What you doing here?" she chimed. Her smile seemed genuine.

"I came for the kids."

"The kids? Is everything okay?" She stepped aside, so that I could enter the house.

"Everything's fine. I just miss my babies."

"I thought I had them til Sunday?"

"Well, I'm here today."

Her expression indicated that my words stung.

I kissed her cheek. "I'm sorry, Janice. I just need the children home with me."

"Well, you should've called before coming. They're out somewhere with James."

"Where?"

"I have no idea. They left early this morning."

She turned and hurried toward the kitchen.

I followed. "Didn't you ask where they were going?"

"No." Her pace was quick. She entered the kitchen with me on her heels. "You know, Carol, the kids were supposed to stay until Sunday. If I would've known you were coming, I would've asked." Her tone carried the tone that my foster mother used to have.

I sat at the kitchen table and bit my lip.

"It's unfair of you to pop up and cut our time short. We have plans for the weekend."

"What plans?"

"To start, the barbecue we have planned for Clarence's 64th birthday."

"Janice, Clarence's birthday isn't for another week."

"Duh-I know that, but the kids are here this weekend. I was gonna call to see if you wanted to come by, but, I guess I won't have to now."

I sat back in my seat, deflated. She was right. I couldn't very well dismiss the children's plans.

"I thought you were all stressed out?" she asked.

"I never claimed to be anything. You did."

Janice tended to a Crock Pot, bubbling on the stove. She had kept herself up over her sixty-one years, but her oversized dresses, which look like robes, give her a grandmotherly look. She stuffed one hand in a mitt, lifted the pot's lid, and fanned away steam. She adjusted the flame. "Carol, don't be so stubborn. Them kids are fine. You act like we might eat 'em or something." I watched her place the lid back on the pot and wondered. When she turned around, our eyes met.

"What's in the pot?" I asked.

Her lips twisted at one comer. "Twin soup."

Janice had not lied about their plans for a barbecue. A huge amount of Clarence's family and friends were gathered. I wondered if Janice could be using the party as an excuse to keep the children longer. Too many grown folks were scattered around the small home for it to be the children's idea. Every adult had a paper plate of food and a drink, somewhere nearby.

I stationed myself at the far comer of the room, where I could view the entire place. A crowd of people was out front where the grill had been stationed. There was no backyard. I could hear the chatter from outside above the old Smokey hit "Cruising," the children's Play Station, and the card game that had broken out, almost immediately, after the first few guests had arrived. The alcohol was plentiful, the food quite edible, and the company compatible-one great combo to pulling off a successful barbecue. And so far, there's been a festive mood.

I was seated in a wingback, trying to melt James with one of my stares. If there were reality to heat vision, then he'd be a huge glob of melted dung.

He was with a cousin, a beady-eyed ex-con with a flashy, pinkie ring to match a sinister smile. I had met the cousin once before, before his lengthy stay upstate. I didn't trust Cousin Flashy then, and knowing James' recent state of mind, I trust him even less now. The two have been in deep conversation for the past half hour. It was time for me to break that mess up.

I sprang from my seat, smoothed over my skirt, and sashayed to interrupt their confab. "Whassup, cuz?" I asked, my smile as phony as silicone breast.

"Ain't nothin', lil cuz. Whassup with you?"

"Nothing. Excuse us." I spun to face James. "Can I speak to you for a minute?"

James' once manicured goatee was now worn raggedly. Now, aware of his problem, I could see the differences in him. His sunken cheeks, weight loss, and glazed eyes were sad.

James has seen my forced smile before and now he looked concerned. "Yeah, sure."

"In private," I added. Before James could answer, I was dragging him upstairs by the hand. I peeped back at Cousin Flashy. His smile wasn't so bright. He was smirking.

In the bathroom, I spoke my mind. "Why you fuckin' with his no-good ass, James? You know he ain't about shit."

"Who?" he asked, dumbfounded.

"Don't play."

"He family. I'm not supposed to deal with my own family?"

"That's not what I'm saying."

"Then why you all bent outta shape? All he wanna know is if they hiring at the site."

I twisted my lips to the side. "And that's it, huh?"

"Yeah. That's it."

I didn't want to look at him, so I eyed the pink and blue towels and wash cloths hanging from a rack beneath a window. The bathroom was small, so we were within a few steps from one another.

"I saw you buying cocaine last night." My tone was matter in fact.

His eyes darted away from me. "What the fuck…you following me now?"

"No."

"You must be."

"Well, I'm not."

There was silence. Our eyes were locked. I wasn't about to be the one to back down.

Beyond the bathroom door, an uproar of

laughter broke the spell we were under.

James backed away and sat on the edge of the bathtub and ran a weathered hand through his, now, semi-afro.

I stooped in front of him with a heavy heart. I felt bad for him, even sorrier for our children. "Baby. You need to go away from here-now. It's the only way," I pleaded.

He nodded. "Don't you think I know that, Carol? I don't need you to tell me that."

"Then just go, James. Get yourself some help, baby."

He shook his head. "I don't know if I can."

I tilted his chin up, forced him to look me in the eyes. "What do you mean, you don't know if you can?"

He pushed my hand from beneath his chin. His stare became icy. "I don't wanna stop getting high!" he spat.

"What?" A tiny laugh escaped me. "Yeah, right. You talking crazy now, James. You can't be that damn weak."

He twisted his head to me so quickly, I could've sworn I heard his neck snap. "Carol, get the hell outta my face, ok?"

I stood looking down at whom I used to respect as my man, then I slapped the hell out of him. "You ain't shit, James! Nothing!"

He grabbed my left wrist midair and squeezed tightly before throwing it to my side.

I pointed my finger in his face. "You willing to smoke that shit and throw away our family?"

He only stared at me and rubbed the cheek I had slapped.

I honestly believed that, if we weren't at his mother's place, he'd try and beat the shit out of me. I was crushed. "What am I supposed to do, James? What am I supposed to do about your children?"

His no-good ass continued his staring and rubbing his beaten down face.

Tears began welling in my eyes, but I simply refused to let any fall. His arrogant ass would probably think that my tears are for him. I was so full of rage that my one swift kick to his groin, let him know.

He dropped to the linoleum just as quickly as my foot was back on the floor.

I stormed from the bathroom, down the stairs, and out the front door. Every eye had followed my vapors as I stomped by. The sight of my children brought my march to a halt. "Come on, kids, get your things. We're leaving."

Kia and Kelly were combing dolls' hairs, and Kevin had his hand-held video game in his lap.

"Aw, Mommy!" the twins yelled.

"I said, get your stuff!" I barked.

Although I hadn't said a thing about James, Kevin, and I connected. I could tell he knew. "Where's your stuff, Kevin?" I asked.

"In Pop-pop room,"

I was relieved his stuff wasn't upstairs, no telling what James would do to me now-regardless, whose house we were in. "Go get 'em. And hurry up," I said. I had completely forgotten about the twenty or so eyes that were trained on me. The tone I had taken with the children hadn't occurred to me until they had gone to do as I told them. "Is there a problem!" I snapped at all the eyes.

Slowly, men, women, and children's eyes turned away from me.

When James emerged at the entrance with a killer's eyes, I felt like running, then I remembered my babies.

"Why you doing this, Carol? Why you taking the kids?"

"Because they're mine."

"They're mine, too."

"Not for long. You got what you want!"

Every eye was on us.

Behind James, Janice had ventured outside.

"What the hell going on out here!" she yelled.

I stared at James, waited for him to answer. I saw the nervousness in his stare and posture. He was quietly pleading with me not to tell his dirty, little secret. It was then I realized that Janice didn't know of her son's issues.

"Somebody better tell me something!" Janice roared. "Carol, where you takin' them kids?"

My eyes never left James'. Now he was daring me to break his mother's heart. "We gotta go, Janice. I'll let your son tell you why."

She spun James by the arm in her direction. His eyes remained on me. "Boy, what have you done?" she scolded.

Children began snickering and relatives were filing from the doorway to enjoy the ruckus.

"Nothing. She just trippin, that's all."

"Ain't no-damn-body trippin'. He's the one trippin'—or should I say, skitsin?"

James stepped within a foot of me and pointed his finger in my face. "Don't fuck with me, Carol!"

"Get your hand out of my face, James." I pushed his hand down.

He put it back.

I pushed it away.

"Get your hand outta that girl's face, James," said Janice.

He must've realized the eyes that were watching, because he decided to have the last word, by giving me the finger and walking off.

I refused to go out like that. He would lose this fight. "That's why your black ass on crack!" I shouted, hearing the words echo across the courtyard and reverb back to me.

James stopped in his tracks and sighed, never turned around, just walked into the house.

Janice's eyes turned to mine.

I closed mine tightly and nodded to her that it was true.

# CHAPTER 17

# WESLEY

In the past, I would have been near the stage, where Benny is, tossing dollars at a creamy skinned stripper. Instead, I was on a barstool, sipping on a cold Corona.

Blue Velvet was packed, as it always is, on M-W-F nights. Its crowd, not the ideal, business types men in their thirties, the young, powerful drug dealers and entrepreneurs.

I surveyed the young faces behind Polo shades and other designer frames. Oversized Kani. Fubu. "Black is Best" sweatshirts and baggy jeans are the norm. Scattered about, businessmen, poised on bar stools, gawking at the thick boned dancers but their dress style gave them an out-of-place look. The younger, aggressive patrons favored all of the dancers' attentions. They were the ones flashing the cash.

Mirrors were everywhere—walls of them. A silver, ball-shaped chandelier whirled colorful reflections of stars and hearts to pace the music thumping through wall speakers. An old Patra cut was on at the moment.

Stacks was beside me, stool-dancing like he always does. He claims dancing is for suckers.

I sipped my Corona, with one eye on Benny. He was already drunk, had been when he and Stacks had picked me up for this One- Time-Special, Janet Jacme lookalike appearance.

Benny has a serious thing for the Porn Queen, Janet Jacme. I've seen her in magazines only, but that was more than two years ago. I'm not high on porno flicks, but my brothers have been bitching about me, somehow, becoming too "uppity." That's the word Stacks had used. Me, I don't see a major change in attitude; however, I do find myself replacing club hopping, crap games, and tricking with: books, classes, and studying. These are the things which now occupy my time, but when I try telling my siblings this—I don't know if it's stupidity or what— they refuse to grasp my sincerity.

The music stopped and applause filled the club when a brown-skinned sistah, who'd been dancing, scooped her earnings to her small bosom and clicked away in three-inch pumps, carrying a monstrous booty.

"Yo, dawg, you shoulda been at the Mann with me and B when Patra did her thing. That shit was dope. She had niggahs tryna climb the stage." Stacks spoke with his Heineken swinging.

I've heard the Patra story before, but each time it would change. "Stacks, you told me already."

"Oh, yeah. But still, girly-girl was butt ball naked."

A short redbone with a nose ring and hair down to her booty, took to the stage, scandalous in a canary yellow G-string and top. The classic Earth, Wind &Fire cut "After the Love is Gone" surrounded us.

The red bone began her tease by licking a forefinger and touching her, supposedly, sizzling rump.

Benny came stumbling back to the bar. "Whew! A niggah be broke in an hour," he boasted, like being broke would be a good thing.

"How much you give that hoochie?" Stacks asked.

"A little somethin', somethin'. You know-gotta support our women. Ain't that right, partner?" he directed at me.

I smiled. "Can never have enough thong, right?"

"And you know this!"

"But you could've gave that to somebody more

deserving," I added.

Benny snatched up the Heineken that I had been watching for him. "Don't start that self-righteous shit. Brotha just tryna have some fun." He and Stacks touched fist.

"Oh, it's like that, huh?" I asked.

They both gave me you-don't-know looks and spun toward the stage.

I swigged my beer and joined them.

The dancer had positioned herself at the stage's edge, gyrating her hips and running a long, pink tongue over cherry lips. Her eyes were the sexiest of gray, made me look elsewhere out of fear of possibly emptying my pockets to her.

I happened to turn into the faces of two brothas posted near the front door. Both had menacing stares. Their snarls were meant to chump a brotha. Both were casually dressed. Timbs and leather. One was a blue-black complexion with a scraggly beard, the other one sported a low cut and was beardless. Both were gritting hard as hell.

I tapped Benny, on the sly, then had to damn near punch him to grab his attention from the stage.

"Yo, what's up?" he asked.

"Don't look, but niggahs grittin real hard."

"Where?" His eyes wandered from me a bit.

"By the door."

He nodded then relayed the message to Stacks.

Stacks nodded.

I swigged my beer and turned back to the front door.

The two guys were gone.

Red bone was leaving the stage with a cash loaded G-string.

"Where they at?" Stacks asked finally, turning around.

"Niggah, them fools gone. They coulda blasted our asses, messin with your late butt," Benny scolded.

"Them fools know me up in here. They ain't jumpin' outta no jets," Stacks replied.

I set my beer down, knowing I was through drinking for the night. If something kicks off, I wanted to meet it sober.

Blue Velvet's lights were dimmed to where silhouettes could only be made out. Sade's "By Your Side" filtered through the speakers along with the mellow voice of the club's emcee, introducing the Janet Jacme lookalike to the stage.

Just her outline, strutting toward the stage, had the house barking and whistling. I wondered if the previous dancers were mumbling "bitch" under their breaths because of the rock star applause she was receiving.

The stage lights had been altered with soft yellows and reds, casting a radiant glow onto the queen's bronze skin. Jet black hair, permed to meet her bronze shoulders. Light brown eyes and perfect lips for seductive suggesting. Leopard and fishnet seemed to be melted onto her curvaceous figure. She was all that's been advertised. "Sex on stage."

Benny was already pushing past people, trying to make it to the stage.

Stacks and I started cracking up.

Benny's done a lot of hilarious things in the past, but his determined expression to be near Janet was tops.

Halfway through Janet's act, a banana appeared out of nowhere. The tricks she began doing, to some, would seem unbelievable.

Benny, at front stage, continued dishing out bills. I would be player hatin' if I said that Janet didn't have it going on. She could definitely raise hell amongst brothas- and plenty of sistahs, too.

She ended her One-Time-Only performance with a five-dollar photo op. My younger brother returned with fifty-dollars' worth of photos. "Here, take these." He pushed three of the photos at me.

I checked them out with Stacks hanging over my shoulder.

"These definitely not going in the photo album," I said.

It was after eleven when dancers began taking the stage for their second sets. There was another club that Janet is supposed to be appearing at, in just a few hours, and Benny wanted to beat her there, so that his face would be among the first she'd see. He says he wants to show her how loyal he is as a fan. It seemed like stalking to me, and she might need to consider calling the cops on his perverted ass.

Outside, felt alienated after the dim lights and nudity. The night was warm, the sky holding pinholes of light.

We turned onto 53$^{rd}$ & Walnut, where Benny had parked his ride. "You ain't spend a fuckin dime. The least you can do is pay the cover charge," Benny was telling Stacks.

"I ain't paying for shit. If you wanna see that hoe, then you better pay your own way in."

"You got me, Wes?" Benny asked.

"You still got some Cheddar on you, right?"

"Yeah, but I need it for tips."

"Don't give that niggah shit, Wes."

"Shut up, Stacks. I'm asking Wes. So, whassup, big bro? You got me?"

I stopped walking, and so did they. "You gotta

control yourself, B."

"This shit ain't about nothing, Wes. We got tons of this shit."

"Then why your broke ass can't pay your cover charge?" Stacks asked.

"Shut up," Benny snapped.

We started walking again.

"I got you, B, but you gotta slow your drunken ass roll, partner."

"Cool. I'ma chill."

I gave Benny a dap.

"Damn, Wes! You dumb as shit." That was Stacks. He's always complaining that I show Benny favoritism. He was pointing and carrying on. "You always do that. I can't get shit, but you give this fool the world."

All I could do is display a smile, as they had complained. Nothing's changed with us. We've had this kind of spat as children. Now, they're more for fun, a remembrance of our childhood.

At the car, Benny went to the driver's side while Stacks and I stayed on the curb, bickering. When the first "BANG" rang out, we flinched. At the sound of the second bullet smashing into the car, we ducked.

"Get Down! Get Down!" Stacks started yelling. He snatched a Glock from his waistband and squeezed off two rounds in the direction the shots had come from.

It dawned on me that "we" were the targets, and that Benny was on the other side of the car exposed.

Stacks must have realized the same thing because we both began inching around to the driver's side. Stacks was hollering Benny's name, but Benny hadn't answered back. Stacks raised Kamikaze like and began reeling off rounds at the shadows that had ambushed us.

Seconds later, the only shots that rang out were coming from Stacks' gun. The night was again quiet, and he was back beside me. We were staring down at Benny's still body, slumped against the car door, keys tightly gripped. The photos he had taken at the club were scattered all around him, and his eyes were wide open, like he had died of shock, but the pool of blood he was in, indicated otherwise.

My legs buckled and I fell to my knees beside him. I looked up at Stacks, who had begun pacing wildly, spitting obscenities like a well-rehearsed speech. "Benny-get up," I pleaded as I cradled his head in my arm and stroked his cheek. "Don't do this, B, please. Please, get up!" I hurriedly gathered the photos and shoved them under his nose. "Here, B. Get up." I hoped to see the smile I had seen just minutes before.

Stacks fell to his knees beside me, his eyes leaked like a running faucet.

I held my dead brother in my arms, forgetting about the blood oozing on me. In the night, I heard the whining of approaching sirens and the chatter of people who were venturing outdoors. A woman was screaming as if it were her child who'd been shot. My eyes fell to the gun hanging from Stacks' fingertips. "Get rid of the gun," I mumbled. Stacks seemed stunned. I snatched the Glock and hurled it down a sewage drain a few feet away. I pulled Benny's arm over my shoulder and lifted him from the ground.

When the police headlights hit us, we were carrying Benny down the middle of the street. We were covered with my brother's blood.

It was near dawn when the police allowed Stacks and me to go home. That's how the pudgy sergeant had said it, too. "Go home!"

He had dismissed us like we had no right to ask questions about our brother's murder.

Stacks and Benny had evolved into well-known dealers in the city, and according to the attitudes of the police department, Benny was just, one less dealer on the streets.

We were at my crib, Stacks, and me, ready to crash on the carpet, next to our fifths of Seagram. We had showered and changed into sweats and had been spending the rest of dawn reminiscing. We had spoken about our futures-futures without Benny.

I was surprised to learn that Stacks couldn't read or write. And I was pleased to hear him admit, being proud of me for having left the coke game.

I've made the mistake of looking at Stacks in the same context I apply to myself. I now understand why he's so true to the "coke game." The game is all he knows and ever wants to know. He does his learning from watching and adapting to the trade. Everything else around him is just bullshit.

I was sure that Benny's death will spark a new fire in his heart. He and Benny hadn't been just brothers-they had been partners.

# CHAPTER 18

# CAROL

I was poised for war the minute I slammed down the telephone receiver. She had told me that her name was Pamela Winthrop-Wesley's fiancée for the past year. She said she wanted to make me aware that Wesley is taken, and if I had any self-respect, I'd find my own damn man. I'm still trying to figure out how she got my number. I already know how she's made my ass whipping list. What kind of name is Winthrop, anyway?

Covert pleasure seems to always contain a sort of grief. Wesley had not mentioned anyone named Pamela, but that's not what I was taking issue with. My issues are with me.

I should not have become involved with

someone until I was more comfortable with my emotions.

I'd been scrambling around the house, trying to rid the impeccable name of Pamela Winthrop from my mind. She became the focus point of my day.

I cleaned house, cooked dinner, three hours too early, and even visited with neighbors, something that is rare of me. Once you make yourself available to neighbors in the hood, it becomes routine for stop-ins.

I continued to tell myself that Winthrop's call was no big deal. But not until I was on my way to collect the twins, did I admit that I'd been truly bothered, and that my feelings for Wesley were strong and lingering.

I rounded the bend, from Glenwood Avenue to Edgley Street, crossed to the other side to avoid a Doberman that kept leaping onto the fence, barking, what I assumed are obscenities in dog language. My nerves were already shot. With what's going on in my life, I might have kneeled, eye to eye with the dog, and vented right back at it.

I crossed Diamond Street, wondering if Winthrop could be psychotic enough to run me down with a Miata she may have gotten for her twentieth-something birthday.

I looked both ways before crossing the street.

Lisa and Elaine were at the school's entrance

with their youngest girls, off to the side, enjoying a set of patty cake. Elaine had the nerve to have crowded her big ass into some Daisy Dukes, made me wonder if her home had mirrors. "She know she wrong," I mumbled to myself, met Lisa with a smile and gave Elaine a small, "Hey, girl." It was obvious that they had been gossiping about someone, because Lisa returned to their confab with, "-Anyway, that's just what they do-they haters." She turned back to me and pointed. "Oooh, I wanna talk to you."

I looked at my homegirl, confused.

"Excuse us, Elaine," Lisa said. "I got a bone to pick with this fluffy."

I was certain Lisa had found out about Wesley. Fluffy is our codeword for "hoe."

"I have to go to the market anyway, girl, but I'ma call you about so-and-so," Elaine said.

"Mm-hm. You do that," Lisa replied, without taking her eyes from me.

Awkwardness settled in me for interrupting their discussion, because Elaine wobbled off with the posture of a woman dissed. Nonetheless, I waved bye-bye to her cellulite and smiled at her daughter.

"I'm upset with you. You know that, right?"

I wasn't about to volunteer any information, so I put on an innocent face.

"Hooker, don't look at me all funny. Who is he?"

I had to smile. Lisa had a way of insulting you but making it seem so amusing. Between Lisa and Liz, I don't know who is the realist. With them, nothing's ever sugar coated.

"He? What he?"

She rolled her eyes. "Carol, you know damn well you can't tell Tonya shit."

I should have known. "Since when do Tonya know anything?"

"Since she also told me about you and James breaking up."

"Damn. Did she put my shit on the Internet?"

While Lisa and I waited on our girls, I told her about Wesley, James' cheating, and Winthrop's phone call.

Lisa rolled gray eyes at me. "Carol, you know you my ace, but you had to be blind not to know that James was cheating."

"You knew?"

"Pun-lease, child, if I would'a knew, you would'a knew-but all the signs seem like they were there. Honey, you gotta be sharp nowadays. Bitches'll steal your man so fast...honeyyy..." She looked away from me then turned back. "I didn't wanna say nothing about James getting high, 'cause I wasn't sure. No need getting my girl all worried, right?" She said it like she wanted forgiveness.

I let her chew her bottom lip for a while. "Right," I finally answered, feeling as if Lisa had betrayed me. Or was I beginning to doubt everyone? My willingness to trust people at their word seems to slowly be diminishing.

I was glad when the twins emerged-runny noses and all. Although Lisa and I are tight, I couldn't help but think she'd taped the words "dumb bitch" to my back as I hustled the twins away. I felt some-kinda-way about people knowing more of my business than I do. I couldn't wait to get home so that I could call and chew Tonya's ass out. Even if I would've, eventually, told Lisa, that decision should have been left up to me.

It's only been a few days since the twins have seen James. Already, the twins were missing him. Each time a van would drive by us, they'd compare the van to their daddy's. It was awful knowing that them missing him will only worsen. They had heard me call their father a crack head at the cookout, but still, they were unaware of how his addiction will affect their lives.

I had explained to the twins that their father was sick and have to go away to some doctors, but even that had been met with emotions about: when can they visit him? can they send him drawings? Can they call?

I'd been able to dance around their questions easily, but with Kevin, there was no way to hide James choosing cocaine over his family; regardless how I might try and dress it up.

After picking up Kevin, I rushed the twins home to bathe the thick filth from their bodies. It would not surprise me one bit to discover that they had been wrestling on the school's hallway floors.

Kevin was in his room, and I could hear his Sega going berserk. I figured I'd give him an hour to unwound before I begin preaching homework.

Bored, I checked my voice mail. There were no messages. Just as I plopped down on the sofa to relax, the phone rang. It was Wesley.

My boredom quickly transformed to interest, because I've been monitoring our minutes together over the past few days, plus, I wanted answers concerning Pamela Winthrop.

"I need to see you," Wesley said.

"Yeah, well, I need to see you, too. A woman called me saying she's your fiancée, a Pamela Winthrop."

There was a pause.

"That's one reason we need to talk."

"Don't you think you should've told me that you have a fiancée?"

"I don't. Can I see you?"

"Is there really anything to say?"

"Yes."

Whatever Wesley needed to say to me, must have been important. He provided the twenty-five dollars to pay Tonya to babysit, picked my sister up, and sat quietly while I chewed her out for putting my business in the street. He was also closed mouthed during the drive to his place.

I was nervous throughout the ride. It was my first time seeing Wesley so tensed. His one-word replies to any questions, Tonya or I had asked, hinted that something heavy was on his mind.

When we entered his place, I was sure something was wrong. His place was a mess. Cartons and brown boxes were lying everywhere, his television was boxed, and his stereo was divided between the sofa and love chair. Newspaper littered the coffee table.

It was obvious he'd been packing, and my gripes about Winthrop suddenly seemed moot. Any idea of breaking it off with him, I could forget. He was dumping me.

I looked around at the boxes, then at him. "What's all this?" I asked.

He scanned the room as if it were his first time seeing the mess. "I'm leaving Philly."

I bit my bottom lip, pushed aside a box, and

squeezed down onto a comer of the sofa. I didn't want him to see me buckle. "For how long?"

"I don't know." The way he shook his head when he said it, could have meant forever.

I covered my scream with a palm and swallowed some anger.

"Too many ghost, Carol…"

"What ghost?" I shot back, surprised at my tone. I thought an answer was about to come from his mouth, then I realized, he was fighting back tears. "What the hell is going on, Wesley?"

He sniffed and shook his head. "Benny was killed last night."

My palm captured my sigh. "Oh, my god. I am so sorry." I fought to raise from the sofa to comfort him, but his words had the effect of nails, made my issues with Winthrop and him leaving seem petty. I managed to lift from the sofa to embrace him. We both shared our tears.

The bedroom was quiet, dark-except for the moon's glow shouldering a comer at the far side. The red glow from the digital clock read: 1:09 a.m. We were fully clothed on top of the bedspread, holding hands, talking. I had shared with him, during our date to Atlantic City, now it was Wesley's turn to share with me.

I felt sure Wesley was doing just as I've been doing, painting mental pictures of our discussion on our black canvas. "I used to think that my life was a motion picture," Wesley was saying. "I would always come out on top-never lose or make the wrong decisions. I guess it's no wonder my life's been filled with anguish and disappointment. No matter how much good I want to do; God always seems to have other plans."

"Don't I know it. I used to wanna be a daggone mountain climber." I confessed, something I've never told anyone.

We giggled.

"You joking, right?"

"Nope. I did. I used to fantasize about what it was like at the top if I'd be able to touch heaven or grab God's hand. I wanted to be near the angels."

"I guess, in some ways you are a mountain climber."

"Uh-uh, not me. I found out I'm scared of heights when I was twelve."

"Not in that sense. I'm talking about the struggles you've overcome growing up a teenage mom, Kevin's situation, James, the fact that you're a Black woman about to rediscover yourself academically--and I'm sure I haven't even touched on the skeletons.

I squeezed his hand. "I don't have skeletons."

"Everybody has skeletons."

"Not me. I've faced mine," I lied, knowing full

well that no one conquers every demon. If someone has, I'd like to begin a new life with that soul.

We were silent for a while. I guess we were searching our past. "I don't want to leave you, Carol-not that we're a couple or anything, but, I do think we might have made a good run at it."

I turned his face to me. "Then don't go." In the darkness, I could barely make out his features, but through his words, I could see his soul.

"I have to."

"No, you don't. You're only running from what happened."

"If I don't go, I'll be spending the rest of my life in prison. I won't be able to live in Philly without looking for revenge."

Again, we lay silent. It occurred to me that he'd be leaving school. "What about school?"

"I'll transfer."

So, that was it, I thought. His mind has been made up. "I gotta pee."

In the bathroom's mirror, I searched for hints of the child, before the children, the abuse, dejection, and love. Things would be far more pleasing if God gave us all just one opportunity to be reborn-not only in Christ, but in life.

I splashed cold water on my face, did my deed,

sat there long enough for Wesley to holler and ask if I were "ok." I cleaned up and told myself that I wouldn't beg him to stay. I'd already asked, despite my resolve to pursue a relationship while my emotions were fragile.

With Wesley mourning Benny's death, I wanted to be there for him in any way that I could. I also wanted to share with him a hunger for other things besides relief from misfortunes.

Back in the bedroom, I stripped to my panties and bra and slid between the sheets.

"You staying the night?" Wesley asked.

"Mm-hm." I watched Wesley undress then join me. His skin was warm and smooth against mine. I kissed him softly on the lips and smiled. "Good night, baby," I whispered, then closed my eyes and wrapped my limbs around him. I melted into the rhythm of his breathing until I drifted off.

The telephone jarred us awake at 7:20 a.m., according to the clock/radio on the nightstand. I was on the side where the phone was, so I fumbled for the receiver, found it, and passed it to Wesley.

I pulled free a numb arm when he sat up.

His conversation had been brief-some uh-huhs, yeahs, and okays. I sat up when he rolled out of bed. "Where you off to?" I questioned.

"I gotta meet Stacks. You can chill if you want. I

won't be long."

"Meet him where? It's seven-thirty."

"Don't worry. I'll be right back. Go back to sleep. I'll bring back some breakfast."

And I did. Opened my eyes again when I heard the front door close. I laid there for a while until the realization of being in a man's home-alone-forced me to jump up and reach for the telephone and check in.

The clan had survived the night, and I'd survived Tonya's tongue lashing and teasing. I had done a lot of smiling and jousting, while we spoke, but hung up feeling guilty after speaking with Kia. I could only imagine what she was wearing this morning.

Last night's darkness had hidden the chaos I was now faced with looking at. I had to step over T-shirts, books, and papers just to get to the bathroom.

I finger-brushed with Aim, showered, and dried off with one of two towels I found on a rack behind the bathroom's door.

After dressing, I fidgeted with the buttons on the clock-radio until Alicia Keyes' "Fallen" filled the room. Her words and melody wavered throughout my insides, and instinctively, I began picking up clothes, books, and some of the other mess scattered across the bedroom's floor. I had no idea where the items should go, so I began tossing them into a large box in a corner. I remade the bed, changed the blanket, white sheets in favor of gray sheets, with huge Tic Tac Toe printings. They were ugly, but clean. I picked up jackets from a wingback and hung them up.

Shoes and sneakers were everywhere, boxes atop of boxes. At the foot of the closet was where most of them were stacked. I began stacking those that weren't. Fila, Nike, Reebok, seemed to be Wesley's favorite choices in sneakers. Brutini, Armani, and Stacy Adams appeared to be his choice of shoes.

I remembered hearing something about telling a lot about a man by what he wears on his feet. I began opening the boxes' one by one, trying to analyze Wesley from each shoe I would come across.

I wanted to know all I could about Wesley and wondered if a shoe's curve means this or that. Does a flashy shoe mean flamboyant? Or does a plain shoe mean boring?

As I dug deeper into Wesley's shoe collection, I found myself turning to the sneakers. It was easy to see what you want in a man, because in every shoe, I saw a bit of Wesley's personality.

I was nearing the last of the shoes when I picked up an Armani box. Its heft was different, much heavier than the others. I lifted its lid and saw it contained newspaper clippings, old clippings with stained, yellowing paper. I read the first of them, my mind soon reminded by its words. I snatched a handful of clippings and was shocked to find the layers of cash beneath them. I turned my attention back to the articles. Just as I'd done the first time I read them, I let my tears drip onto the article.

The articles were all about Kevin. About how he'd been shot on his way to school, and how unfortunate it was that a promise of the community would never walk again. I looked back to the layers of cash in the box. Stuffed in a slot, between the cash and the box was a stack of plain, white envelopes. My hands began to tremble.

# CHAPTER 19

# CAROL

What seemed to be a thousand questions entered my mind at once, a thousand questions with two-thousand answers that needed deciphering. I held in my hands facts. The money and clippings are proof. His brothers. His background. The years of envelopes, stuffed with money, arriving at my home. Us meeting because of Kevin, all proves that Wesley is no accident. He'd planted himself into my life.

I dumped the box's contents onto the bed. Beneath the money were photos of me and Kevin at the van stop. The pictures had been taken over a year ago, I knew because they were of me with extensions.

I stuffed everything back into the shoe box and

stomped down to the living room. Uncertainty. Disappointment. Betrayal. Rage-mixed with-Hope. Belief. Denial. All of these things overwhelmed me while I stared at traces of my family's misery.

It was still unclear to me why Wesley would have the clippings, photos, and money. But, I had every intention on finding out the truth.

I set the box on the coffee table, in clear view, and parked myself on the sofa. I crossed my legs and began swinging my foot back and forth.

That's the position I was holding when Wesley returned looking strained. Tiredness was in his eyes, then surprise when he saw the Armani box. I pointed to it. "What the hell is that? I know you haven't been following me and my son?"

He clasped both hands behind his head and tucked his lips.

"What's going on, Wesley?" I demanded.

He only stared at me, like he would run if I lifted from the sofa.

I wanted to see if that were so and stood.

He didn't flee, but he did, however, lay a forearm on the wall and rest his head on it. "Why'd you go through my stuff, Carol?"

"Don't hand me that shit! Answer the damn question!"

He spun toward me. "Why'd you do this, Carol?"

I pulled the lid from the shoe box and held the clippings out to him. "What's this? How long have you been following us?"

"I'm not following you."

"Not now! Hell, you already had your thrills. You got to play with the real thing!"

"It's not even like that."

"Then tell me what it's like. Where'd these pictures come from?" I snatched the photos out of the box with the same hand I held the clippings in. My anger was on the brink. I slung the photos and clippings to the floor. I was ready to explode at any minute. I think Wesley was counting the seconds.

His eyes were clear puddles, and a single teardrop dripped onto the shag carpet. He looked like a tortured man. "I want to be honest," he began. "I want to be a better person than I had been a long time ago, when I had done some of the worst things in my life."

I stood quiet. Listening. Waiting.

He put his back to the wall and slid down it, sat there and spoke to me as if out of a memory. "I'm in love with you, Carol-I know that's not what you wanna hear, but I need you to know this first." He wiped a tear away. "I can never right what wrongs I've done-ever- and I know you forgiving me will probably never happen."

While Wesley was speaking, my anger rose and fell. My tears ran freely and my heart swelled then ruptured. I could not believe what I was hearing. Wesley. Murder, both in the same sentence-and my son having been shot in the process.

It was horrifying to think of the nerve it had taken for him to fuck "me" for comfort. I was too stunned to move, too shocked to do anything but relive the grief that-not just anyone had caused-Wesley had caused.

There was nothing Wesley could say to destroy the barrier of hatred building inside of me. His lips were moving, but not a sound could reach me. I'd ventured to another place, where moments became silent and rushed. I was no longer in control of my actions, and with my newfound hatred, I plunged forward, hurling punches, kicks, cursing and clawing.

He balled into a shell.

Again, and again I kicked and punched him, until I finally tired and fell to the floor beside him, delirious and spent, unable to raise my arms above my head and pull myself up from the floor.

For several minutes, we laid there eerie in our plated futures, knowing that neither would be in the other's.

I conjured the strength to lift myself, my hopes,

and dignity from the floor and stumble to the front door. There was no need to look back, didn't have to. I'd always see Wesley's face when I watch my son spin the tires on his wheelchair. It would have been easier not knowing who had crippled my son, having a nobody to point my anger at. Now, that nobody has a face, a name, a scent, a feel, and a charm that I'd enjoyed and had made love to. I wished it all gone, wanted that empty nobody back. But now that emptiness will forever be replaced with the memory of weeks of loving at my cripple son's expense.

I slammed the door to Wesley's feelings. I believe guilt will never allow me to forget how not to trust.

# CHAPTER 20

# WESLEY

It's been two weeks since Benny's body had been laid to rest, and I still haven't heard from Carol. I can't say that I'm surprised about not hearing from her, but I am surprised, as well as grateful to her for not calling the police on me-especially not that morning. I had felt so horribly that morning that I might have broken down and confessed to anything they would have asked me.

Pam helped me stuff my duffel bag into the Volvo's trunk. I slammed down the hood.

Pam rewarded me with a peck before hurrying back into my place for more of my things. She was excited about me accepting her father's job offer, not mentioning having me at arm's length. She returned with an armful of magazines and CD's.

"Why you packing the car with this stuff? I told you I was renting a U-Haul."

"We're going to need something to read and listen to, right?"

"All that?"

Pam carried about twenty CD's and ten magazines. She tossed it all in the backseat. "It's a long ride."

"If you say so."

"I say so. Are you going to miss Philly?"

"I doubt it."

Pam had some business to handle before we could leave the city. We headed north, through Germantown and Mount Airy, to a fabric distributor in Montgomery County.

Pam had her fashion career planned out. She'd begin by designing sleek, exotic dresses and blouses for women, and playful, urban boss wear for both sexes.

While she spoke with a company representative, I wandered a block away to the mall, not looking to buy anything, just thinking about how I had altered Carol's life. My fingerprints are all over her and Kevin's futures, and regardless of any restitution I've given them, any condolences or redemption on my part, grief will always follow them.

I returned to the fabric company just as Pam was exiting it.

Her eyes were dancing.

"Did everything go ok?"

"Yep. I'll be receiving my first batch of material in a week. My dad's going to be excited."

"What about your mom?"

"Oh, she'll be happy, too, but not truly happy until I'm married. I think you should be prepared. She's kinda old school, so, don't be alarmed if she waits on you, hand and foot."

"I can handle that."

Pam turned her lips up at me. "I bet you can."

We headed back Northside with Missy Elliot banging from the car speakers. Pam had ditched both shoes and had a pedicured foot up on the dash. She was flipping through the pages of a "For Men" mag. She had reached the photo spread of Elise Neil. "She's cute and all that, but she should know better."

"Know better than…what?"

"To pose in her underwear."

"It's good exposure."

"I can see that." She closed the magazine and tossed it in the back seat. "Are you gonna feed me?"

"Sure. What kinda grub you want?"

"A Philly cheese steak to go."

We made the twenty-minute drive to Pat's Steaks, a straight ride south on Delaware Avenue, into the Italian part of the city. I preferred Jim's Steaks, myself, but Pam had insisted. Now, I was stuck staring at a seven-dollar sandwich. I had no intention on eating.

I wrapped it up and sipped my Mountain Dew.

"You not eating?" Pam asked.

"Too greasy." I held the sandwich out to her. "You think you can bang two of them?"

"Yeah, right-and tear this figure up." She lifted one side of her rump from the seat to show me.

We were outside, on a sidewalk patio watching the traffic flow by. I listened to her ramble on about historical sites in Atlanta, while she snatched huge bites from her cheese steak between sentences.

She had wolfed her sandwich down in record time then walked to the trash can, clinging the sandwich wrapper with a pinkie, her Styrofoam cup in the same hand, while stuffing the butt of the sandwich in her mouth with the other.

"You ready to roll?" I asked.

"Mm-hm."

We were minutes away from turning onto the Ben Franklin bridge when my pager went off. It was Stacks. I called him on the cell phone.

"Where you at?" he asked. There was an

excitement in his voice that I haven't heard in weeks.

"Downtown."

"Turn around."

"For what?"

"I found out who killed Benny."

I swerved and nearly hit a parked car.

Pam looked at me like I was crazy and buckled her seatbelt.

"Who did it?" I asked.

"I'll tell you when you get here. I'm 'bout ready to blast them fools."

"Don't do anything stupid, Stacks. I'm on my way." I hung up and made a U-turn.

Disappointment covered Pam's face "What's wrong? Where are we going?" she asked.

"I'm taking you to my place til later."

"Why?"

"Stacks is trippin."

After dropping Pam off, I rushed over to Stack's crib, hoping he had waited. His car was in its parking spot. I pulled in behind it. Before I could exit the car, Stacks was down the front stairs, pulling on a jacket.

Fie slammed the car's door when he was inside, made the entire car rock.

"You got heat on you, don't you?"

"Damn right!"

I pulled from the curb with visions of Benny's dead body in my arms. It was two years ago all over again, only there's two of us this time.

Stacks pulled a dock 19 from his waistband and held it out to me. "You might need this."

I laid the gun on my lap. "Who was it?" I asked.

"Two dudes, supposed to be Bittles cousins. I got a guy that sell weight on that side. He say them niggahs was drinkin' and braggin' 'bout that shit."

For the first time, I saw Stacks, the man, no longer the kid I used to push around. His eyes were determined, and a huge vein bulged from his forehead. "How the hell they know we did Bittles?" I asked.

"I'm not even sweatin' how they found out. Them niggahs walkin' dead."

"Hold up, hold up!" I pulled the car into a parking spot and cut the engine off. I turned back to Stacks. "Do you know what these dudes look like?"

"Nah. My man gonna point 'em out."

"And you just gonna start shooting, huh?"

"You damn right!"

I pulled a Newport from my pack and lit it up, eyeballing a rundown tenement, then Stacks. He'd been watching me.

"What?" he asked.

"Who'd you tell about Bittles, Stacks?"

"Nobody."

"Don't lie to me, Stacks. This shit ain't no game. Nobody saw shit that morning, so, somebody had to say something."

Stacks focused on an elderly man. His thoughts were elsewhere. "Calvin knew," he said finally.

"Fuck!" I shouted, slapping the steering wheel. "That's like broadcasting that shit over the radio."

"Benny told that fool. You know they was tight at one time. When we opened the house on Van Pelt, shit fell off. I don't know who else know."

I dragged my smoke then tossed it out of the window. I felt lost, trapped between good and evil.

It would be stupid to rush across town and murder two guys that someone, whom I've never seen before, points out. I'd made the mistake of rushing to revenge before. I wasn't about to repeat. "I'm not doing this," I said. I handed Stacks back the gun. "And neither are you."

"You trippin'."

I started the car and eased into traffic. "I'm serious, Stacks. I'm not with this no more."

His face became taunt. "Don't start bitchin. Them niggahs killed B."

"I know that!" I shouted. "Don't you think I know that shit?"

"You ain't actin' like it!"

I fought to calm myself down. "Stacks, can't you see that this shit is inhuman, making monsters out of us? There's gotta be another way to do this shit, without making us open targets. I've been running from this hell for two years. I'm just not built for killing."

"Let me out the car, then. I'll do this shit, myself."

"Hell no, Stacks. Think. It's not like this thing has to be done right away. Prison is packed with motherfuckers doing shit on the whim. Let's be smart and come out on top. It's time to get out of the game, like we had talked about when we first started."

Stacks was angry, but he was listening. That's about all that I could hope for. I had circled back to Stack's crib. "Not fly from the cuff, ok?"

He paused before nodding.

"I'm serious, Stacks. Let's handle this my way. Put the guns in the spot, and let's go see your man."

Two hours later, I was back at the crib, where Pam had been roasting. Her legs were crossed and her foot kicking. Her lips were pushed way out. She was upset about us having to delay going to Atlanta. "What's one day?" I had asked. But Pam's so spoiled to the bone that she was, probably, more concerned with having to call her parents and explain that we'll be a day postponed.

She stopped kicking long enough to shun away my kiss.

"Don't touch me," she warned.

"How long do you plan to be upset?"

"Until we're on the highway, or you tell me what's this 'thing' you have to take care of."

"I can't say. I promised Stacks."

She went back to her kicking.

I woke up tangled in Pam's limbs-her security blanket. I was almost certain she sensed danger around the comer, but what she may not know is that my troubles can be fixed with a simple phone call.

Her eyes fluttered open while I was easing from her grasp. "Where you going?" she asked.

"I have some calls to make."

"What's wrong with this phone?" Her eyes pointed to the beside phone.

"Didn't want to wake you."

"I wasn't sleep."

"You looked sleep to me."

I telephoned Stacks from the bedside.

Stacks had already been awake when I phoned him a half hour ago. He said he's been up since last night, and that we should meet about our problem.

"I thought we decided on that?"

"You decided, not me," had been his reply.

Now, at 9:10 a.m., I found myself drumming on his front door, peeking through his peephole.

He answered the door, wearing his no-rap face, talking on his cell phone.

I followed him into the living room and waited til' he had folded his phone. What happened?"

"Them niggahs got what they hands call for." His demeanor was defiant. He stood like some mafia don who had executed an enemy.

"Again-what happened?"

"Ten Gs and it got done."

We both sat quietly for a minute. As much as I wanted to argue over his impatience, I couldn't. What's been done, has been done. Besides, to chastise his actions would show a lack of respect to Benny.

"I'm leaving town today."

He nodded. "I guess it's just me now?"

"Never that. All you have to do is pick up the phone."

"Not the same." He smiled. "Big college man, now. I always understood, though. I'ma miss all the shit me, you, and B used to do."

"What about the business? You staying in?"

"I thought about that. Maybe it is time to get out while I can."

I nodded. "That'll be one less thing I'll have to

worry about."

"Me and you, both. I already know the game'll kill you if you let it-that's why I'm takin' my small fortune and gettin' ghost."

"You can always go back to school," I suggested.

Stacks' expression said yeah-the-fuck-right.

"It's a suggestion," I added.

"And so is a cruise to Jamaica. I'm booked for this afternoon."

"Stop lying!"

"No shit. Me and big girl been planning this shit for a while."

"That's what's up."

I thought it ironic that I'm the one struggling through college and catching grief, and Stacks, as uneducated as he may be, is headed to the islands. My pager interrupted us. It was Pam. "I better to roll up out here before Pam hunts a brotha down."

"Sis, still jockin hard, huh?"

"Like a heat-seeking missile."

Stacks and I shared a warm embrace before I left his place.

I called Pam from my cell phone and asked her to be ready to roll when I arrive.

She was, too, outside with her large bag, hanging from her shoulder. At this point, Pam seemed more concerned with getting me out of the city-limit, before I changed my mind, rather than where I've been.

I helped with her bag before breaking more bad news to her.

"I have two more stops to make, first."

She tsked while climbing into the passenger seat.

"Well three," I added, and sped into the house to use the bathroom.

My next stop was the garage. Magic was in his office. He slid a Blacktail in his desk drawer and smiled up at me.

I tossed him the keys to my place. "It ain't much but it's better than here," I said.

It hadn't taken much to convince Magic to sublease my place-just in case Atlanta doesn't work out.

"I'll keep the place smellin fresh," he said.

"Just keep your hoochies in check."

"I'ma do that, too." He came from around the desk and awkwardly embraced me. He also walked to the car and insisted Pam give him a goodbye hug as well.

After we had gone, Pam said she thought he had felt her up.

"He probably did," I told her.

I wanted to say my last goodbyes to Carol and Kevin, and used, getting something to eat as my excuse to park in "my spot." Pam knows I hate to eat and drive, so, I sat there, picking at my cheese hoagie-waiting, hoping to be able to erase my last memory of Carol, and replace it with how I became so fond of her to begin with.

Occasionally, I would glance at Pam to see if she had become suspicious. She hadn't. She was too busy tearing into her tuna sandwich and munching on plain chips.

Pam had just crumbled her sandwich wrapper when Carol turned onto Diamond Street, carrying a handled, JCPenney's shopping bag.

Carol wore tight, blue jeans, white Reeboks, and a long sleeve blue blouse. She appeared too young to have three children and so much stress in her life.

"Are you going to finish that?" Pam asked.

"I'm almost done."

"You barely touched it."

I looked down at the near-whole sandwich. "I'm not as hungry as I thought."

Pam pushed open the car door and walked to a nearby trash can.

Pam's leaving enabled me to dissect Carol for signs of what I'd done to her life. She appeared as strong and capable as always.

Upon Pam returning, I bit my sandwich.

She tsked when she saw me eating, grabbed a

stack of CD's and began calling out artists' names.

I continued watching Carol until the van arrived, and she and Kevin turned into the project. I started the car and noticed that Pam had been watching me.

"That was her, wasn't it?" she asked.

I didn't respond, just drifted into traffic, headed southbound.

# CHAPTER 21

# CAROL

I could have easily called the police on Wesley, but the reality is, Wesley being jailed would gain nothing from no one. No comfort. No retribution. Only grief for my son, who would have to relive the incident through a trial and discover that I had been sexually and emotionally involved with the man responsible for crippling him. The fact that Kevin had been shot by a once-lost spirit, influenced my decision as well.

In the little time Wesley and I had spent together, I understood and believed why and whom he's become. Life in the ghetto has its price tag. We all make mistakes, some more tragic than others, but mistakes, nonetheless.

I turned onto Diamond Street, and like I've been

doing for two weeks, looked to where Wesley's car had been parked when we first met. My heartbeat skipped when I saw it was there, and I felt an anger-pang when a slim woman, who I assumed to be Pamela Winthrop, emerge from the car and saunter to the trash. It was difficult dealing with, but I managed to keep a straight face, my roar buried deep, and my eyes turning every-which-way except where my ex-lover sat, watching.

I eyed Winthrop returning to the car and wondered why he would bring her to our meeting place. I've had two weeks to think about questions that I needed answers to. Each time I would try to piece together the puzzle, a piece always seems to be missing.

I was so engrossed in my thoughts that I hadn't noticed the van until it had eased in front of me. I sighed in relief because it blocked Wesley's view of me.

I couldn't get behind Kevin's chair to push, quick enough. With every step I took to distance myself from Wesley, I felt closer to accomplishing something, and confident that the worst for my children's lives, as well as my own, has past-and I've been given some insurance to prove just that.

I turned into the project and slowed my pace.

Kevin looked over his shoulder at me. "Where's KK?"

"At your Grand mom's. James is going in a rehab

today. He wanted to say bye. You want to say bye, too?"

"Only if ifs for good."

I popped him upside the head.

"Ow!"

We walked in silence for a while.

"Kevin, would you be upset if I went back to school?"

He looked back at me. "You for real?"

"Yeah, I am. Welfare ain't cutting it, and now the twins are old enough to fend for themselves more-well, I figured I'd give it a shot."

Kevin's grin was wide.

"I guess that means yes, huh?"

He nodded. "You gonna need me to help you with your homework?"

I popped him upside the head. "You can't even do your own, boy."

He sat rubbing his head, grinning.

As we turned the bend, leading to our block, the teenage girl, that had been waving and speaking to Kevin, was there with two other young girls. They were huddled.

As we passed by, she waved at me then shyly dropped a folded sheet of loose-leaf paper on Kevin's lap. She and her girlfriends trotted away, giggling suspiciously.

I shook my head and looked at Kevin's gaped

mouth and curious eyes.

He snatched up the note and began reading. His lips moved with each word and he blushed as he read.

"Kevin got a girrrlfriend," I teased.

"Uh-uh."

"Yes, you doooo," I countered childishly.

He looked back at me smiling.

I kissed his forehead. "Don't worry, I won't tell your sisters."

He kept on smiling. I don't think I've ever seen him so happy.

I left Kevin at a neighbor's; whose son was mesmerized at Kevin's ability to manipulate a Sega. I caught a hack into Center City and asked him to wait for me outside of PSFS Savings Bank.

Every month, for the past two years, I've been making the trip. And like always, I stood in the first line, where an old, freckled face woman, with the nameplate of Mrs. Crawford, greeted me.

"What can I do for you today, Miss Shavers? Will you be making your usual deposit?"

"No, ma'am, not today." I reached into the JCPenney's bag I'd brought along, and pulled out the Armani shoe box, I'd received in the mail. I dumped the contents of the box on the counter. "I'd like to make a deposit into Kevin Shavers' account."

Mrs. Crawford's eyes widened, and her hand flew to her fake, pearl necklace. "Oh, my. Just give me a moment, please?" The teller left and returned with the manager, a thin fellow with sunken eyes, a curved mustache and wire-rim specs.

"Hello, Miss Shavers, my name is Carl Baldwin. I'm the bank's manager. I understand you'd like to make a substantially large deposit?" His eyes were glued to the stacks of bills on the counter.

"Yes. I'd like to deposit fifty-thousand dollars into my son's account."

"Certainly, ma'am." He nodded to Mrs. Crawford to collect the cash from the counter. "If you won't mind stepping over here, please?" He directed me to a fleet of desks where "special" customers are attended to.

I concluded my business with the bank, feeling comfortable about there being "some" financial stability in my children's futures.

Wesley, having given Kevin the money, could only be one way of him fighting his demons. Hopefully, him graduating college and making a difference in society will help him face and possibly conquer some of his other ghosts as well.

As for myself, I begin refresher courses at St. Joseph's during the evenings. I think it's time I begin

setting an example for my twins.
I know my ride is uphill from here.

# THE END...

# PUBLISHER'S CREDITS

**Story by:** David C Stewart

**Edit/Text formation by:** David C Stewart/Kerry Watson

**Cover Concept:** David C Stewart

**Cover Graphics by:** Kerry Watson (**www.fiverr.com/kerrywatson**)

UP NEXT…

# CHAPTER 1

# CAROL

My eyes wandered around my new office, but always seemed to rest on the gold nameplate on my scarred, mahogany desk.

My son, Kevin, had given me the nameplate a week ago, a day after I accepted the position at William Penn high school as its students' guidance counselor. It's still unbelievable to me what I've been able to achieve so far, but it had taken hard work at a diligent pace to get to this point. I had struggled through numerous awkward situations which many of the less fortunate students, here at the school, had gone through themselves and some who are still experiencing difficulties; plus, I'm where I have had some schooling myself. Now I'm back and anxious to try and assist those students I feel might need guidance.

My eyes again rested on the nameplate then on the bare egg-white walls and two metal file cabinets tucked in one corner.

I struggled to yank open the middle drawer of my desk. A note had been left inside. *"You asked for it."* the note read. It was signed by Mrs. Burns, an English instructor, who's been teaching at the school even before I was a student here. I checked the rest of the drawers for more surprises. They were empty. I settled into my chair and closed my eyes, thanked the Lord for his blessing to lift me from welfare and guide me to my feet. "God is good," I said aloud, ending my prayer.

At the small window, I surveyed a busy Broad Street. My childhood appeared behind my eyes so I pushed away my thoughts and dragged a box of personal items across the floor, items I hope will spruce up the empty office. My Certificate of bachelor's degree in Sociology and my Masters in Guidance Counseling from the University of Pennsylvania were the first items I grabbed. I smiled at the framed degrees before searching for the right places to hang them. "Not bad for a single mom from the projects," I said aloud. I decided to hang them directly on the wall behind the desk and above where my shoulders will be when I'll be counseling teens.

I pulled another item from the box. It was a photo of myself and my three children. The twelve-year old twins, Kia and Kelly, and Kevin who'll be eighteen in December. I sat the framed photo on the desk just as a knock came at the door. Before I answered, Mrs. Burns stuck her salt and pepper head inside.

"Oh, good. You're here. Just checking. I wanted to know if you'd join me for lunch in the cafeteria?"

"Sure."

"Good. I'll hold us a table." She stepped inside. "Do you need anything more?"

"No. Thank you. I think the tour you gave me last week informed me plenty."

"Wonderful then." Her wide, brown eyes sparkled with delight. She spun in her black, floral dress and waved on her way out. "Don't hesitate to ask for anything," she threw over her shoulder.

The school's second floor hallway was cluttered with chattering teens giggling while mulling between classes. Their screaming shook my nerves, but I just kept moving and shaking my head and pushed through the crowds, listening, trying to decipher the beat-box noises, rapping, and young girls degrading other young girls by referring to them as bitches. Some girls covered their mouths when they noticed me eyeballing them. Then there were others, teenagers who kept on cussing as if they were grown alcoholics. Ninety percent of William Penn's students are minority; and it shows amidst the sea of black faces and the fashion show being exhibited. Baggy jeans and Timberlands for the boys and low-rider jeans and belly shirts for the girls. My eye for street fashion hadn't just developed. I'd been raised in ghettos most of my life, so, what I was observing was anything but unusual to me. I understood how brandishing high fashion can lessen the dislikes of black youths, can cause an urban youth to feel less unimportant amongst their peers and better about being without material things they assume their lives should possess.

I was passing the girls' bathroom when I noticed three girls eyeing me suspiciously. I decided to begin my reputation, "Is there a problem?" I asked.

"If it was, you'd know," one sassed.

I grinned, stepped toward the bathroom door. All three straightened their slouching.

"Somebody's using the bathroom," another said.

I split their line of defense. "I'm sure there's room for one more."

I entered the bathroom and was stifled by thick cigarette and marijuana smoke. The smoke was so thick, I fanned a hand across my face, blinked several times to ease the burning in my eyes.

Shock was on the faces of the ten or so girls who began stubbing their smokes and pretending to be doing makeup. Within seconds, the bathroom was nearly clear of students except for two girls. One girl I recognized from the Hank Gathers Community Center where I volunteer some weekends. She still fingered a cigarette. Her friend fingered a joint. They were quiet, staring at me as if I'd intruded on their turf, I hadn't expected this. - Now, I had little idea what to say. I said what my teachers had said to me when I used to hang in the bathrooms. "Don't you two have classes or something?" I managed. My heart sank when I noticed one girl's belly. I turned away to erase the flashbacks of my own past.

"It's fourth period lunch. Duh…" remarked the thin girl with slanted eyes and caramel skin. She stubbed out her joint and tucked it in her palm.

I held out my hand.

She gritted me up and down then rolled her eyes. "I'll talk to you later, girl," she said to her pregnant friend then started by me.

I stepped in front of her with my palm still out. Eye to eye we stood, sizing each other up. I had her by a couple of inches and outweighed her by twenty or so pounds. My heart was thumping, mostly from anticipation.

"Give it to her," said the pregnant girl.

Our eyes were still locked. When I reached for the joint, she let it drop to the floor.

"Oops," she slurred then passed by me with you ain't-said-nothing eyes.

I turned to the pregnant girl. "And you."

"And me what?"

"You plan on putting that cigarette out?"

She dragged the cigarette once more before letting it fall to the checkered linoleum floor, stumped it out with the toe of her black Reebok. "I know you, don't I?" she asked. "You work for the rec center, right?"

"No. I work here."

She wobbled to the sink and splashed water on her redbone skin.

"How old are you?" I asked.

She dried her face with some tissue. "Please, don't start preaching' 'bout no cigarette."

"I asked because I would like to know."

"Fourteen," she shrugged.

I folded my arms across my chest. "And your name is what?"

She tsked before rolling her eyes. "Felicia Knight."

I nodded as if I already knew her. "Well, Miss Knight, don't you think it's time you eased up with the nicotine and give the child you're carrying a chance?"

She didn't answer, just raised a palm, and walked by me. "Excuse me, Miss Knight," I called after her.

She stopped and spun. "Look, lady, I heard it all before, okay? I'd appreciate it if you just do what it is you do around here…monitor halls, bathrooms, or whatever. Don't even try preaching to me because you don't even know how many times, I heard those tired-behind lines." She spun back around and snatched open the bathroom door. "I got classes."

She left me there, staring at the door and wondering if I should've taken this job, wondering if I were cut out to shape the minds of young adults and prepare them for life beyond high school. I took a deep breath and exhaled. Time will tell.

Lunch with Mrs. Burns was awkward. She still lunches in the student cafeteria just as she had done when I was a student here. To be seated with her and sharing lunch as peers was intimidating. Sitting with her had me self-conscience about how I'd like to be perceived by the students as the newest staff member, a staff member that will have to gain students' trust to be effective at my job.

Mrs. Burns had been pointing out those she deemed to be "the bad kids." It wasn't her choices that bothered me so much as it was her conviction of having already counted them out.

The crow's feet at the corners of her eyes shown deeper as she was squinting with each word. She wore too much makeup, as she always has, and to me, with hearing her speak and watching her demeanor, I can see why some of the children feel intimidated by her.

"Look at that one." Mrs. Burns pointed with a cold stare. She was singling out Felicia, who'd entered the cafeteria with a group of four girls. They sat at one of the longer tables across the aisle from us. The conversation she and I had earlier in the bathroom came to mind. I bit into the cold burger I'd been nursing.

"They're all the same," said Mrs. Burns. "Babies having babies. Boys. Boys or babies. It doesn't matter. Kids today need to be ashamed of themselves."

"Do you know her?" I asked.

"I've seen her around. She and that dropout, Hasim Riley, be hugged up so much, you'd think they were Siamese twins."

"Is that whose baby she's carrying?"

"Who's to know. As fast as you think who's with who things change."

"Is that how you felt about me when I used to walk around this school pregnant?"

She fingered her neatly folded handkerchief and patted two red lips. "Probably. But you turned out well, now didn't you? I guess there are some exceptions, as there always are. But not many I suppose." She stood and smoothed her flowered dress. "There's ten minutes before the bell sounds. I like to beat the crowd. Are you situated?"

I nodded and remained seated.

"You were such a good student." She smiled warmly. "I'm pleased you've come back to help but take some advice. Don't become too involved in the children's' lives. It'll only bring you grief."

With that said, Mrs. Burns made her exit. For the life of me, I couldn't figure out if she were for the students or against them. I gave her the benefit of doubt. However, she had displayed a lack of confidence in whether there is hope for this new generation.

I spent the rest of my afternoon settling in my office until the 2:45 bell rang, signaling the end of the school's day. Staff would linger and mingle until 3:30, but I had been summoned to the principal's office.

Mr. Epps, the school's principal, is a small man with soft eyes and a warm smile. At five-foot-three inches, we would stand eye to eye, but he chose to speak with me from behind his desk in a too large leather chair.

I sat across from him.

"So, how did it go…your first day I mean?

"Well. Slow, but much like I thought it would. I haven't had time to review many of the children's files, but I will."

"Splendid. Glad you weren't spooked."

"Spooked?"

He grinned and leaned forward. Well, maybe spooked was the wrong word to use. What I mean is that your job at this school is one of necessity, Miss Shavers. As a first-year counselor with an enormous case load and equal responsibilities, it can be a bit intimidating."

I fought down my wanting to agree and sat quietly.

"I can remember my own initial impression of the school. But why bring that up. What's important is the perception you bring, this school's integrity, and its students. That's why I've chosen you for this job, out of love for these students." He stood and came around to the front of the desk. He rubbed his stubbled beard. His eyes were shinning. "You have what no other candidate for the position possessed. A purpose."

"Excuse me?"

"You know…purpose. A reason for wanting to see these children succeed. You've been in their shoes as well as in the trenches. You know their problems more-so than any book education can teach at any university."

I considered his words. His confidence in me nearly exceeded my own.

He returned to his leather chair. "Am I'm wrong?" he asked.

A tingling trickled through me. I knew that I had something to offer the students and knowing that Mr. Epps believes it as well is inspiring. Nothing teaches like real-life experience. What my college degree has taught me is how to implant the seeds in their minds. What seeds to plant and in which soil to plant them will be my hardest task. Some seeds may only produce weeds, and my experiences will have to guide me in order to produce flowers. No one understands a child of the ghetto better than a parent of a ghetto child.

Mr. Epps and I spoke for thirty minutes. I left the school assured that my "purpose" for seeking out my new career was achievable.

I had parked my leased Altima across from my office window.

As I eased the car into traffic, I gazed up at the window and blushed. I felt accomplished, so different from my old self. No longer will I have to depend on public assistance, public housing, or any man to motivate or mold me into a satisfied woman. Gratified is how I felt to be independent, and it had only taken five and a half years of educating myself to achieve this sensation.

Of course, those years had not been at all easy—not with three children and a drug addicted babies' daddy all vying for attention.

I turned off Broad Street and slipped a CD in the dash. Maxwell's "Let's Stay Home Tonight" engulfed me. Immediately, I felt relaxed and I allowed the music to swallow me whole while the smoothness of the ride to mellowed me from the tensions of the first day on the job.

The neighborhood I'd moved into wasn't a huge step from the projects, where I used to live, but it's a step up, nonetheless. We've lived in the Germantown section of Philadelphia for two years, and already the advantages have outweighed the disadvantages by far. My number one consideration for moving here had been the crime rate. It's been a far less headache than when I was in the projects, simply because the poverty rate is less. Many of the homes on my street are owned by so-called middle-class families. As I am, most residents rent to own, and I figure if I'm thirty-one now, by the time I'm forty, I'll own my home outright. I've already begun renovating the two-story home by appealing to the city for vouchers to have the home wheelchair accessible for Kevin.

I stepped onto my front porch and cringed from the music thumping inside. On many occasions I've asked Kevin to respect our adjoining neighbors. I was near deafened by DMX's lyrics when I opened the door. I squinted, dropped my briefcase in the living room and bypassed the twins, sitting Indian style, on the living room floor playing jacks. I clicked the off button on the stereo and surveyed the living room. It was a mess. Bookbags and jackets covered the sofa and chairs. A mountain of penny candies lie scattered on the coffee table. Neither twin seemed enthused to have me home. They continued their game. "Where's Kevin?" I asked.

"Upstairs," they sang in unison.

"Ya'll get up from there and hang those jackets up. Take those bookbags to your rooms and tell Kevin I said to come down here."

Both girls stood, arguing over their game. I wondered if they'd say hello.

"Mommy, Miss Diane said she gonna be late picking' us up tomorrow from school. She gotta be at the doctor," said Kelly.

"How late?"

"I don't know," she shrugged as she gathered her jacket and bookbag then headed upstairs.

"Have you lost your tongue, Kia?" I asked.

"No."

"Then can you at least say hello?"

"Hi, Mom."

"'Hi, Mom,'" I mimicked as I passed through the dining room in route to the kitchen -- the largest room in the house. I had been surprised by the kitchen's enormity. It's one main reason why I had decided to purchase the home. I poured myself a glass of apple Snapple and started dinner. I was pulling the wrapping from a family-size pack of lamb chops, I'd set out to defrost this morning, when Kevin entered the kitchen.

Kevin sat tall in his wheelchair. He was his father's image with short, wavy hair and a thin build. His shoulders had widened since had begun lifting weights, but his smile still possessed its child-like innocence.

"How was it?" he asked.

"Strange. It would have been better if I knew that I could trust you not to blast the music while I'm gone."

Kevin rolled to where I stood and smiled. "Sorry."

"Mm-hm. I bet."

"I am. I went upstairs right before you got in. Plus…"

I cut his words short. Kevin, please…"

"Okay, okay. I'll put headphones on."

"Thank you." I turned back to the stove.

"I can make KK sandwiches if you want," Kevin offered.

KK is Kevin's nickname for the twins.

"No. It's okay. They had sandwiches three times this week already. Plus, you should be trying to get every meal possible. When you're on campus, you'll be missing these." I turned and blew him a kiss.

Kevin is so much like his father, Langston, who'd been killed in a car crash early during my pregnancy with Kevin. I had been thirteen then. Langston's death had crushed me.

"I'ma miss your cooking, Mom, but I'm still looking forward to being on my own for a while."

"You sure you know what you're asking for? Temple's a tough school. It's even tougher living on campus."

"I'll be fine."

The twins rushed into the kitchen; both were out of breath. "Mom, Kia pushed…pushed me…pushed me over the bed and

cursed."

"Uh-uh, Mom. She storying! She mad 'cause…'cause she lost in jacks."

"Uh-uh. No, I didn't."

"Yes, you did."

I rested a hand on the counter and one on my hip. Lately, the girls would argue over anything. Games. TV. Clothes. Oh, Lord, can they argue over clothes. I used to buy them identical outfits until last year. That's when the fighting really escalated from shoves to wrestling then punches. Kia's always been more aggressive and is usually the one who I chastise most. "Did you two do your homework yet?"

"No," Kia answered. Kelly shook her head.

How could they be alike and yet so different? I thought. "Then I want the two of you to take your narrow behinds upstairs, and get it done. Do I make myself clear?" They nodded.

"I don't want to see your faces or hear you until I call you for dinner. I'm tired of the fighting."

They pouted then moped from the kitchen. I returned to dinner.

"It's been that kind a day, huh?" asked Kevin.

"No. But it doesn't make sense the way they argue."

"They're probably tired of looking at each other. Every time they look in the mirror, they see each other's face."

"Thank goodness. I don't know if I could take two Kevins."

We both smiled.

After dinner, I went over the girls' homework with them. Math mostly I felt good about how both have grasped the concept of mathematics, and the fact that they compete against one another to learn the most. It suits me simply fine. One is always showing off, anxious to tell the other how to do a problem. Both are a trip.

Kevin retired to the computer in his room, and after I showered, I retired to my room as well. I had brought home a few of the students' files, those who I planned on speaking with tomorrow, students' whose files bear red dots next to their names. The previous counselor had taken "special" interest in these students, and from what I could tell, just from reading the few files I've read already, she had no choice. I found myself wondering about Felicia. Tomorrow I'll look over her file, too. Maybe I'll give her my own red dot. There has to be a story there.

# ALSO BY THE AUTHOR...

## About the Author

Keith Hayden enjoys writing, learning, and creating. He aims to entertain and educate readers through his science fiction and fantasy works.